Bedevilling

Murray and Tidswell Paranormal Investigations

Book Five

J.E. Nice

First published in Great Britain in 2023 by
Write Into The Woods Publishing.

A CIP catalogue record for this book
is available from the British Library.

ISBN 978-1-912903-44-3

Cover design and typesetting by Write into the Woods.

www.writeintothewoods.com
www.jenice.co.uk

Other Books By J.E. Nice

The Last War Series:
Matter Of Time
Despite Our Enemies
In My Bones
With A Scream

Murray And Tidswell
Paranormal Investigations:
Beginnings
Becoming
Belonging
Bewitching
Bedevilling

No Masters Or Kings:
No Masters Or Kings
In Feverish Haste

Find them all at www.jenice.co.uk

JOIN US IN THE WOODS
for news, early access and freebies at
www.jenice.co.uk

For the people just trying to hang on.

Better times are coming.

1

Mullarky

At times like these, one had to wonder if modern, newly built houses produced this amount of dust. Mullarky assumed not. With their lack of dust, however, came a lack of character. Mullarky liked personality in his home. In fact, he rather liked personality in his life in general. Just not too much. He preferred the personality of the cottage and flowers over the personalities of people. Most people, anyway. He paused his dusting to listen to the quiet of the cottage and there came the sound of shifting upstairs.

With a sigh, he continued transferring the dust from one surface to another, until movement caught his eye. Ambling over to the living room window, Mullarky peered over the window sill to watch a man on the other side of the small fence that marked the boundary of the cottage's front garden. The man had his hands deep in his pockets and was staring down at the ground as he scuffed his feet over the dirt. Was he going for a walk in the woods? The path that led to the wooded entrance was right outside the cottage, and for good reason.

No, Mullarky knew from one look that this man wasn't just out for a stroll, a dog walk or hike. He was too busy scuffing a particular area of ground and his lips were moving. Mullarky narrowed his eyes and sharpened his ears.

The man was muttering to himself.

Mullarky's gaze dropped to the ground where the man was standing, lifting up on tiptoes to get a better look. The man dropped to a crouch and brushed away the fallen leaves, laying his palm flat on the broken path where weeds and grass pushed their way through.

Swallowing hard, Mullarky turned away and sank down to the floor until he was sitting, his back against the wall beneath the window.

The man was paying far too much attention to the ancient crossroads. It had been a long time since the crossroads had caught the eye of anyone. Or, at least, it had been a long time since the spring, when that witch had wandered from the woods and noticed the crossroads, doing as the man was doing now: crouching and brushing away the detritus that hid where the paths crossed.

Witches. Mullarky would have spat if he wasn't the one responsible for cleaning the floor. She had disturbed the ground. This was her fault.

Was this man a witch? Or wizard?

Mullarky closed his eyes and a pain instantly stabbed at him in the forehead. With a gasp, he opened them and then, with trembling limbs, lifted himself back to his feet to peer out of the window once more.

The man was still there. Such pain he was in, although he was not a wizard, nor fae, nor any other magical creature that Mullarky could ascertain. He was human. A human in an extraordinary amount of pain and panic, staring down at the ancient crossroads, muttering to himself.

Mullarky squeezed the duster in his hands.

This wouldn't do. This wouldn't do at all.

As he straightened, considering the possibility of marching out there right then and confronting the poor man, he heard Mauve leaving her bed upstairs. Flinching back, Mullarky studied the man as he straightened and turned. For the slightest of moments, their eyes met through the window and the man hesitated. Mullarky waited, wondering if the sight of him would bring the man to his senses. But then there was the sound of footsteps on the stairs and Mullarky reluctantly left the window.

Erica

Erica Murray sighed as they wandered into the grand dining hall of the Georgian townhouse.

'Still not decided what to do?' Jess asked, staring down at the 'phone in her hand. On the screen, words flickered and jumbled.

'No. What would you do?' Erica asked, hands on her hips as she surveyed the darkened room. She was tempted to put on the light, but there seemed little point. Jess followed as she moved around the room and out through a door that led to a beautifully sleek, modern kitchen.

'Honestly? I think I'd move in with Alfie.'

Erica sighed again. It had become a bad habit.

'I can't,' she murmured.

'Why not? The amount your landlord has put your rent up by is insane. I couldn't afford that with

Marshall, not with Ruby in tow, I have no idea how you're supposed to afford it on your own.'

'I think I'd be able to afford it if I had a well-paying career,' Erica mumbled, gazing around the kitchen and opening a door onto a pantry. She closed the door again and wandered over to another, finding herself back in the hallway. 'We need more clients,' she told Jess.

'Yeah.'

'That's one option. Grow the business more.'

'Well, I mean, I think we should be doing that anyway,' Jess pointed out.

'Yes, but quicker. So I can afford rent. The other option is to move back in with my parents.'

'Or...in with Alfie,' Jess repeated.

Erica pursed her lips and opened a door on the right. Darkness greeted them. Jess peered over her shoulder and gave a small tut.

'I can't move in with Alfie. I'll be unreachable. What if something happens? What if you need to get hold of me? Or my parents need me? Or Gran? I won't know anything about it until Alfie does and then I'll still need him to hold my hand just to get back. It's not practical.'

'I thought you said if you married Alfie, you could come and go as you please? Is this the cellar they mentioned?' Jess asked.

Erica looked at the wooden steps leading down into darkness.

'Has to be,' she said. 'Ready?' The cellar was where the client was certain all of the noises were coming from. Erica had decided to work the house from top to bottom, which, considering it was three floors plus an attic and a cellar, was a lot of work.

'To go down into a dark cellar that's supposedly haunted? Sure, why not.'

Erica grinned, glancing back to Jess over her shoulder. A year ago Jess would have been quaking in her shoes, now she was practically nonchalant. Jess had come so far since they'd started their paranormal investigation business, and Erica had a feeling her friend knew just as much as she did about this job.

Pulling out her phone and tapping on the torch, Erica slowly made her way into the darkness.

'Can't we just put the light on?' Jess hissed from behind.

'Not yet,' Erica murmured back. Then she stopped and held up a hand. Jess smashed into the back of her.

'Ow!'

'I gestured to stop.'

'Yes, and if we'd put the light on, I would have seen it.'

Erica opened her mouth to admit defeat when she heard the noise again.

'What is that?' she murmured.

Jess showed Erica her phone and the app on the screen that wasn't doing much.

They made their way carefully down the stairs to discover a large laundry and storage room leading onto another dark room through an open door.

'Boiler making noise?' Jess suggested, pointing to the combi-boiler in the corner of the laundry room.

They both pulled a face. It hadn't been a boiler noise.

'Something's not right about this,' said Erica, and then, loud enough to make Jess jump, 'Hello? Is anyone there?'

Jess gave Erica a light smack on the arm.

There came no answer. Erica moved towards the darkened room when there came a scuttling noise and then the sound of breathing.

Jess was at Erica's shoulder instantly.

'Doesn't sound like a spirit, demon or imp to me,' she whispered.

The women exchanged a look.

'That's the only way into the cellar, right?' Erica asked loudly.

'Yup,' said Jess. 'And from the history of this place, there's never been another way in.'

The noise sounded again: a light scuffle and then – was that a giggle?

Erica rolled her eyes.

'Oh spirits!' she cried. Jess stared at her with wide eyes. 'My name is Erica. If you are here, please make yourself known.'

A muffled sound came from the darkened room

and Erica leaned forward, found the light switch and then narrowed her eyes against the brightness.

It was a cinema room with plush red velvet chairs and a large screen on the wall opposite them. Over to the right was a table with slushie and popcorn machines.

Jess whistled.

'Oh, to have money.'

Erica scoffed and moved into the room, checking down the three rows of seats, and then turning back to Jess and opening her arms. There was no one there.

Jess was looking over their heads, studying the ceiling. There was no hatch, no ladder, no straying ceiling panel, nothing to suggest foul play. And yet someone had been moving in this room and giggling about it.

Erica sat in one of the red velvet cinema seats and glanced back to Jess.

'What do you think?'

'I don't know,' said Jess. 'It's odd, right?'

Erica nodded.

'Definitely odd. And nothing out of the ordinary came up on the plans?'

'Nope.'

'But this place was owned by merchants once upon a time, right?'

'We're in Clifton,' Jess pointed out. 'Safe to say we're standing in a cellar once owned by one of the top Bristol merchants. I couldn't find much information in such a short time, so I don't know what they were selling. But given where we are, I can take an educated guess.'

Again, they exchanged a look.

Jess looked down at her feet.

'Perhaps someone buried under the floor? I've been listening to history podcasts with stories of slave owners burying their slaves under their cellars.' Jess shuddered. 'That was in America, but still. Who knows what rich people get up to in their cellars.'

Erica shook her head, studying the room thoughtfully.

'Eating popcorn and drinking slushies, apparently,' she mumbled. She stood and walked up and down the rows of seats, searching beneath and around them.

Both women straightened and froze at the sound of footsteps.

Jess slowly turned to Erica.

'Someone going up the cellar stairs,' she murmured.

Erica nodded and gestured for Jess to go ahead and check it out. Jess stared at her dumbfounded and then repeated the gesture.

'What does that mean?' she hissed.

Erica went to sigh but caught herself and held it in. Pushing past Jess, she led the way back into the dark laundry room and shone her torch on the stairs. Then, in a burst of energy, she ran up the steps, her feet making a racket against the wood. At the top she stopped and jumped left and right, searching. Then she looked back down to Jess with a frown.

'No one here.'

Lips pursed, Jess followed Erica at a much slower pace. She'd given up on the app, closing it to turn on her torch instead. As she climbed the steps, her hand trailed along the wall.

She stopped about five steps down from the top. 'Huh.'

'What?' Erica joined her and they both stared at the wall beside the steps where there was an obvious wooden cupboard door. Erica flicked on the cellar light and they both blinked as their eyes adjusted.

'I did say we should have just turned on the light,' Jess mumbled, switching off her torch.

'You need to remember to take things slowly,' said Erica, opening the cupboard door and using her torch to peer inside. A broad smile grew on her face and then she gave Jess a nudge. Jess looked into the supposed cupboard and sighed.

'Love it,' she murmured. 'I absolutely could not live here, but I love it.'

'Right?' Erica closed the door. 'Time to meet with the client.'

'She won't be happy,' said Jess. 'I get the feeling she's one of those who might put up a fight about paying.'

'Well, that's how rich people stay rich, isn't it,' said Erica, walking back up the steps.

Erica and Jess found Marjorie Bellows in her living room, sitting on the sofa, scrolling on her phone. She jumped up when the women walked in.

'Did you find anything?' she asked. Her skin was pale, but it had been pale when she'd opened the front door. Erica assumed that was just her complexion. A pretty woman in her forties wearing an expensive dress, smelling of expensive perfume, but the bags under her eyes gave her away. She'd tried to cover them with makeup, but it didn't take much for the façade to fall. Just as it did in that moment, as her twelve-year-old son appeared at the door.

'Mum? Is it over yet?'

Marjorie held out an arm but her son stayed put, staring at Erica and Jess. Erica stared back hard.

'I think we should have a chat,' said Jess in her best professional, soothing voice. She gestured for their client to take a seat and then suggested that her son join them.

'Oh, I don't think so,' Marjorie began.

'I think he'll find it interesting,' said Jess, pointing for the boy to sit beside his mother. He did so and Erica narrowed her eyes slightly. Did he waver? Was that a flicker of something?

'You're right about your cellar,' Jess began. 'That's where most of the activity is taking place.'

'So, there is a ghost?' asked the boy.

Erica caught his eye and smiled in such a way that the boy's own smile faded and he sat back.

'Not exactly,' Jess explained.

'Then what is it? Please don't tell me it's the boiler making noises. Boilers don't sound like children running up and down the stairs,' said Marjorie. 'My husband is wrong about that. Isn't he?'

'It isn't your boiler,' said Erica, her gaze still on the client's son. 'I actually wonder if we should show you.' She glanced at Jess, who nodded.

Together, they led Marjorie and her son to the top of the cellar stairs and opened the cupboard door.

'Do you use this at all?' Erica asked.

'It's just a little storage cupboard. It's in a strange place, yes. But I never gave it much thought. We don't keep anything in there, but I used to keep...' Marjorie's voice faded away as she peered into the cupboard. 'What the hell is that?'

'You're not used to seeing it like this?' Erica hazarded.

The woman simply shook her head, staring into the cupboard that was less a cupboard and more a tunnel that led beneath the ground floor of the house.

'This has always been here?' she breathed.

'A hidden tunnel.' Jess nodded. 'My best guess is that it was created by a previous owner for secret storage. Perhaps even by the original merchant who had this place built.' Her words were speeding up; she was getting far too excited by the history of the place.

Erica watched Marjorie and interjected before Jess could get carried away. 'It's where the noises are coming from,' she said gently.

Marjorie snapped up to look at Erica, then she straightened, turning away from the cupboard door and hugging herself tightly. As she moved away, her son was revealed, standing at the top of the stairs. Erica eyed him.

'Did you know this existed?' she asked, keeping her tone innocent.

His eyes widened a fraction and then, a little too late, he shook his head.

'What does this mean?' Marjorie looked to Jess.

'Let's go back and sit down,' Jess suggested, herding everyone back up to the living room. Once they were seated, she glanced at Erica and said, 'Mrs Bellows, your house isn't haunted.'

Marjorie frowned.

'But the noises. And that...that tunnel!'

'There are no spirits in this house, Mrs Bellows,' said Erica gently. 'No spirits, no demon, no malevolent presences.'

'Which is a shame, given the history of the house,' Jess added.

'But what you do have, however, is a son who I imagine enjoys a good prank.'

All three women looked at the boy and he sank back into the sofa he had been perched on.

'You?' his mother whispered.

'You've been hearing a child giggling and running up and down the stairs,' Erica continued. 'We heard it too. It certainly wasn't a spirit.'

'How do you know?' Marjorie asked defiantly.

'Because we've met the things you're worried about,' Jess told her. 'The things that giggle and don't sound quite right. The things that run up and down stairs when there's nothing there. The things that hover over your head and breathe down your neck. Or pinch and scratch at your child's legs.'

'And we've also met a young man who thought it would be a good idea to carve symbols into trees and ended up summoning a demon into this world. It killed a girl,' said Erica, making eye contact with the boy. 'There's nothing strange in your house, Mrs Bellows, but I did notice the Ouija board up-stairs.'

Marjorie started and glanced at her son.

'Oh, I...' She sighed. 'That was supposed to be a surprise. For your birthday,' she told him.

He did his best not to react, but both Erica and Jess noticed the edge of excitement that filled his eyes.

'Throw it away,' Erica suggested. 'Better yet, I'll buy it off you.'

Marjorie's features hardened.

'What? Absolutely not.'

'Mrs Bellows, Ouija boards can be incredibly dangerous. Use them enough, keep opening that door, and you don't know who will walk through. Right now, there aren't any spirits here, but there will be if you use that board. And it won't just be a spirit. Chances are something much stronger will come through. And it won't run up and down the cellar stairs giggling. It won't even crawl through that tunnel and try to scare you. It will haunt your dreams. It will pin you down as you sleep and bind your chest so you can't breathe. It will follow your son like a shadow throughout his life, making him miserable.' Erica stopped as Jess put a subtle hand on her knee.

Marjorie Bellows, her eyes brimming, stood up.

'I think it's time you left. Please.'

3
Jess

Erica walked out of Marjorie's beautiful townhouse and waited on the pavement for Jess.

'I'm sorry,' Jess told their client at the front door. 'We didn't mean to scare you. You have a stunning house, and it's wonderful that the noises you're hearing are your son playing pranks rather than anything seriously scary. Although you might want to get a builder to check out that tunnel. I know I would. It's just...we really have seen some scary stuff, Mrs Bellows. If you change your mind about not using the Ouija board, just let me know. We'll happily buy it off you if it means we can keep people safe from it.'

'It's a collector's item,' Marjorie said.

Jess flinched.

'Like I said, we'll buy it from you.' She passed Marjorie her business card with her contact details and her mouth became dry as she prepared to say what she had to. 'I'll be in touch with our invoice.'

Marjorie's eyes darted back to her.

'But you didn't do anything.'

Jess sighed inwardly.

'Do you feel better knowing that there isn't a spirit in the house?'

'I don't feel better being told my son has been playing jokes on us.'

'If it wasn't for this survey, you wouldn't know about that tunnel. Imagine if your son had become trapped.' Jess stopped herself, her tongue sticking to the roof of her mouth. It didn't bear thinking about.

Marjorie softened a little.

'It's just the price of the survey,' said Jess. 'We don't charge for things we haven't done. And I'll include an offer for the Ouija board, see what you think.'

Marjorie gave a nod, which Jess took as an excuse to turn away and join Erica on the road. The door was closed firmly behind her, the sound making her wince.

'Well, that went well,' said Erica as Jess reached her.

Jess let out the sigh she'd been holding in.

'More clients,' she mumbled. 'Better clients.'

'Oh, come on. You've been dying to look in these houses for years,' said Erica, gesturing to the Georgian townhouses either side of them. 'Don't tell me you didn't enjoy that.'

Jess beamed.

'Wasn't it gorgeous? Just need to win the lottery and me, Marshall and Ruby could move right in. That tunnel was fascinating. I get the feeling Mrs Bellows didn't feel the same, though.'

'Don't buy a house full of history if you don't want surprises,' said Erica. 'I imagine we'll get a call back at some point, once her kid's played with that Ouija board.'

'It's a collector's item, don't you know.'

Erica grinned.

'I bet. If it really is old, and she hasn't been dupped, then that's worse. Chances are there's already something attached to it.'

Jess frowned.

'Wouldn't we have felt it? Wouldn't *you* have felt it?'

'Maybe,' Erica agreed. 'I guess we have to hope for the best.'

'Pfft.' Jess threw an arm around Erica's shoulders as the car came into view. 'But how will we grow the business if rich people don't summon angry spirits and ask us for help?'

Erica laughed and unlocked her sky blue Mini Cooper. They climbed into the car and Jess lent her head back as Erica started the ignition.

'When are you going to move in with Alfie?' she asked, a smile playing on her lips.

Erica shot her a look before pulling out onto the road.

'How's the wedding planning going?'

Jess's smile fell and she groaned.

'Mum keeps making it bigger and bigger. I keep suggesting to Marshall that we just elope, but he wants my parents to like him so badly.'

'He's practically renovating their house for them, what more can he do?' Erica said as they drove out of Clifton.

'I actually think he might be starting to come around to the idea,' Jess continued softly. 'Paul's wedding last weekend was an eyesore.'

Erica smiled.

'Do you regret going to your ex's wedding?'

'A little,' Jess admitted. 'It was weird. A lot of people giving me a lot of strange looks. But Ruby had to be there, for her dad's wedding. And I just couldn't put her through all of that alone. I tell you what was nice, though.' She turned her head to look at Erica. 'Being able to introduce Marshall to all of Paul's stuffy relatives who never did like me. They were either annoyed that I had a man who could actually fix things or I think they were a little intimidated by his size.' Jess chuckled. 'Or maybe it was all in my head.'

'Either way, Marshall made it bearable.'

'Exactly.'

Erica glanced at Jess.

'Your wedding will be amazing, you know. Whatever you choose to do.'

Jess sighed. It was true that there was still time.

No deposits had been paid yet.

'We're visiting my parents this weekend. Marshall offered to help with some house stuff and Mum suggested we bring Ruby and have a proper Halloween weekend.'

'Oh, I forgot it's Halloween on Sunday.' Erica pulled a face.

'Should be the best time of year for business. We should be doing more,' Jess pointed out.

Erica shrugged.

'What can we do? The hotel is closed while they fix that flooding problem. We couldn't hold a paranormal investigation night there if we wanted to.'

Jess looked at Erica.

'Don't we want to? It'd be fun.'

Erica remained quiet. Jess shifted so that she could look at her friend better.

'What's going on?' she asked.

'I don't know,' said Erica. 'I'm just tired, I guess. This running a business thing is hard. Hustling for clients is hard. Especially when you do the work and they don't want to hear the outcome. Should we be lying? Should we have told Mrs Bellows that there was a spirit?'

'Of course not.' Jess looked out at the Downs as they drove past, the large trees dropping their golden and red leaves. She loved this time of year. When they'd driven there that morning there had been a low level mist over the grass. 'You need a break,' she added gently, still staring out of the window at the dog walkers and joggers. 'Why don't you come with us this weekend?'

Erica pulled a face.

'To help your parents with the house?'

'No. No, no. There's a fair happening on the high street. Come to that with me and Ruby. We'll eat toffee apples and go on some silly rides. It'll be fun.'

'I could stay in a hotel,' said Erica wistfully.

'You could. And you could bring Alfie,' Jess suggested, gently elbowing her friend.

Erica laughed.

'I'm not sure he'd like to stay in a hotel, but I could ask him. It would be fun. Go on then. I'm in. I'll check out if I can find a hotel room when we're back. If you're sure that's okay?'

'Of course it is!' Jess looked ahead with a satisfied smile.

Erica glanced at her.

'You want me to talk your mum out of a big wedding, don't you.'

'No! But, you know, if the topic of conversation comes up, then that might be good of you,' Jess said slowly. 'Maid of honour.'

Erica pulled a face, then laughed.

'Maid of honour, huh?'

'With a big, flouncy dress.' Jess nodded.

Erica barked a laugh.

'Okay, okay! You win. I'll try and talk to your mum. I'll have your back. But there'll be toffee apples, right?'

'All the toffee apples, candy floss and burgers you want.' Jess held out her fist and Erica bumped it in agreement.

'Was that very old of us?' Erica asked after a moment.

'Nah, we're cool,' said Jess, before they both burst into laughter.

4
Rick

Rick Cavanagh was already regretting his choice. Not that it had fully been his choice. His old boss had somewhat forced his hand. Which was probably why they weren't trusting him to go out on his own yet.

'Morning, Sandra.'

The receptionist glanced up at him briefly and then, eyes back on the screen, she grumbled, 'You're still not allowed out, Detective.'

Rick stopped on his way to the doors, heaving a deep sigh. Turning on Sandra, he leant on her desk.

'C'mon. You know they're keeping me here against my will. This isn't right.'

She shrugged.

'Who are you going to tell? The police?' She barked a laugh and then went back to her screen.

Rick's gaze drifted down to her desk.

'I was forced here, you know. Kidnapped.'

Sandra didn't respond.

'Blackmailed, more like,' Rick corrected himself. 'It was a form of kidnap.'

'You'd know more about that than me, Detective,' Sandra muttered.

Rick watched her for a moment before glancing back down to her desk. There was a notebook and pen, a pile of post, a pot of pens and elastic bands, the phone, the key to the top drawer...

'Haven't you ever just wanted to disappear, Sandra? That's all I wanted to do. But DCI Burns made me choose...'

'Hmm.'

Rick glanced back up to Sandra.

'Stay in this twisted place or go to prison.'

'Poor you, being offered a great paying job with a pension.'

Rick frowned.

'I have to act as if I'm above the law.'

Sandra shrugged and began tapping at her keyboard.

'And you get paid a decent amount for it.' She stopped and looked up at Rick. 'Look, I know. You screwed up, went back in time, met your wife when you shouldn't have, ruined your own timeline, lost everything you love and face a prison sentence because of it. And yet, here you are with a second chance, a good job and a future. Maybe if you could just see the opportunity being handed to you, they'd let you out of that door, on assignment, and you can stop bothering me. Or, and this is just a suggestion, Rick, you could go and complain to someone else.' She returned to her computer.

Rick stared at her, a lump growing in his throat.

'Thanks for summing it all up so nicely,' he mumbled.

'Sorry to be harsh.'

'No, no. That's what people around here do, right?' Rick pushed off the reception desk and moved away, past a tall plant, as if heading towards the lifts. He paused, hidden by the leaves of the fern, and watched Sandra relax. She shook her head to herself, sighed, lifted her tea mug, found it empty and quietly swore. Rick's stomach flipped as she rolled her chair back and walked away from reception, towards the nearest kitchenette, shoes tapping on the tiled floor.

Rick didn't hesitate.

Springing forward, he reached the desk and immediately found the key. Unlocking the top drawer, he slipped out the piece of paper he'd noticed Sandra putting inside only the day before, then he closed and locked the drawer, replaced the key and was gone before Sandra returned.

That had been the easy bit.

Rick hummed to himself in the lift as it glided up the building. There was a ding and the doors opened on the fifth floor. Striding with purpose, Rick found DCI Burns at his desk. The tall, lanky man was frowning, but that was nothing new.

'Sir? May I have a word?'

Burns glanced up at Rick and a hint of a smile touched the corners of his lips.

'Sure.'

Burns led Rick to a small meeting room and shut the door behind them.

'Have you come to your senses yet? Or do I need to book another six months of training?'

Rick shuddered inwardly.

'No, thank you, sir. I would like an assignment.'

Burns gave Rick an appraising look.

'Fine.' He sat back. 'You'll be teamed up with one of my experienced detectives.'

Rick almost spluttered.

'I have experience, sir.'

'Not enough and not in this branch,' said Burns. His gaze lifted slowly to meet Rick's. 'And you won't be given a time travel device until your third assignment.'

Rick's stomach twisted. He nodded.

'That's fine.'

'Can't have you disappearing on us.'

'No. Sir.'

'Not that it's that easy anymore. We've learned lessons from you, Cavanagh. The devices have been altered.'

'Yes, sir.'

'Good. Well, go back to your room and I'll email you the assignment details.' Burns stood and held out a hand. 'I'm glad you've finally come to your senses, Cavanagh. I was truly worried I was going to have to arrest you.'

Rick forced a smile and shook the man's hand.

'I'm sorry it took so long, sir.'

Burns grinned and gave an almost playful shrug, opening the door and letting Rick out first. As they wandered back to Burns's desk, Rick made some pleasant small talk and then headed back towards the lift, to the second floor where his room was.

Instead, he stepped off the lift on the sixth floor and hurried down the corridor, pulling the slip of paper he'd found in Sandra's desk from his pocket.

Stopping outside a door marked 'Storage', his lifted the paper and punched in the entry code to the door's security system. The door opened and Rick entered, closing it behind him. For a moment, he stood in the darkness, breathing hard.

Moving slowly, fingers groping, he found the light switch and allowed his eyes to adjust. Around him were shelves and shelves of boxes and, up ahead, was a safe. Ignoring the shelves, Rick crouched in front of the safe and lifted the piece of paper again. He entered the number on the keypad and the safe made a horrendous noise as it told him access was denied.

'Shit.'

He tried another number.

Access denied.

He tried again.

Access denied.

'Shit, shit, shit.'

There was one more number and then he'd be out of options.

The door to the safe swung open and Rick clapped a hand over his mouth to stop himself laughing with relief. Inside was a cardboard box overflowing with the shiny time travel devices used by the police force and secret service. Rick took the top one and straightened as the door to the cupboard opened.

There was a short pause as the newcomer made sense of what they were seeing and then, 'You know, I had a feeling you'd be here.'

'Sorry, sir,' said Rick, slapping the device onto his wrist and turning to face DCI Burns. 'But you know I can't stay.'

'Next time I see you – and I will see you again soon, Cavanagh – I'm going to arrest you.'

Rick pushed the right buttons, overriding the alterations as instructed by a drunken colleague one night, gave the device a twist and, with a mock salute to DCI Burns, vanished in a flash of bright light.

5

Erica

'You lied to me.'

'Pish! I'd never lie to you,' said Minerva, handing the end of a banner to Erica, standing on the top of a stepladder.

'Nope. You lied to me. It dawned on me the other day.'

'What did I lie about?'

Erica tied the end of the banner in place and leaned back to check her work. Happy with the banner's placement, she made her way back down and put her hands on her hips as her grandmother stared at her.

'You said that if you married the fae, you'd become one of them and immortal.'

Minerva frowned.

'When did I say that?'

'When you first told me about Alfie.'

Realisation grew like a light in Minerva's eyes and then she burst out laughing, making Erica jump.

'Did I say that? Oh, Erica, my love. I'm sorry. Your mother was so against you ever meeting Alfie, I probably thought that was a good compromise. You know, you can meet him but it's not like you'll want to marry him. Because if you do, you'll become one of them. Or whatever.' Minerva dismissed the concept with a wave of her hand.

Erica studied her as Minerva looked up at the banner.

'Why haven't you married Eolande, then?'

Minerva pursed her lips.

'I don't like it.'

Erica frowned.

'Marriage?'

'What? No. The banner. No one needs to be reminded that I'm ninety.' Minerva grimaced.

Erica smiled, looking back to the HAPPY 90TH BIRTHDAY banner hanging across her parents' living room.

'I think they do, Gran. Otherwise how will they know that you're ninety? You look a good twenty years younger and you act about seventy years younger.'

'Why would anyone want to be reminded that they're ninety?' Minerva declared, hands on her hips. 'And I look thirty years younger, thank you very much.'

Erica laughed and gave her grandmother a quick hug, filling her nostrils with Minerva's scent of sage, sandalwood and toffee.

'So why haven't you married Eolande?'

'Why would I?' Minerva sniffed, turning her attention to the balloon decorations.

'Because you love each other and so that you can travel between her world and this world on your own?' Erica waited for her grandmother's reaction.

Minerva moved her eyes to look at Erica without turning her head.

'Alfie told you that?'

Erica nodded.

'Are you going to marry him?' Minerva hissed, glancing over her shoulder to the door and where Erica's mother was bustling around the kitchen.

'I don't know,' said Erica when in fact she'd meant to say no.

Minerva's eyes widened.

'Is there a reason you haven't married Eolande?'

Her grandmother shook her head.

'No reason whatsoever.'

'What? It's never come up?' Erica raised an eyebrow. She couldn't imagine Eolande not suggesting marriage to Minerva, their love was palpable.

Minerva shrugged.

'It's only recently that it's become just the two of us.'

'What does that mean?'

Minerva gave Erica a playful look.

'What do you think it means?'

Slowly, a look of disgust grew on Erica's face and her grandmother laughed. 'Oh, don't be such a prude! You haven't been tempted to try any of the other fae in bed? Trust me, after decades of marriage, you want to have your cake and eat it.'

'And Eolande was okay with that?'

'No,' said Minerva gently. 'But it was something that I needed and she understood. She's asked me to marry her many times,' she continued quietly. 'Maybe it'll be time to say yes soon.'

Erica followed her gaze back up to the banner, a ball of dread dropping into her gut.

'What does that mean?' she whispered, not sure if she wanted the answer.

The shadow that had fallen across the room lifted as Minerva turned back to her with bright eyes and a wide smile.

'I smell cake baking,' she announced. 'Let's go see if your mum needs help with the icing.'

With that, Minerva Warner left the room and Erica watched her go, feeling a deep need for Alfie's arms to be around her. Instead, Daisy the elderly golden Labrador wandered into the room and looked up hopefully, tail wagging.

'Hello, my lovely one,' said Erica, crouching and giving the dog a cuddle. Daisy licked her cheek and Erica laughed, wiping it away and ruffling the old dog's ears, kissing her head.

When Erica followed her grandmother into the kitchen, she found her mother making cups of tea while the cake cooled. Bramley, the family's young black Labrador, sat on his bed obediently, his eyes on the cake, drool gathering at his lips.

Minerva sat at the large table and looked away quickly when Erica appeared. Erica frowned at her.

'I think you should move back in here,' said her mother.

Erica narrowed her eyes at Minerva and her grandmother made a show of avoiding her.

'Oh? Why do you think that? What's Gran been saying?'

Esther sighed and turned on her daughter.

'If you can't afford the rent, I'd rather you move back in with us than marry Alfie.'

Erica almost laughed, but held it together.

'I'm not marrying Alfie, Mum.' She gave her grandmother a playful admonishing look and Minerva pulled a face. 'If I ever get married, it'll be for love,' Erica continued. 'I'm certainly not marrying a fae just because his house is rent free.'

'How much are deposits these days?' Minerva asked gently. 'I could give you your inheritance early.'

Erica shook her head.

'Buying a house is out of the question.'

'She wouldn't get a mortgage in this economy, Mum,' Esther agreed. 'Which is why you should move back here. Save your money, pay us some token rent. Other people your age are doing it. It's nothing to be ashamed of.'

It wasn't, and yet the idea of being in her mid-thirties and still living with her parents hurt a little.

'We just need to grow the business, that's all. We're working on it.'

The women in her family were hardly subtle, so Erica saw the look Esther and Minerva exchanged.

'Anyway, it's good to know I won't turn immortal if I do choose to marry Alfie. Although I'm sure they don't believe in divorce.'

Minerva shrugged as Erica sat beside her.

'Not all fae relationships last. They don't have divorce, as such, but marriages can end amicably. I wouldn't worry about that. And no, you won't become immortal. But if you live in their world, bound to one of them like that, you will begin ageing slower.' Minerva twisted a loose thread from her skirt in her lap.

'Oh yeah. I heard about that.'

Minerva glanced up at Erica.

'The woman who tried to drug me,' Erica explained. 'Alfie's lovely neighbour. Remember?' Erica's stomach remembered, turning at the memory.

'Another reason that you are absolutely not moving in with that man,' said Esther, placing a mug of tea in front of her mother. 'Tea?'

Erica shook her head.

'No, thanks. I should be heading off.'

'Work?' asked Minerva.

Erica hesitated for a little too long and Minerva's eyes lit up.

'If you're going to the cemetery, I'd love a lift.'

'No!' Both Erica and Minerva flinched as Esther raised her voice. 'We have a birthday party to plan, Mum. You can go to the cemetery afterwards.'

'Pfft. I don't even want a birthday party.' Minerva crossed her arms and Esther, flustered, threw her hands up.

'What? Why? You said you wanted a party!'

'We bought a banner and everything,' said Erica, trying to keep the grin from her face.

'I'm making a massive cake, Mum!' Esther pointed at the practice cake on the side, waiting patiently.

'Oh, yes, well, obviously I want the cake, love.'

'She hates the banner,' Erica told her mother. 'She doesn't want to be reminded that she's ninety.'

Esther softened.

'Well, no. None of us do, to be honest.'

There was a silence, broken by Bramley barking as the front door opened and closed. The kitchen was suddenly bereft of dogs as they ran to greet Erica's father. He entered the kitchen holding a bag higher than Bramley was jumping and muttering to the dog to get down.

Esther took the bag from him and he sat with a huff before finally noticing the silence amongst the women, looking up from Erica to Minerva and, finally, to his wife.

'Am I interrupting?'

'No,' said Esther, looking through the bag's contents. 'Mum doesn't want a birthday party anymore and doesn't want anyone knowing she's ninety, and your daughter is apparently talking about marrying Alfie just so she has somewhere to live.'

Erica's stomach turned and she snapped up to look at her father as his eyes widened at her. He opened his mouth, but she got there first.

'She's joking, Dad. I'm not marrying Alfie.'

'You can move back in with us,' John told her. 'It's really no problem.'

Erica warmed as his eyes softened. He glanced at Esther's back and then gave Erica a small, secret smile. She smiled back.

'I haven't figured out what I'm doing yet.'

'They just need to grow the business,' Minerva declared. 'Which you're doing, aren't you?'

'We are,' said Erica. 'Everything's going to be fine.' Except that she'd been saying that so often recently that she hardly believed it anymore. 'Right. I'd best be off. I can take the banner down later, if you'd like?' she asked Minerva and Esther.

The two women looked at one another and then Esther relented.

'Fine. No banner. Do you want a party without a banner?'

Minerva thought on this, sipping her tea.

'Oh, go on then. Eolande and Alfie are coming, though.'

Esther sighed but nodded. She could hardly argue.

'No other fae, though. Right?' Erica checked.

Minerva shook her head.

'Just those two. Sure you can't give me a lift?'

'Mum, the cake, remember? Do you want to help me ice it and then taste test it?' Esther asked, taking cake ingredients out of the bag her husband had given her.

Minerva stopped and blinked. Erica watched, bemused.

'Fine! I'll stay.' Minerva shooed Erica away. 'Go enjoy the cemetery without me.'

Erica's parents both turned to her.

'Don't worry, I'm going to meet Jess,' she told them. 'We have work to do.' She picked up her coat on the way out, along with her bag and keys, pausing to give both of the dogs a quick goodbye cuddle.

When in her Mini Cooper, she took a moment to gather herself before driving to the cemetery.

Alfie was waiting for her. Sitting on the steps that led up to the community run café next to the chapel that now held events and yoga classes. Erica allowed herself a moment to take in the cemetery gardens, developed by the Victorians before being abandoned and left to overgrow, and then rediscovered and tidied up by the local community. The autumn sunshine was peeking through the trees, lighting up the gravestones covered in ivy. There was a fresh smell in the air along with a waft of coffee. Erica's stomach grumbled and she approached Alfie, watching him watching her.

He stood and held out a hand to her. She took it and, without a word, he pressed the back of her hand against his lips. His blue eyes were darker in the autumn light, the breeze lifting his brown hair, long enough to curl about his ears. He wore what seemed to be the only items in his wardrobe: jeans and a white shirt with the top buttons undone. His boots were muddy, as were the bottom of his jeans. He didn't feel the cold, not in the same way Erica did.

His hand brushed over the small of her back, against her thick coat, as she stepped past him and into the shelter of the café.

'Coffee?' he asked.

'Please.' Erica found a table for two in the corner and pulled off her coat. A few minutes later, Alfie arrived with a plate holding a raspberry croissant. Erica grinned and leaned over to kiss his cheek.

'What a day,' she said, pulling the croissant in half and stuffing some into her mouth.

Alfie watched, his eyes dancing.

'Oh?'

'My parents think I'm going to marry you just to

have somewhere to live.'

Alfie started.

'Not because you're madly in love with me?'

Erica chewed quietly as their coffees were placed in front of them. Alfie thanked the woman who had brought them and she flushed a little. Erica narrowed her eyes ever so slightly.

'I don't think they're ready to hear that I'm madly in love with you, yet,' she murmured, swallowing.

Alfie grinned and took her hand to place another kiss on her crumb-covered fingers.

'Hey. How do you fancy a weekend away with me? Over Halloween? There's a fair on the high street in Chipping Briar, where Jess's parents live. They're going up at the weekend so Marshall can help with the house and Jess wondered if we fancied going to the fair with them?'

Alfie ran his finger over the rim of his coffee cup.

'We'd stay in a hotel,' Erica added.

His eyes lifted to hers.

'Or a B and B. Whatever.'

Alfie blinked thoughtfully.

'It's a big step, isn't it? To go away for a weekend together?'

Erica laughed.

'I don't know. I just thought it might be fun. Share a hotel bed, get away from here for a bit.'

Alfie studied her, his blue eyes softening. Eventually, he nodded.

'All right. I do like the idea of having you in a hotel bed.' He winked and Erica did her best to ignore him as a warmth grew in her belly. She inadvertently leaned into him, stuffing more croissant into her mouth.

6

Jess

Jess was contemplating opening a bottle of wine, or maybe a beer, when her phone beeped. It was a message from Erica.

Big yes to Halloween weekend at the fair. Alfie's coming. I've found a hotel on the high street but all others are booked. See you later for work meeting?

Jess sighed in relief and tapped out a reply.

That's great! We're heading up Friday night so just let me know when you're around.
And yes to later. I've got some big ideas. Think we need to brainstorm to get you your rent.

She hit send and looked up at her laptop screen, immediately faced with her mother's email of wedding venues and links to dresses. She glanced at the fridge, newly stocked with beer from the latest weekly shop. She was just about to stand up and go look at the bottles – just look at them – when her phone beeped again.

Yes please! I have some ideas too. My parents are now worried I'm going to marry Alfie and move into his world. How did my life come to this?

Jess laughed out loud and Bubbles, her Bernese mountain dog, looked up from her bed.

Oh, poor you. A powerful, kind man is in love with you and wants to marry you. Your parents will come around.

She waited as the dots indicated Erica was typing out a reply.

I am NOT marrying Alfie. See you later.

Jess laughed again and then placed down her phone and stared at the fridge. She had to pick up Ruby in an hour, there was no way she could have a beer. Or a glass of wine. Not yet.

Sighing, she stood and began making herself a coffee. Bubbles watched, her head on her bed, between her paws.

'Oh.' Jess rushed back to her phone as the coffee

machine whirred.

Forgot to say. Mrs Bellows has paid her invoice. Hurray! But won't sell the Ouija board.

She returned to the coffee machine and by the time she'd sat back down with her drink, Erica had replied.

No problem. Hopefully she'll call us back if the Ouija board goes wrong. Got rent money to find!

Jess smiled and sent a thumbs up emoji. Then she sipped her coffee, closed her mother's email with more force than was needed, and pulled up the spreadsheet she'd started full of business ideas and plans.

It pained her that they were missing out on business opportunities this Halloween, but it wasn't for lack of trying. Other companies had already covered the best ghost tour spots in the city, and their main hotel client was closed for refurbishments – they were just as annoyed as Erica and Jess about the loss in revenue, the flooding hadn't exactly been on their business plan.

Still, they were scrabbling, almost desperately. Jess could see that. Ghost tours in the city centre weren't their thing. Tours around the hotel were better, and they could do with more clients like that, but even so, there was something not quite right about it.

'We need a USP,' Jess told Bubbles. 'A niche. A gap in the market. Something that is just ours.' She blew out air and sipped her coffee again. Was it possible to read too many business books? She seemed to know all the words but still not quite have the ideas.

Maybe Erica would have a clue about what to do next.

The problem was, the only way to make money as paranormal investigators, it seemed, was to hold investigation nights and tours. They were fun for a while, but they lost their shine quickly. Not to mention Erica didn't enjoy annoying the spirits with so many visitors.

All of their major and most interesting cases had been unpaid. The terrifying demon in the woods, the imp in her parents' house, the truth behind the fae seducing teenagers over the bluebells into another world, the power of a coven of women against a poltergeist.

In hindsight, those had been the most exciting experiences. If exciting was the right word. Her nightmares about demons in the woods and angry spirits in her daughter's bedroom were starting to wane. In fact, they'd lessened the night after the imp left her parents' house, and that was something Jess couldn't stop thinking about. Had the imp taken some of her nightmares with it? Had it helped her? Or had she simply figured out how to process all of the terrifying things she'd seen?

Considering how the imp had left, Jess had expected Ruby to suffer more nightmares. It was true that her five-year-old had her quiet moments, when Jess would catch her staring off into space, away in her own world, but when Ruby came back to them, she was her usual bouncy self.

Still, Jess had kept her promise to Marshall and found both her and Ruby a therapist. Ruby was under strict instructions not to tell the therapist too much, though. The little girl had nodded and declared that not everyone would understand the things they had seen: not everyone was a witch.

Jess smiled to herself, sipping her coffee.

A key turned in the front door and Bubbles leapt from her bed, tail wagging. Jess clinked her tooth on her coffee mug and gave the drink an accusing look.

'Hello?'

Jess stood and moved to the kitchen door, leaning against the frame as she watched her fiancé place down a tool bag and give the dog a big cuddle.

'You're home early,' she told Marshall.

The big man, half as broad as he was tall, by her front door looked up with a grin.

'Finished my last job early. Thought I'd come pick up Ruby with you.'

Jess's heart skipped.

'Because you're gorgeous and amazing,' she told him with a wink.

Marshall's eyes grazed over her.

'Had a good day?' he asked, his voice a little rougher.

Something stirred inside Jess.

'Yeah. Erica and Alfie are coming to the Chipping Briar fair with us, for the weekend. They booked a hotel room.'

'Oh, lucky them.' Marshall approached Jess.

'Hmm. And my mum has sent me an email full of links to wedding venues and dresses.'

Marshall nodded, reaching out to envelop Jess in a hug.

'That's nice,' he murmured, breathing in her hair.

'And you've got great timing. My fancy man only just left.'

'Sounds good.' Marshall moved back Jess's hair and kissed the soft skin on her neck. Jess shivered as Marshall straightened. 'Wait. What?'

She laughed, taking his hand and leading him towards the stairs.

'Just wanted to check you were listening.'

'So, no fancy man?'

'No.'

'But your mum did send an email of wedding stuff?'

'Yep.'

Marshall sighed, kicking off his boots and hurrying Jess up the stairs.

'Back in a bit, Bubs!' Jess called to the dog.

'Hey! Longer than a bit,' Marshall complained.

Jess wasn't sure if half an hour constituted 'a bit', but thirty minutes later she was making two coffees in the kitchen while Marshall had a shower. Bubbles had been given a chew and was happily lying on her bed.

Waking up her laptop, Jess went back to the spreadsheet of business ideas. Erica was coming over in a couple of hours and Jess didn't have as much to share as she'd hoped.

Marshall appeared topless, some water droplets still on his close shaven head. They vanished as he pulled a clean t-shirt on and Jess watched the thick muscles in his chest and arms become covered.

'Do we need to talk about the wedding stuff?' he asked, moving to the coffee machine to finish what Jess had started.

'Probably.'

'Do you like anything your mum sent?'

'I haven't really looked.'

Marshall glanced over to her.

'Why not?'

Jess sighed.

'Why can't we just elope?'

Marshall grinned.

'We can. If you want. But I'm kinda hoping this will be my only wedding and I want to really celebrate finding you. It took me a while, you know.

I was beginning to think I wouldn't manage it.'

Jess grinned, the heat in her body rising. She wandered over to him, wrapping her arms around his waist, her fingers slipping under his t-shirt to the warm, clean skin beneath. He hugged her, planting a kiss on the top of her head.

'We can have a big wedding if you want one,' she murmured into him.

'Not a big one,' he corrected. 'But a fun one.'

Jess smiled and kissed his chest.

'We can do that. I've already asked Erica to be on Mum Patrol, try to get her to listen to me about the size of the whole thing.'

They parted and Marshall handed her a coffee.

'Want some help with business ideas?' he offered.

'Oh yes, please!' Jess cried, dragging him over to the table and the laptop. 'This business was your idea, come help me make some money.'

2

Connor

'Would it kill you to empty the washing machine?'

Connor flinched but otherwise didn't move from his seat on the sofa, game controller in hand. His girlfriend, Maggie, appeared at the doorway, one hand slowly stroking the large bump of her belly. 'Connor.'

'Sorry. I'll do it now.' Connor didn't move, his eyes fixed on the screen.

'Connor!'

'What? I said I'll do it now.'

'But you're not doing it now. You're playing your stupid game.'

'Well, I won't be able to play the stupid game when the baby comes, will I? You keep reminding me of that. And I need to relax.'

The controller was snatched from his hand and on the screen there was an explosion of flames. Connor sighed and looked up at his girlfriend.

'You need to relax? I'm growing and carrying

another human life.' She pointed to the bump. 'And while I'm growing a whole other human, I'm cleaning the flat and washing your underwear and tidying up after you, and I just...' Maggie stopped, closed her eyes and took a deep breath. 'Do you know how exhausting you are?' she murmured, turning away and waddling back to the flat's tiny kitchen and the washing machine.

Connor stared at the floor that she'd vacuumed that morning. She'd been calling him exhausting for a while now. Before she got pregnant. That had been an accident, and a huge shock to them both. Still, back then Connor hadn't had the same doomed sensation that she was about to leave him. Now that feeling was on his shoulders every day.

She didn't want a baby with him. She didn't want to be with him. He was exhausting.

Connor's gaze lifted to the TV screen where his respawned avatar was waiting for him to have another go.

If only having another go was that easy.

He'd been laid off from his job two whole months ago and it seemed that everyone else was in the same boat. Jobs were not just hard to come by, they were becoming endangered. And Connor just didn't measure up. Not compared to all those applicants with degrees, living at home with their parents, without a baby on the way, willing to work for lower salaries if it gave them a foothold.

The recruitment agencies were useless; they

never called him back. The job centre was worse; rude and condescending. He'd worked it out, done the research, added up the salaries available to someone like him. Connor would need two jobs just to stay afloat. He'd never see Maggie or his new baby.

She'd be better off if she did leave him. She could find someone better, someone who could provide.

Then, only the day before, the estate agency had informed them that their rent was going up. Again.

That had thrown his sums out of kilter. Now he'd need three jobs. There just weren't enough hours.

Connor balled his hands into fists, forcing back the threatening tears. Maggie, done with the laundry, wandered past to the bedroom.

'I'm sorry, Mags,' he murmured as she disappeared.

'I know.'

'I'll fix it,' he told the empty room. He couldn't hold down three jobs, not without killing himself, but there was another option. On the outskirts of the woods, on Halloween night, was Connor's last hope.

8

Erica

'Why don't you move back in with your parents and then unofficially move in with me?' Alfie offered as he led Erica through his village to the door that led back to Erica's world. The fae world was everything the fae were: lush, seductive, charming. The village was essentially wide dirt roads lined with ancient trees that had been fashioned into houses. The forest that surrounded the village was brimming with life. Now that autumn had arrived, the bright colours of this world had changed from shades of green to gold and red. The browns were still deep and, when the sun shone, the sky was still the brightest of blues. The same blue as Alfie's eyes. Today, however, rain was coming and the dark, blue-grey clouds that lined the sky were heavy with atmosphere, crackling with potential.

'Am I going to miss a storm?' Erica asked, staring

up at them.

Alfie followed her gaze.

'No. I don't think so. Just rain. Are you ignoring my question?'

Erica looked back down, avoiding eye contact with any of Alfie's neighbours as they wandered along. The bag on her back was growing heavier, although not as heavy as it would be when she stepped back into her own world.

'No. I'm not ignoring you. It's an idea. But I'd still be stuck here, wouldn't I. No way for anyone to contact me and the only way out is if you're there to hold my hand?' Erica looked down at their clasped hands. He wouldn't even let her wander around the village without him holding onto her. Not yet. He claimed it was too dangerous still, and after his neighbour had poisoned her earlier in the year, she believed him.

Alfie sighed.

'This was fun, though. And it's stupid to spend so many nights here when you're paying all that rent.'

Erica smiled. He was making such an effort to truly understand the concept of rent and housing markets. Alfie had built his own home, with help from some friends. Often a fae's father would help, but Alfie's father was human and had stayed back in Erica's world. She glanced at him sideways. He wouldn't tell her how long ago his father had died, only that he had led a good, long life.

'You're right,' she admitted. 'It would be more

cost effective to move back in with my parents.'

Alfie pulled a face.

'But you spend so many nights here with me already. What difference would it really make if you moved here?'

'If I moved here, would I be able to leave the house and walk around without you?' Erica held up their clasped hands for emphasis.

Alfie gave a huff.

'Yes,' he managed, reluctantly. 'Your grandmother does.'

'I can't imagine anyone trying to drug my grandmother.'

Alfie smiled.

'You'd be surprised,' he told her. 'But Minerva has developed something of a reputation.'

'But I haven't?'

'Not yet.' Alfie squeezed her hand and slowed as they reached the doorway between worlds. They paused as Erica looked back to the village, breathing in the clean air. Finally, she gave a nod and they stepped back into her world.

The colours faded, the air became thick and filled with the noise of the nearby road. Alfie watched Erica as she tried not to react.

'Move in with me,' he whispered.

'Stop it,' she warned, walking away from him to find the path that would lead them out of the small woodland. Grinning, Alfie followed, pushing his hands deep into his pockets and glancing around them. 'Want to practise talking to the trees?'

Erica shook her head, brushing her fingers over the trunk of an ash as she passed it.

'I think I'm getting pretty good.'

There was a silence, and then Alfie asked, 'We could go check the old gateway? See if it's still closed.'

'I'm sure it is,' said Erica.

Behind her, Alfie puffed out an exhale.

'Sex against a tree?'

Erica barked a laugh and turned back to him, offering her hand. Alfie took it sheepishly and they left the woods still clasping one another.

'What is with you?' she asked. 'You have me. You win. I'm yours.'

Alfie squeezed her fingers.

'Not yet,' he murmured. 'You haven't told Rick your decision. You haven't moved in with me. You haven't agreed to marry me yet.'

'Yet? Like you're so sure that I will agree.'

Alfie smiled his most charming smile and kissed the back of Erica's hand.

'I can see the future, remember.'

'And you can see us getting married, can you?'

Alfie only grinned, moving to wrap an arm around her waist as they found a residential road and wandered along it to where Erica's car was parked. Erica unlocked it and turned to Alfie. He kissed her lips softly, enough to make her consider ditching her client meeting and running back to the woods with him.

'I love you,' she murmured.

He smiled and kissed her again.

'Tell the time traveller and then marry me,' he whispered, slowly backing away and turning to walk home, hands deep in his jean pockets.

Erica watched him go, sighing deeply, desperate to follow him. Shaking herself as he glanced over his shoulder to her before disappearing from view, she got into her car, started the ignition and tried to put her brain into work mode.

'Thought you weren't coming for a moment there,' Jess murmured as she and Erica walked up the steps to the theatre an hour later.

'Of course I was coming. This could be a great new client,' Erica whispered back. 'The client who could pay my rent.'

Jess gave a shaky inhale.

'Sorry I was late,' Erica added. 'Alfie...' She shrugged, as if that was all that needed to be said.

Jess grinned.

'Alfie, huh? I get that. Marshall came home early yesterday, an hour before school let out.'

Erica laughed.

'I did wonder. You seemed a little flustered when I came round. Did you make it to Ruby in time?'

'Just about.' Jess looked up at the entrance doors and then tried to open one. It was locked. She rapped lightly on the glass, peering inside to the dark foyer. 'Did you look at the book I gave you last night? Or were you and Alfie too busy?'

'No, no. I looked at it. It's interesting. I'll give it a proper read and we can sit down and go through it together, make a plan to follow.'

'It's an easy read,' said Jess. 'Shouldn't take long. And it's got some really interesting ideas about growing businesses that work for any industry. You never know. We really have to stick to what we stand for, you know? I think that's really important. It's what will make us stand out.'

Erica nodded but didn't reply. A man had appeared on the other side of the glass and was unlocking the door.

'Hi there,' said Jess as soon as the door was open. 'Jess Tidswell, and this is my colleague, Erica Murray. From Murray and Tidswell Paranormal Investigations. Are you Tim?'

The man was a little taller than Erica with hazel eyes and hair to match. His black rimmed glasses slid down his nose as he looked at them both, and he pushed them back up as he gave a wonky smile.

'Of course. Please, come on in. Yes, I'm Tim. Welcome to our theatre.'

He wore something of a pale blue suit, although it was relaxed with the shirt not tucked in all the way around and the top buttons undone.

'Thank you.' Erica and Jess followed him inside and he locked the door behind them.

It was the usual theatre foyer, with plush red carpet that had seen better days, a ticket office to one side, a concessionary stand closed up with the sweets locked away, and to the left was a door leading into a bar area. In front of them were further stairs, presumably leading to the theatre.

'This is lovely,' Jess remarked, smiling at Tim.

'Thank you. We certainly love it. The building is very old and I believe it's been a theatre for at least a hundred years.'

'Wow.'

'Yes. It closed down for a while in those years, then a community campaign brought it back when developers were threatening to turn it into flats.'

Erica smiled to herself as she gazed up at the ceiling and down the walls.

'What made you reach out to us?' she asked. 'Has anyone had any experiences?'

'Oh yes. There's been quite a few. There's definitely something here. I myself have heard voices when I know I've been alone, and I saw the shadow of a figure once but, again, I was here alone.' Tim shuddered. 'It's really creepy. We don't like to be here on our own much anymore, but so far whatever's here seems to be friendly. We thought it would be nice to see once and for all if there actually is something or someone, and maybe who they are.'

Jess nodded. Erica looked into the bar area from the foyer, listening. No, not the bar. Nor the foyer. She looked up the steps and tilted her head, feeling for something that was mostly instinct.

'Where did you see the figure and hear the voices? Was it more than one voice?' she asked.

Tim followed her gaze.

'Ah, yes. Backstage for the voices but in the gods for the figure. Would you like a tour?'

'Yes, please,' said Jess, her smile completely failing to hide any excitement.

Tim led them up the stairs and then through a door on the left which opened onto a staircase.

'Am I right that you can do a sort of paranormal investigation to see if we have anything here immediately?' he asked as they climbed.

'Yes, although it depends on what you're after,' said Jess, right behind him.

'And there's a fee for that?'

'There is. I believe I attached our rates to the email I sent you?'

'Oh, yes. It wasn't as much as I thought, although I was surprised there was a fee at all. I guess I always assumed paranormal investigators were in it for the love of it. You know, finding out the truth and all that.'

There was a short pause and then Erica replied, 'We know the truth, and unfortunately Bristol is a ridiculously expensive city to live in.'

'Oh, tell me about it. My landlord's just put my rent up.'

'Same,' said Erica.

'I keep joking that maybe I'll move in here for a

while and not tell the owners, but I don't want to do that if it's haunted.' Tim gave a short, nervous laugh and Jess glanced back to Erica over her shoulder with a smirk.

'I don't blame you,' said Erica, glad that she had more options than moving into her place of work without her employer knowing.

'When you say you know the truth,' said Tim as they reached the top of the stairs and he opened the door, ushering them through. 'Do you mean you know for definite that ghosts exist?'

They were in the gods, and a short walk down the corridor revealed the vastness of the little theatre, reaching out below them from the steep seats. Erica hesitated as her mind swam. There were three bunches of seats, each with five rows, separated by steps. Along the top corridor was a door leading to toilets and another to a fire escape and presumably another flight of stairs.

Erica turned her head sharply as something dark flashed across the corner of her eye. There was nothing there, not even a shadow against the dark red walls lit by dim Victorian style electric lamps.

'Everything okay?' Jess murmured.

Erica nodded, eyes still scanning the top right of the gods. Jess cautiously moved down the steps to look out over the theatre. 'It's beautiful,' she whispered under her breath.

'Spirits definitely exist,' Erica told Tim, not taking her eyes from where she could have sworn she'd seen something move. Goosebumps lifted on her arms and a chilled breeze swept across her right arm and only her right arm. 'In many different forms,' she continued. 'I know because I grew up around them. I know because I often talk to them. My grandmother taught me how. They were in her house when I was growing up. Jess knows because they've been inside her house, haunting her daughter's bedroom.' Erica turned to look at Tim. 'When would you like us to do the survey?'

Jess

Jess snapped round to look at Erica at the top of the stairs. What was she doing?

She opened her mouth to protest, or say something reassuring to the client, but Tim got there first.

'Do you think there's something here?' he asked matter-of-factly.

Jess looked back to Erica.

'There's definitely something here,' said Erica. 'I just saw a shadow move, but there's no one else up here, is there.' It wasn't a question but Tim shook his head anyway. 'There's a chill when there's no reason to be one.' Erica rubbed her right arm and finally met Jess's eyes. 'Do you feel anything?'

Jess opened and closed her mouth, glancing down to the theatre below.

'I saw the shadow too,' came Tim's voice. 'It wasn't a figure, though. Not the same thing I saw before. I see shadows darting around all the time, I just thought it was my eyes playing tricks.'

Erica gave a small smile.

'It could be,' she told him. 'Maybe my eyes are playing tricks on me.' She looked down at Jess. 'Shall we check backstage?'

'Wait,' said Tim. 'You can do the investigation now? How long would it take?'

Again, Jess opened and closed her mouth, waiting for the professional answer to find her lips. She couldn't feel anything. Why was it that sometimes she could and sometimes she couldn't? She'd felt the demon in the woods, she'd felt something in her parents' house, although whether that had been the shadows, the spirit or the imp, she couldn't be sure. Perhaps that was it. She couldn't feel the spirits, but she could sense the demons.

Wonderful. That was great.

Jess sighed inwardly and willed the spirit in the gods to reveal itself to her. Just for a moment. An unscary moment, preferably.

Nothing happened.

'An hour, maybe two, for a preliminary survey. That's the basic price on our rate card,' Erica explained. 'We can do that and see what comes up, then see what you want to do from there. A more in-depth survey will take longer and cost a little more, but it may not be needed.'

Tim nodded thoughtfully.

'The cheaper option, please. The shorter one. We're a bit tight on cash, to be honest.' He grimaced. 'When can you do it?'

Jess and Erica studied one another.

'Now?' Jess offered. 'Or at a time more convenient to you.'

'Doesn't it need to be dark?' Tim asked, pulling a face.

'Night is usually the quietest, it makes it easier to hear voices and things, but during the day can work equally as well. We just have to know who else is here and what's going on. Any construction work nearby, any staff meetings, any planned works, that sort of stuff.'

'Oh, well, let's do it now then. That would be great.' Tim grinned. 'Erm, how does it work? What can I do?'

'Show us where you heard the voices,' Erica suggested. 'And tell me the stories of other things people have experienced here.'

Tim agreed and led Erica back to the stairs down to the foyer. Jess followed hurriedly, not wanting to be left alone with a spirit she couldn't see, which was ridiculous considering her job. She slowed at the door, hitting a timer on her phone to start the survey and smiling to herself. As she looked up to the gods one more time, a darkness shifted in the corner.

Heart jolting, Jess froze. She looked down the stairs to Erica and Tim's diminishing voices and then, for some reason she couldn't fathom, she stepped back into the gods. Approaching where she'd seen the patch of darkness, she called out, 'Hello? Is anyone there?'

The darkness lifted and there was nothing and no one. Jess stood there for a while, waiting. She pulled up the dictation app on her phone and set it to record.

'Hello? We don't want to hurt you or cause any trouble. We just want to say hello. This machine here can record your voice so I can hear it. Please answer me if you can. What is your name?' Jess left a long pause and then said, 'Thank you.'

She stopped herself from running out of the gods and down the stairs, but she kept her eyes forward, refusing to look back.

Erica and Tim were at the bottom, waiting for her. Erica smiled.

'Did you see something?'

'A shadow that was moving with nothing to cause it,' Jess explained, holding up her phone. 'I tried to make contact.'

'Did you? Make contact?' Tim's eyes widened.

'I'm not sure yet. We'll find out at the end of the survey when I play this back,' Jess explained.

'Oh, can you record a ghost's voice on your phone?'

Erica and Jess looked at Tim and his cheeks flushed a little. 'I like watching paranormal investigation shows sometimes. Especially this close to

Halloween.'

Jess grinned.

'Yes, exactly. Believe it or not, there are now apps for that.' She glanced at Erica, who gave a subtle shrug. 'Do you want to join us on the survey, Tim?'

His eyes widened further.

'Is that okay?'

'Of course,' said Erica. 'It'd be good to have someone who knows where they're going and all the stories.'

Tim clapped his hands excitedly and then bounded forward, leading them into the theatre.

'Great,' said Jess, pulling out a tablet from her bag and turning it on. 'Before we get going, we just have the survey contract to be signed. Hang on.'

They waited as she opened her contract template, filled in the details and then signed it before passing it to Tim. He read it through, nodded and signed.

Shoving the tablet back into her bag, Jess nodded to Erica. 'Let's go.'

Tim led them through the theatre, past the rows of red velvet seats, quietly telling them a story of one particular play being interrupted at exactly the same point every night until eventually the cast refused to go out on stage. The play's run had to be cut short and the theatre was forced to refund tickets.

'Honestly, we've been struggling for a while,' Tim admitted as they reached the stage and paused.

Jess looked around curiously; she'd never been this close to a theatre stage before. Erica, on the other hand, was focusing on something above them in the gods.

'What was it that interrupted the play every night?' Erica asked gently.

Tim and Jess both followed her gaze and Tim gave a sharp intake of breath as a shadow in the gods moved.

'There's definitely no one up there,' he murmured, perhaps more to himself than to them. 'Is there. No. We didn't see anyone.' He shivered and glanced at Jess. 'I've never seen that much activity in such a short space of time.'

'Sorry,' said Erica. 'That might be our fault.' She turned to look up at the stage. 'What was interrupting the play?'

'Singing,' said Tim. 'Someone singing, but we checked and it definitely wasn't anyone in the audience. It was coming from backstage. But no one backstage could hear it. Only the people on the stage and in the first few rows of the audience.'

'People at the back couldn't hear it?' Jess checked.

Tim shook his head.

'Can we get onto the stage?' Erica asked. 'And backstage, of course.'

Tim led them onto the stage and after a quick check of the curtains, walls and floor, staring up at the ceiling, Erica quickly asked to go backstage.

Behind the stage was a labyrinth. Jess stuck close to the others for fear of getting lost.

There was a narrow corridor leading off to small rooms behind closed doors, although Tim opened a few to explain their functions. Each time, Erica glanced around and then moved on.

Jess tried to take a moment to feel anything for herself, but she wasn't as practised as Erica and she needed more time. Just as she was starting to settle, Erica would move on, taking Tim with her.

They reached the side of the stage and Erica stopped suddenly without warning. Jess had to bounce on her toes to stop herself from careering into the back of her.

Instead of asking what had made Erica stop, Jess took the opportunity to settle herself. She quietened her breathing, focusing on her inhales and exhales, as both Erica and Alfie had taught her. Then she did what could only be explained as spiritually reaching out, a technique that Minerva had told her about. Eyes closed, Jess allowed her mind to wander, reaching out to the stage beyond and the space around them.

When she opened her eyes there was the indistinct figure of a woman in a long dress standing in the middle of the stage, looking out onto the empty seats.

Jess held her breath.

'Has anyone ever died here?' Erica asked quietly, staring at the same figure.

'Not that I know of,' said Tim, oblivious to the apparition standing on the stage.

'How about an actress, or a singer, I suppose,' Erica ventured. 'Blonde hair, a long flowing blue dress.'

'Like Cinderella,' Jess hazarded.

Tim frowned thoughtfully.

'There is a story that before the theatre was closed, decades ago, if not longer, there was a singer who would perform here. She was blonde. There's a black and white photo of her in the foyer. You can't tell what colour her dress is, though. Her husband used to beat her. It was said that the stage was her happy place because he couldn't touch her there. He killed her, but not here. Why?'

Jess sighed.

That was the problem with spirits. Their stories were generally ones of sadness.

'Bring your phone,' Erica murmured to Jess, and then to Tim she said, 'Would you mind staying here for a moment?'

She stepped out onto the stage, Jess close behind with her phone out, bringing up the dictation app and pressing record.

'Hi there,' said Erica gently once they were a comfortable distance from the spirit. 'My name's Erica. This is my friend Jess. We understand that you're a singer?'

The figure of the woman vanished, slowly dissipating into the air.

Neither Erica nor Jess moved.

'We don't want to cause you any harm, but we would really appreciate it if you could talk to us,' Erica continued. 'I understand that appearing like that costs you a lot of energy. I imagine singing does as well, now. My friend here has a machine that can record your voice so we can hear you. I would love it if you could just tell me your name?'

They waited in the echoing silence for a minute and then Erica turned to Jess and gave a subtle nod.

'Thank you,' she told the empty stage.

Jess followed Erica back to where Tim was waiting, a sceptical look about his eyes. She fiddled with the app while Erica described what they'd seen on the stage. Still, Tim didn't seem sure.

'Let's see if we picked anything up,' said Erica.

'We probably won't be able to hear anything until I've got it on my laptop and messed with the levels,' Jess explained. They fell quiet and she hit the play button.

'I would love it if you could just tell me your name?' came Erica's voice.

There was silence, and then static, and then, '*Crysss...*'

Tim slapped a hand over his mouth.

The sound turned back to static and Jess locked her phone.

'As I said, we might hear more when I get it on my laptop.'

Tim shook his head, eyes wide.

'No. No. Hang on.' He turned and rushed away, pausing to gesture for them to follow.

They hurried through the theatre, following Tim, until they were back in the foyer. Embarrassingly out of breath, Jess struggled to keep her breathing normal as Tim disappeared and reappeared a moment later holding a framed photo. He passed it to Erica, who smiled and showed it to Jess.

There, in black and white, was the woman they'd seen standing on the stage, long blonde hair flowing down her shoulders as she smiled and sang. Her dress was grey, given the nature of the photo, but it was easy to imagine it being blue.

Beneath the photo was lettering from an old typewriter.

'Crystal Rose, singer.

1896.'

'That's what we heard,' Tim said in the rush. 'That's what the voice said. On your recording. It said "Crys", Crystal, right?' He looked up at them. 'There was a ghost on the stage.'

Jess was fiddling with her phone again.

'Crystal Rose was on the stage,' Erica agreed.

Jess replayed the recording, and this time they huddled together, getting their ears as close to the held up phone as they could.

'...Tell us your name?' came Erica's voice.

'*Crysss...*'

Tim looked up at them.

'This is amazing,' he breathed. He stood back, chest heaving as he processed everything. 'You see, the reason we called you in – the real reason – is because we're struggling and we thought...maybe... do you run ghost tours? Is that a thing?'

Jess and Erica exchanged a private smile.

'It is,' said Jess.

'But we'll need to do some preliminary work first before we can agree,' Erica cautioned.

Jess nodded.

'How much would it cost?'

'Don't worry,' said Jess, pulling out her tablet again. 'We work with you to make sure it's profitable for both of us. But you have to understand that your theatre is indeed haunted, and the last thing we want to do is annoy or scare the spirits who are here. We'll be working with them as much as with you.'

Tim nodded and gave a shrug.

'Sure. Whatever.'

'Shall we go discuss the options?' Jess asked.

'Yes. In the bar. I'll get us some coffees.'

'None for me, thanks,' said Erica. 'I'd like to go back to the stage, if that's okay? Do some of the preliminary checks now?'

Tim shrugged again.

'Sure.'

Once Tim's back was turned, Erica and Jess did a silent celebration together before Jess followed

him into the bar and Erica ventured back into the
theatre to find their singing spirit.

10

Rick

Rick didn't have time. The irony was not lost on him. He'd flashed to another time, barely checking the year, realised he'd gone back too far and took a deep breath. Around him were fields and somewhere close by the Romans were building a city. Adjusting the device, he prayed to whoever was listening and disappeared again in a flash of bright light.

When he landed, squinting his eyes against the wind and the colours dancing in front of him, he found himself in Bristol at around the right time.

He could have hired a car, but that would leave a paper trail. So instead, he found a taxi.

The journey was spent trying to coax his heart down from his throat. He'd had a plan, he'd been thinking about this for a long time, but now he was here, he wondered if it was the right thing.

Rick smiled to himself. Of course it was the right

thing. Right then, it was the only thing.

He paid the taxi driver with a flash of his bank card, not caring if it worked, and stepped out of the car to face the detached house belonging to Erica's parents.

She might not live there anymore. In fact, since their timelines had been ruined – by him – it was almost as if he didn't know her anymore. But that wasn't true. She was still Erica Murray, the same Erica he'd fallen in love with. The same Erica he'd married and had a baby with.

Taking a deep breath that did nothing to steady him, Rick walked up the gravel driveway and tentatively knocked on the door before he could talk himself out of it. Erica's Mini wasn't there, but her parents' cars were.

Esther opened the door and stared at him wide eyed.

'Hi,' he murmured, giving a weak wave.

Erica's mother opened her mouth but no words came.

'Who is it, love?'

This time it was Rick's eyes that widened. Minerva Warner appeared behind Esther, less frail than he remembered, but much more alive too.

Erica's grandmother looked him up and down as Esther turned to her and simply said, 'Rick.'

Minerva raised an eyebrow.

'The time travelling future supposed husband?'

The 'supposed' hurt, like being stabbed in the

gut, and Rick took a sharp intake of breath.

'You'd best come in,' said Minerva.

'Erm. No?' said Esther, turning on her mother. 'He can't come in. Erica isn't here.'

'So? We're here. And I'd like to talk to the boy. Come in,' Minerva told Rick.

Rick watched Esther, waiting to see what she would do. Sucking on her teeth, Esther let Rick into the house. The smell of polish and dog and sage hit him as he stepped inside and Minerva led him into the kitchen.

'Where's the dog? Dogs,' Rick quietly corrected himself.

It was Esther's turn to look as if she'd been stabbed by his words. He apologised quickly and she gave a small smile, waving his apology away.

'My husband is out with the dogs,' she told him.

'Make us some tea, Esther, love,' said Minerva. 'And you, sit here.' She gestured to a chair at the large table.

Rick did as he was told. Minerva sat opposite and studied him as Esther brewed the tea. Trying not to squirm, Rick stared at the table in front of him, unable to keep eye contact with Erica's grand-mother.

Eventually, she said, 'So, you're the man who claims to be my granddaughter's husband in the future. A time travelling detective.'

Rick gave a weak smile.

'I'm not a detective anymore.' His voice came out

with a croak and he was grateful when Esther placed a cup of tea in front of him. 'I'm in trouble and I don't know what to do.'

Minerva's brow creased as she frowned, thanking Esther for her own cup of tea.

Esther didn't join them. She leaned back against the worktop, out of the way but in earshot, sipping her drink.

'Is this to do with Erica?' Minerva asked.

'I don't know,' said Rick honestly. His lifted his gaze to Minerva. 'I get the feeling I've lost her. And if that's true, then maybe I should just go back and accept my fate. I need to know.'

Minerva gave a sharp single nod.

'She'll be home soon,' said Minerva, throwing a glance over his shoulder to Esther. Rick heard Esther rummaging with something, probably sending Erica a message. 'In the meantime, tell me what you're running from.'

Everything inside Rick relaxed, whether that was thanks to Esther's tea or Minerva's demeanour, he didn't know, but regardless, the words spilled out.

Erica

It took longer than it should have for Erica to open the door to her parents' house. She'd sat in the car for a while, on their driveway, staring at her mother's message again.

Come here asap. Rick is talking to your gran.

Whatever was waiting for her on the other side of the door, this was the time Erica had been waiting for. It was time to tell Rick the truth about her feelings. When she let out a long breath, it came with a shudder.

Finally, clenching her eyes shut and trying hard not to think about, and therefore summon, Alfie, she opened her parents' front door and walked in.

Her father must have been out with the dogs because no barking or wagging tails greeted her.

Instead, there was her grandmother's calm but stern voice.

'Erica? Is that you?'

She wasn't sure she could speak, let alone call out. So she simply walked into the kitchen to find her mother, grandmother and Rick Cavanagh looking at her. Erica's gaze went immediately to Rick's and they stared at each other, until he seemed to read her mind and looked away, fiddling with the empty cup in front of him on the table.

'I'll make some more tea,' said Esther gently.

Minerva gestured to the seat beside Rick, and Erica sat.

'You two need to talk,' said Minerva, giving her granddaughter a pointed look. 'Honestly. Truthfully. And, if need be' – she turned to Rick – 'remember everything I told you. It was lovely to finally meet you, Mr Cavanagh.'

Rick smiled.

'And you, Mrs Warner. A real pleasure.'

Minerva smiled as Esther placed cups of tea in front of Erica and Rick, and then the women left them alone in the kitchen, closing the door behind them.

'Hi,' said Rick after an awkward moment of silence.

Erica stared at him, taking in his light brown hair and soft blue eyes. Something stirred inside her, but it wasn't as strong as it had been. The pull she'd felt towards him when they'd first accidentally met at the wrong time was gone. There was something different about him, as if they were different people, no longing fitting together.

'Hi,' she murmured. 'I've been wondering how to contact you. I hoped you'd show up.'

Rick smiled and shuffled his chair closer, moving to reach for her hands and then seemingly thinking better of it.

'It's all gone wrong, Ricci,' he said quietly, and Erica's chest tightened painfully. 'I think it's time.' He reached into a pocket inside his long brown coat, a hidden one on the inside against his chest, and pulled out a gleaming golden pocket watch.

Erica's eyes widened a little and she stared at the watch as Rick placed it on the table between them.

'Alfie gave me this,' he murmured.

'I know. You told me,' said Erica breathlessly, practically sitting on her hands to stop herself from reaching out to touch it. 'His father gave it to him.'

Rick stared at her.

'I know. He told me, back in Victorian London. How do you know?'

Erica looked up and met his eyes.

'Present day Alfie told me. You met Victorian London Alfie? What was he doing in London?'

Rick tilted his head so slightly it was almost imperceptible.

'You're choosing him, aren't you.'

It wasn't a question and it took the wind out of Erica. She opened her mouth to protest but there were no words. Instead, she looked back to the watch. Even the small sigh that she forced through hurt her chest.

Rick gave a deep sigh and sat back.

'Well. There we go.'

'It's not...' Erica began and then stopped. 'I still...' She fidgeted and finally caved, reaching out for the watch. The gold detail was intricate and the second hand gently ticked time away.

'I'm not even sure it works as Alfie said,' Rick murmured.

'He said it chimes on my birthday.' Erica smiled, brushing her thumb over it.

'That would have been handy when we were married.'

Erica's heart gave a jolt and she looked up to Rick.

'I wish things were different,' she whispered.

He smiled and shook his head.

'No you don't. You're happy. I can tell. I know what you're like when you're happy, Ricci. I used to be the one making you happy.' His smile fell. 'He does make you happy?'

Erica nodded, staring down at the watch.

'And he keeps you safe?'

Erica nodded again.

'When we first met, I thought it would be you. But now, every time we meet, I... It's like we both change every time. Like we drift further and further away. Which is ridiculous. As if the first time we met, we already knew each other. Like we were...meant to be. And now...' Erica bit her bottom lip as tears threatened to spill. 'Love is supposed to be the reverse of that, isn't it?' She glanced up to find him watching her with soft eyes, a gentle smile on his lips. He reached out and brushed a tear from her cheek when it fell as she blinked.

'I should never have left. I should have stayed here with you,' he whispered.

Erica shook her head.

'As far as you knew, you had a wife and baby to get back to. You couldn't have stayed.'

'Then I should have come back the moment I found out what a mess I'd made.'

Erica didn't have a response for that. Yes, he should have. But if he had, then maybe she wouldn't have Alfie right now. Maybe she wouldn't be as happy in the relationship. Maybe she'd have always wondered.

She sniffed.

'There's just no winning here, is there. I honestly don't want to hurt you. That's the last thing I want. And how can I ever know if I'm making the right choice? I can't. I don't know what your version of me was really feeling. I have no idea where I'd be happiest. I just...' She met his eyes. 'I'm so sorry.'

Rick's lip quivered but he didn't cry. Somehow he was managing to hold everything together while silent tears dropped down Erica's cheeks.

'We probably should have had this conversation

earlier,' he said, his voice breaking slightly. 'Thank you for telling me. And being honest. I appreciate it.'

Erica nodded, wiping her face with the edge of her sleeve.

'Is that what you came back for?' she asked.

There was a pause before Rick nodded, and Erica narrowed her eyes.

'What trouble are you in?'

Rick laughed.

'Never could keep anything from you.'

Their eyes met for one glorious moment, sending a pang through Erica that cut so deep she couldn't breathe.

'I'm okay,' he told her, lying. She could tell. 'Actually, your grandmother has been a big help. I'll be okay.'

'Can I do anything?' Erica asked, placing the watch back on the table.

Rick smiled and leaned close.

'Be happy,' he told her. 'Do what makes you happy. Have an amazing, happy life.'

Without thinking, Erica pushed forward and their lips met. It wasn't quite like their first kiss; the tension wasn't right. But still, it was warm and soft, and Erica found herself holding onto him for longer than she should have.

When the kiss broke, they bumped noses and smiled into one another.

'I'm going to miss you, time traveller,' Erica

whispered.

'You'll always be with me,' Rick told her. 'I'm never going to stop loving you.'

Erica frowned and moved back enough so that she could look into his eyes.

'No. I want you to stop loving me. You have to be happy too. Go and follow Gran's advice, because I know whatever she's told you, it's the right thing to do, and then go and be happy. Be you. Have a happy and amazing life.'

Rick smiled and leaned forward to kiss her again.

'Goodbye, Erica Murray,' he murmured.

'Goodbye, Rick Cavanagh.'

One last kiss, and then Rick pulled away, turned the device on his wrist, and Erica shielded her eyes as he vanished in the now familiar flash of white light.

When she looked back up, colours dancing in front of her eyes, she was alone in the kitchen.

The tightness in her chest made it hard to breathe. She couldn't move.

A knock at the front door made her jump and she turned in her chair. Her mother and grandmother, presumably in the next room, didn't move.

After another knock, Erica's body gave a deep sob and she stumbled to her feet and through the house. She opened the front door to find Alfie there, his bright blue eyes soft, his arms reaching out to her. Erica collapsed into him, all of the pain and tears she'd been holding back pouring out, staining his shirt. Still, he held her tight, rocking her slightly, his lips in her hair as she sobbed.

Erica wasn't sure how much time passed before the sobbing quietened. Then it was just her and Alfie, on the floor of her parents' hallway, just by the open front door. Alfie was murmuring into her hair but she couldn't make out the words. Still, it was comforting, as were his strong arms holding her close. She pulled away from him and wiped her face again with her sleeve.

'I'm sorry,' she murmured. 'I shouldn't have done that.'

'Why do you think I'm here?' Alfie told her, brushing her hair from her face and his thumb over her wet cheek.

'Are you all right, sweetheart?' Esther carefully approached, her feet desperate to rush and scoop up her daughter while the rest of her body held back.

Alfie helped Erica up and then she threw herself into her mother's arms, the sobs threatening to return. She swallowed them down and nodded into her mother's shoulder.

'I'm okay. Sorry.'

'Don't be sorry.'

Minerva was standing at the edge of the group. Once she'd ascertained that Erica was all right, she moved into the kitchen and stared at the space Rick had filled.

'Well, that's that,' she said to herself.

'What was going on with him?' Erica asked as they followed Minerva into the kitchen. She took the tissues her mother offered and sat back at the table, trying not to look at Rick's empty chair. 'He wouldn't tell me what trouble he was in.'

Minerva shook her head.

'The future sounds like a damning place,' she said, as if that explained everything. 'But then, it is now as well. He'll be all right. I hope.' Minerva pulled a face. 'I did everything I could for him. As did you,' she added when she caught sight of Erica's expression. 'It's done now, love. It's time to move on. Enjoy life.' She glanced at Alfie.

Erica took a deep, shuddering breath, feeling Alfie's presence behind her. Eyes scanning the table, she stopped.

'The pocket watch is gone.' She looked up to Alfie. 'He left it on the table, but it's gone. It's yours. You should have it back.'

Alfie gave a soft smile and shook his head.

'He still needs it,' he said.

Erica gave him a quizzical look and opened her mouth to ask why when Minerva loudly interrupted any thoughts by asking, 'Is there any cake left?'

12

Jess

'You'd think this would get easier, considering how often we're doing it,' Jess grumbled as she stared at Ruby's selected clothes on her bed.

'It is easy,' said Marshall from the other room.

Jess scooped up the clothes and moved into her and Marshall's bedroom where he was packing a couple of shirts and underwear. Brushing his hands, he gave her a grin and gestured to the bag. 'See.'

Jess blinked at him and then threw Ruby's clothes onto the bed in front of him.

'Great. Now that you're done, you can pack Ruby's bag.'

Marshall laughed.

'Fair enough. It's only a weekend. We don't need much. We never do. You always pack more than we need.'

'Fine. In that case, you're in charge. And this will

be the weekend that she jumps in a muddy puddle and needs another change of clothes, and she won't have any. Then what will you do?'

'Ask to borrow your parents' washing machine?' Marshall suggested.

Jess opened her mouth and then closed it. Damn him.

'It won't be dry in time,' she argued.

'Stick it in their dryer.'

'It'll shrink.'

Marshall exhaled through puffed out cheeks.

'Worse-case scenario, we can buy her more clothes. But honestly? Just let her wear the same clothes two days in a row. It won't hurt her.'

Jess sighed and sat on the bed.

'Oh god! You're impossible to argue with. You don't understand what it's like being a mum. That isn't how it works.'

Marshall sat beside her.

'How am I doing for understanding what it's like being a dad?' he asked quietly, slipping an arm around her waist.

'You're doing brilliantly,' she told him, leaning over to kiss him. 'Now stop questioning me and pack Ruby's bag.

Marshall gave a mock salute and stood, returning to the pile of Ruby's clothes and her designated bag.

Jess looked over her own choice of clothes and sighed. She'd chosen comfortable, warm clothing, with a second set just in case she got talked into sanding or painting something. It didn't happen on every visit – Marshall was the handyman and therefore the one her father wanted to help with the mucky jobs – but that didn't stop them asking her to pick up a paintbrush from time to time. She'd learned her lesson when she'd had to wear one of her father's old t-shirts for fear of ruining a new top she'd bought specifically for the weekend.

'I'm not sure I can do another weekend of wedding talk,' she murmured. 'I wonder if me and Ruby can just spend all day, every day at the fair.'

'Erm, I'd rather you didn't,' said Marshall.

'Oh, come on. You're always busy working with Dad. Are you sure you're okay to go? You've had a busy week.'

'Of course! I'm always happy to help your parents.'

Jess studied her fiancé.

'They love you, you know. You don't have to keep doing this to impress them.'

Marshall chuckled, pushing the last of Ruby's clothes into the bag with a little more force than Jess liked.

'I'm doing it because I enjoy it. It's fun to see the house coming together. Even more fun because your dad spends the time telling me stories about you when you were little.' He glanced up mischievously as Jess slowly turned to look at him.

'He what?'

Marshall laughed.

'The stories I've heard!'

Jess opened her mouth.

'What? You didn't tell me that. What's he told you?'

'Nothing bad.' Marshall laughed again. 'Some embarrassing stuff, but nothing bad. Turns out you were a cute kid. Cute and a bit naughty.' His eyes shone. 'I wonder where Ruby gets it from.'

Jess's heart fluttered.

'Obviously Dad's said nothing that's put you off me. So that's something.'

'Nah. If anything, I think I love you more.' Marshall moved around the bed and wrapped his thick arms around Jess's waist, holding her close, kissing her neck. Then he stopped, pushing his body against hers. 'Wait for it,' he murmured against her skin, his breath tickling her. She smiled, holding him tight.

'Mummy? Marshall? When are we leaving?'

'Like clockwork.' Marshall gave Jess's neck another kiss and then released her.

Bubbles appeared in the bedroom before Ruby, and Jess turned to the dog.

'Oh, Bubbles! You've learned to talk. How clever of you. We're leaving very soon. Do you know where your big sister is?'

Ruby walked into the room giggling.

'Mummy! It was me!'

'Oh. So Bubbles can't talk? I did think that was

strange. We could have quit our jobs and travelled around with her, showing off her skills to everyone. She could have made us a fortune.' Jess crouched and caught Ruby in a bear hug. Ruby grabbed and hugged her back. 'Marshall's packed your bag,' said Jess, releasing her daughter. 'And Bubbles is all packed, I think.' She straightened and tried to think what they'd forgotten.

'It's two nights,' Marshall reminded her. 'We'll be fine. C'mon, Rubes.'

'Hang on!' she cried, running from the room.

Marshall and Jess gathered their own things and left the bedroom, closing the door behind them as Bubbles bounced towards the stairs. Ruby reappeared with a large cuddly dog toy.

'Okay, now I'm ready.'

'Good. Go to the toilet and then shoes on,' Jess informed her, taking the toy.

Ruby headed for the bathroom and Marshall took all of the bags and toy dog from Jess. Once downstairs, Jess moved the bag of Bubbles's food, treats and toys into the hallway, along with her bed.

'Like a military operation. Just for two nights,' she mumbled.

'Have you worked out what you're going to say to your mum about the wedding?' Marshall asked quietly as he strapped on Bubbles's harness.

'Not really, but Erica said she'd help if Mum got a little over excited again. Don't worry, I'll get through.'

'Okay. It doesn't have to be a small-small wedding. At this point, I honestly just want to marry you and start our lives together.'

Jess gave Marshall a look.

'We're already living together.'

He grinned at her.

'Yeah, but married life will be different. And we can have a baby.' He winked at her.

Jess smiled but looked hurriedly back to the stairs to see if Ruby had heard.

'Shh. I haven't talked to Ruby about that yet. I have no idea how she'll react to a baby brother or sister.'

'Oh, she'll love it,' said Marshall, picking up all the bags in one go. 'I don't mind about the wedding, but as much as I love you and want to tell everyone, I really don't think I can do a big wedding.'

'Would a big wedding be like Daddy's? Or bigger?' Jess turned to Ruby as she made her way down the stairs.

'Did you wash your hands?'

Ruby pulled a face of disgust and held up her hands.

'Yes!'

'Good. And Daddy had a very big wedding.'

Ruby pulled another face, sticking out her tongue.

'I don't want a very big wedding.'

'See, it's not just me and you,' said Marshall, gesturing to Ruby's tongue. 'None of us want a big wedding.'

'It was boring,' Ruby declared.

If only it had just been boring. Ruby had spent her father's wedding eating cake and running around with the other children, who were mostly older and weren't that interested in her. Jess and Marshall, on the other hand, had been subjected to adult conversations with people they didn't know and, worse, people Jess did know.

It had been loud and busy and too much.

'It was,' Marshall agreed with Ruby. 'And we want something smaller.'

'And more fun,' said Ruby.

Jess stared at her daughter thoughtfully.

'Have you told Granny you'd like something smaller and fun, Rubes?'

Ruby gave her mother a strange look and shook her head.

Jess smiled.

'Maybe it's time we did tell her.'

'Oh, bringing out all the reinforcements this weekend, huh?'

Jess looked into Marshall's playful eyes.

'She's going to make us set a date soon,' she told him. 'It's time for the big guns.'

Marshall laughed and opened the front door to start packing up the car.

'But we're going to the fair as well, aren't we,' said Ruby as she followed Jess to the car.

Bubbles jumped into the back and Marshall

made sure she was comfortable and safe.

Jess helped Ruby into her car seat.

'Of course. We're going to the fair both days. Especially for Halloween,' said Jess, giving Ruby a tickle.

'I don't have a costume,' Ruby giggled.

'Granny's got you the one you wanted, don't worry.' Jess kissed her daughter's cheek and did a double check of all the fastened straps.

'Is Erica coming?' Ruby asked.

'She is. And Alfie. They're going to join us at the fair.' Jess watched her daughter's face when she mentioned the fae's name, but Ruby didn't react.

'Will they be in costume?'

'I think Alfie's permanently in costume,' Marshall muttered, closing the boot and moving to the driver's door.

'Probably not, sweetie.'

Ruby stuck out her bottom lip.

'They get less chocolate, then.'

Jess laughed.

'Erica's going through a rough time, baby. She can have all the chocolate she wants.'

'But she won't be in costume!'

'Sometimes adults need chocolate when they're not in costume,' said Jess wistfully.

There was a pause, and then Ruby asked, 'Why is she going through a rough time?'

'Because her landlord has put her rent up and she can't afford it. She's going to have to move again.'

'Why?'

Jess hesitated.

'Because her landlord's put up her rent, Rubes.'

'Why?'

Jess pursed her lips.

'Because the housing market is an arse.' She kissed Ruby's forehead and then closed the door before Ruby could drag her into a conversation about the British economy and political situation.

As she climbed into the front passenger seat, Ruby's voice reached her.

'Will Erica be staying with us?'

'No, sweetie. She's getting a hotel with Alfie. I think they're staying on the high street, of all places,' she added quietly to Marshall.

'Probably the only place left,' he murmured.

Jess pulled a face. Rather them than her.

'Oh,' said Ruby.

Jess turned in a seat to peer at her downhearted daughter.

'Why?' she asked, lips twitching with a smile.

'I won't be able to introduce her to the shadows.'

Jess's smile fell and she swallowed on her suddenly dry mouth.

'Oh, I'm sure we can arrange that,' she croaked under her breath as Marshall pulled the car out of the driveway and they began the journey to Chipping Briar.

13
Mullarky

Dusk was turning to night as Mullarky moved from shadow to shadow. The people setting up the fair didn't notice him as he wandered past, his dark eyes watching them build rides that would shake and rattle the historic buildings that lined the street. Mullarky snarled. Horrible modern day contraptions. He'd once had hope that humans would build something remarkable, but instead they'd built monstrosities that left them red and screaming.

Although he knew there was more to humans than this.

Many an evening was spent hiding behind Mauve's chair as she watched the television. He knew about the wars and the poverty, the new laws, the families who were struggling, turning up to marry a person they'd never met and answering questions to earn more money.

The older Mullarky got, the madder the world became.

He could understand why a human might stand outside Mauve's cottage, muttering to themselves as they scoured the ground. Which is why he found himself outside the witch's house.

It was a double-fronted Victorian house that only recently had been on the point of ruin. It hadn't been the witch's house for over a hundred years. Then a couple from elsewhere in the town had purchased it, cleared it of its malevolent presences and made it brighter and cosy.

And they'd started leaving out a saucer of milk again.

It had been a long time since that had happened.

Many in the town would leave out milk and food, presumably for the local wildlife, but this was different. They even used the same saucer that the witch before them had used. It was something of a comfort, knowing that witches had returned to Chipping Briar.

Often, once Mauve was safely asleep, Mullarky would wander through the town to this house. Now he sat, back against the house's front wall, sipping the milk.

Times had certainly changed, but in some ways they were exactly the same. Whereas once men would be falling from the pubs on the high street at this time, drunk and singing and returning home, now young people fell from the pubs and something called a night club. Mullarky didn't know what that was but it seemed to involve deep, throbbing beats and just as much vomit as those drunken men had produced over the centuries.

Mullarky licked the saucer clean and then studied it. There was the crack from where he'd accidentally dropped it, startled when the woman's husband – James, wasn't it? Mullarky wasn't always good with names – had come home late one night, a strange look on his face.

That had been the night Mullarky had realised he'd made an error.

It occurred to him that he was making the same error now, considering what he'd seen from Mauve's window the other day. But no, it was not yet All Hallows' Eve. The human would wait, if he had any idea what he was doing.

Mullarky scoffed.

In his experience, humans had no idea what they were doing. He should return home immediately. But then, that man was exactly the reason he was at the witch's house that night. He needed to speak with her, but how did one such as Mullarky introduce himself to a human for the first time? Especially one who had obviously only recently discovered she was a witch.

The woman did nothing remotely witchy, other than leave the saucer out with full fat milk poured up to the brim. Was that an instinct? Perhaps she didn't wish to embrace who she was, or perhaps she was lazy.

Mullarky carefully placed the saucer down. No, if either of those were true, she would not leave out the saucer of milk.

Deep down inside, the woman knew Mullarky was there. But that didn't mean he could just walk up to the front door and introduce himself.

There would likely be screaming.

Mullarky flinched as bright headlights appeared on him. As quickly as possible, he moved back to the shadows, to the side of the house, and watched curiously.

A car was pulling up. Mullarky's eyes brightened at the sight of the stronger witch stepping out of the car. There were voices as the couple who now owned the witch's house appeared and they hugged, chatting away.

Mullarky sunk back as there came the bark of a dog.

This was a good sign. It was good news.

Mullarky wouldn't necessarily have to introduce himself to a woman who was so newly a witch. No, now he could introduce himself to the witch's daughter, and implore that she help him to save the man's life.

Erica

They could have travelled to Chipping Briar on the Saturday morning, but Erica had a need to get away. A stay in a hotel would be good, she'd decided. It might give her the space she needed to think through her living situation dilemma.

Alfie didn't argue, although he did put up some resistance to travelling there in Erica's car instead of through the woodland of his world. A few months before, they'd discovered the door in his world, outside a neighbouring village, that led to the woods on the edge of Chipping Briar, but Erica knew those woods now.

Travelling by car would be quicker, if nothing else.

The hotel didn't have a car park, but there was a twenty-four hour one nearby so Erica drove slowly around the town until she found a way in.

'It's usually easier,' she told Alfie, who was

staring out of the window from the passenger seat. 'But they've closed the high street because of the fair.'

'Hmm.'

'What? Oh, you're not still sore about us going by car, are you?' Erica found a parking spot and reversed her Mini into it.

'No,' said Alfie. 'Although I don't know what you suddenly have against sex in the woods.'

Erica smiled.

'Nothing,' she told him. 'But if we'd gone through your world, we'd still be there now. In fact, we'd probably be closer to your village than the one near here.'

Alfie grinned.

'Would we be up against a tree or in an open clearing?'

A tingling warmth spread through Erica, blood rushing to her cheeks.

'Stop it. Come on. Let's go find the hotel.'

The car park was surrounded by trees, giving off a glorious golden hue, and they had to walk past the church to get onto the high street. Alfie paused to study the building, cocking his head one way and then the other.

'Pretty, isn't it,' said Erica, stopping next to him.

'Old, too,' Alfie murmured, glancing back over his shoulder, to the direction of the woods. 'Hmm.'

Erica stared at him.

'What?'

'What?' He turned back to her and urged her to keep walking.

'You keep saying "hmm".'

'Do I?'

'Alfie.'

Alfie put a hand on the small of her back and she relented, for now. There wasn't much chance of talking on the high street, anyway. The wide road, built for medieval markets, was filled with people setting up stalls and rides. Most of the road was cordoned off, but they could walk along the wide pavements, dodging the other pedestrians.

At the top of the high street was a tall, grand, white building. Alfie stopped again, although Erica only realised when the pressure from his hand on her back was gone.

'Everything okay?' she asked when Alfie finally joined her.

He nodded, although his expression didn't agree.

'It's an old building.'

Erica gave him a sweet smile.

'Everything's old here, I think.' Slowly, she took his hand and squeezed it. He met her eyes and softened a little. 'C'mon.'

Erica led him into the hotel where they were met with a bright, neutral and modern décor, and a fairly small reception desk. A man was tapping away at a laptop behind the desk. He looked up as they entered.

'Good evening,' he said with a smile, giving them his full attention. 'Booking in?'

'Yes, please,' said Erica. She gave the man her booking details while Alfie studied the framed photos on the wall.

'You're in room five, it's on the first floor. I've given you a room facing the back, but as you can imagine, we're pretty busy this weekend and it's going to be quite noisy. We can only apologise, but given our setting and the age of the building, there isn't much we can do,' the man explained, handing Erica the key for room five. 'Other than a complimentary drink at the bar.' He grinned.

'Oh, lovely. Thank you so much,' said Erica, returning the smile. 'Let's go drop off our bags and get a drink, then, shall we, Alfie?'

'Hmm.'

Erica turned to face the fae who was still studying the photos.

'How old is the building?' he asked the man before Erica could snap at him.

'It's over a hundred years old. It was built to be a bank. Still got the old safes downstairs. Our manager keeps talking about turning the basement into a restaurant and making a feature out of them. I've seen other places doing that. But it's the expense of it all.'

Erica nodded.

'Everything's expensive at the moment. It sounds amazing, though.'

The man nodded, but there was something not quite right in his smile. Erica studied his features and then subtly felt the air in the room.

'Would you like to book dinner?' the man asked.

Erica blinked out of her thoughts.

'Oh, no, not tonight, thank you. We're meeting a friend. Can we book breakfast, though?'

'Of course. Two for breakfast, room five. Erica Murray and...sorry, sir, what was your name?'

Alfie stirred, joining Erica at the desk.

'Alfie.' He gave a quick smile.

'Alfie...?'

Erica waited to see what Alfie would answer. She wasn't even sure that fae had surnames.

'Murray,' Alfie said, flashing Erica a look.

The man nodded.

'Wonderful. I'm Dave. You'll usually find me on reception or back there in the office. Do let me or one of my colleagues know if you have any issues or requests. Please enjoy your stay.'

'Thank you,' said Erica, leading Alfie towards the single lift. Alfie nodded thanks to Dave and then took Erica's bag from her.

Once they were alone in the lift, Alfie sidled closer and breathed in her hair.

'Is there something here? Is that why you keep saying "hmm"?'

Alfie pushed back her hair and kissed her neck.

'I don't know,' came his muffled voice.

Erica made a raspberry noise.

'Rubbish. Tell me what's going on.'

Alfie slid his free hand under her coat and around her waist. Annoyingly, Erica's body responded immediately and her breath caught as his hand roamed over her clothes.

The doors pinged open, but rather than jumping away, Alfie stayed close, breathing warm air over Erica's skin and making her shiver.

'The doors will close again,' she murmured, closing her eyes and leaning into him.

Slowly, Alfie moved away and led her out of the lift. They stopped on the landing.

'This way,' said Erica, reading the sign on the wall. Room five was to the left, opposite room four. She unlocked the door and wandered inside, Alfie right behind her. He dropped the bag on the floor and put his hands on his hips.

'Not bad.'

Erica was already at the window.

'Even got a nice view,' she said, peering out over a small courtyard garden with the tables and chairs stacked under a shelter, waiting for the summer. Beyond, there were crumbling old brick buildings that were probably storage, and then a line of golden trees. Behind those, Erica knew, was the river and then the woodland. She breathed in deep and looked around the room.

'It's nice.'

There was a double bed, beautifully made with white sheets and plump pillows. Opposite was a dressing table and small television. Alfie opened a door to the side and found an en suite. He pulled an impressed expression and went in to investigate.

'The shower's not big enough for two, but I'm sure we'll manage,' came his voice.

Erica laughed and sat on the bed, giving it a testing bounce.

'Well, the bed's big enough for two.'

Alfie reappeared, his eyes grazing over her. He shook his head.

'You're wearing too many clothes.'

'Oh, sorry.' Erica stood and removed her coat, throwing it onto a nearby chair. 'Is this better?'

Alfie gave her an appraising look and then approached slowly. Erica's pulse quickened as she watched him, her eyes darting down to the buttons of his shirt as he reached her. His fingers found the hem of her jeans and undid the button, so she began doing the same to his shirt. Once her jeans were off and he was topless, they stared at one another and grinned.

She reached for his jeans and was interrupted by his need to pull her top over her head. They made it to the bed once they were both completely naked and Erica took a moment to relish the feel of clean, fresh sheets against her skin. Then Alfie was on top of her and all she could feel was him.

Alfie had been right. The shower was too small for

both of them, but that didn't stop them from trying. In the end, they'd had to take it in turns, but they spent the showers chatting and laughing. Erica could only imagine what anyone would think if they could hear them, and she was sure they could. This building wasn't meant to be a hotel, it was hardly soundproof. She'd been as quiet as possible, but fae didn't generally understand the concept of quiet sex.

Once they were dry and dressing, Erica sat at the dressing table brushing her hair while Alfie considered the view from the window.

'I'm going to pop out. Get some fresh air,' he said, not turning to look at her.

She stared at his reflection in the mirror.

'Where are you going?'

His shoulders heaved in a shrug.

'I just want to check something out.'

'The thing you keep "hmming" about?'

Alfie turned and gave her a wicked grin.

'Maybe.'

'Okay. But be safe and don't hurt anyone and be back by seven. We're meeting Jess and her family for dinner.'

'Will do.' Alfie kissed the top of her head as he passed on his way to the door.

'Meet at the pub?' Erica suggested.

'Don't worry,' said Alfie, opening the door. 'I'll find you.'

Erica watched the door close behind him and

gave a deep sigh. How wonderful to be able to wander a strange town at the end of October with no coat on and with no worries for your safety. She glanced down at her empty ring finger, imagining a wedding ring slid on by Alfie, and her heart gave a jolt.

'Shit.'

Rick had given her a promise ring and she hadn't returned it. Would she ever see him again to give it back? Sighing, she went back to sorting her hair. There wasn't much she could do about it now.

The room was quiet without Alfie in it. One of the good things about being able to sense spirits was that Erica was certain she was alone in the room.

A noise filtered through on the edge of her hearing. At first she put it down to the fair outside. Someone had turned on some music. But the more she listened, the slower her movements became, until she stopped so she could listen properly.

It was someone playing the piano, and it wasn't the fair. It couldn't be the fair. It didn't sound right.

Finishing her makeup and grabbing her bag, coat and hotel key, Erica left the room, locking the door behind her. The music was a little louder out in the hallway.

As she followed the sound, the air in front of her shimmered. It was just enough to make anyone think their eyes were tired. Even Erica was tempted to rub hers, but she resisted, not wanting to smudge her makeup and knowing that the shimmer was something else.

She walked slowly down the stairs, pausing every now and then to listen. The music was getting louder.

Out into the communal area of the small hotel, through reception and into the bar where one family were resting at a booth while the father brought over a selection of drinks. Erica glanced at them and then tilted her head, trying to hear over their voices for that music.

She found herself at a door beside the bar bearing a sign, STAFF ONLY.

Erica looked around but the only member of staff was the barman who was ignoring her. The piano music was unmistakably loud now and the floorboards beneath her feet trembled with the vibrations. The barman and family didn't seem bothered by it. Could they hear it?

When the barman's back was turned, Erica tried the door. It opened easily and revealed a wooden staircase that led down to a dark basement.

'Of course,' she mumbled.

A cord hung to her left and she tentatively pulled it. Thankfully the basement below lit up and Erica hurriedly stepped inside and closed the door behind her. As she did so, the music abruptly stopped.

The light wasn't bright and as she stepped carefully down the stairs, she could see why. The basement was a small, square storage area, or at least, that was all she could see. Between the thick walls and piles of tables, chairs and things covered in sheets were obvious pathways leading to other sections.

'Probably to some safes that you wouldn't want to get locked in,' Erica reminded herself.

The area she stood in was lit by a single hanging lightbulb covered in thick dust and old cobwebs.

Below the lightbulb was a piano, half covered with a dust sheet.

The silence of the room was deafening. Erica wandered over to the piano and gingerly pressed one of the white keys. The noise reverberated around the room, making Erica jump.

'Was that you playing?' she asked quietly, looking around the room, peering into the shadows. 'I won't hurt you. I just wanted to say hello. My name's Erica. You play beautifully.'

With a soft smile, Erica left the piano and made her way back up the stairs. As she reached the top step, the piano music began again. Grinning, Erica tried to lean as far as she could without leaving her step, to see the piano and who was playing it. She made it as far as the piano stool, which still stood empty.

Erica gave this some thought and then whispered, 'Beautiful.' She turned off the light and stepped back into the hotel, closing the door behind her. It was time to go meet Jess and her family; the spirit in the basement could wait.

15
Jess

Every time Jess stepped foot inside her parents' new house, she couldn't believe the transformation. Thanks to Marshall's help and her parents' hard work, it had only taken around six months to turn the neglected Victorian house into a beautiful and cosy home. The guilt around the living room window cracking, thanks to the imp, had been awful, but her father had only been glad of an excuse to order the new windows early. They had to be replaced at some point. In the meantime, it had been boarded up while they waited for their expensive, top of the range Victorian-style sash windows to be made. They'd been fitted only the week before, so Jess got a shock when they'd arrived at the house to find the board gone and a beautiful new window in its place.

The living room was once again bathed in sunshine, only this time there were original floorboards instead of the disgusting carpet Marshall and her father had pulled up. The coving and skirting were painted a soft white, and the walls were a calming sage. The fireplace had been restored and added to a little, and as the chimney had been swept during the summer, there was a fire laid, ready to be lit in the evening. New large, comfortable sofas had been purchased and placed around the fireplace, and over the mantel was a large television. In the middle was a coffee table, made by her father, with a glass top specifically so that they could show off the door to the hatch that rested in the floorboards. The hatch that had led them to the witch bottle that had protected the spirit of the house for so many years, holding the imp on the periphery, casting a strange darkness over the house. It was probably the reason the previous family had struggled to sell it, eventually forced to auction it off, much to Jess's parents' joy. They wanted a period fixer-upper, and something deep inside Ginny, Jess's mother, hadn't minded the strangeness of the shadows that moved of their own accord, nor the darkness on the edge of it all.

Most of the other rooms were nearing a stage of completion, too. The carpet in the hallway had been hiding original tiles, which had been revealed and cleaned. All of the walls were freshly painted and Ginny had almost finished making new curtains for each room.

New bathrooms were required, along with a new

kitchen, but for now they'd painted the walls and given everything a good scrub. The rest would come in time.

Yet, the shadows that moved on their own remained, even in the bright, fresh rooms.

'I think I'm beginning to not notice them,' said Ginny, surveying the bedroom she'd made up for Jess and Marshall.

'That's good.' Jess threw her and Marshall's bags onto the bed.

'But every now and then I catch your dad talking to them.'

Jess's eyes widened and her mother gave her a worried look.

'Is that bad?' she asked.

'No. No, I don't think so. I don't think they can hear us. How do you know he's talking to them and not to you?'

Ginny fidgeted.

'I considered that. He was in the bedroom one evening and I could hear him from downstairs. So I came up to see what he was doing and he was merrily chatting to the corner of the room. So I asked him. He's been talking to the shadows for a while now, apparently. He says I should try it.'

Jess watched her mother warily.

'And have you?'

'What? No. Of course not. I'm not about to go around talking to the shadows in my house. That's madness. Isn't it?'

Jess struggled for a moment and was saved by her daughter wandering into the room.

'Mummy, is Bubbles coming to the pub with us?'

'I don't see why not, sweetheart. It's a dog friendly one, isn't it.'

'But we'll be eating,' said Ginny.

'Do you really want her staying here on her own?' Jess asked her mother.

Ginny grimaced.

'Fine. Bubbles can come.'

'She could stay,' said Ruby, climbing onto the bed. 'The shadows would take care of her. But she might miss us.'

Jess and her mother exchanged a glance.

'Do you talk to the shadows too, Ruby?' Ginny asked.

Ruby nodded and lay back on the bed, staring up the ceiling.

'I know them,' she said matter-of-factly.

Jess wasn't sure what to make of that, but she didn't like it.

'Do they talk back to you?' she asked.

Ruby nodded.

'Sometimes.'

'Do they talk back to Dad?' Jess asked her mother.

'I'm not sure,' said Ginny. 'You'll have to ask him. Oh, but do we have to talk about the shadows? I don't want to know any of this. Do they have names? No! Don't tell me. I don't want to know. It's like having roommates. I don't want roommates. We've paid a lot of money to not have roommates.'

Jess tried to hold back the laugh.

'And there's no way to get rid of them?' Ginny turned on her daughter.

'Mum, they're not doing anything bad. If you don't want to acknowledge their existence, then don't. Don't talk to them, don't look at them. I don't think they care. Just ignore them.'

'Wonderful. Can you tell your father that, please.'

Jess smiled and patted the bed.

'Come on, you. Off. Where's Marshall?' she said to Ruby.

'With Grampy.'

'And where's he?'

'In the living room with Bubbles. They're just sitting and talking. It's very boring. When can we go to the fair?'

'I don't think it opens until tomorrow, sweetheart. But we'll go find out soon. Go tell Marshall and Grampy that we're leaving soon, yeah? Time to get ready.'

Ruby bounced up, jumped off the bed and ran down the stairs. Ginny watched her go as Jess sat on the foot of the bed.

'I wish I had her energy,' Ginny murmured.

'Me too. And I would have thought you did, Mum,' said Jess, looking around the room. 'What you've done to this house in six months is nothing short of a miracle.'

Ginny waved her words away.

'That's just because we've been doing all the easy stuff. Flooring and walls are easy. Getting someone in to do the windows was pretty easy too. Now the difficult stuff starts. We've got a designer coming round to look at the kitchen next week.'

'We can help fit it if you want to keep costs down,' Jess offered, lying back just as Ruby had done and staring at the ceiling.

'I'll leave that up to your dad and Marshall. Speaking of Marshall...' Ginny sat beside Jess. 'Did you look at those wedding venues I sent you?'

Jess inhaled deep, held it and then exhaled slowly before answering.

'I did, Mum. I liked a few of them. But, the thing is...' She sat back up and glanced sideways at her mother. 'You know, we've talked about this before. About keeping the wedding small.'

'Yes.'

'And some of those venues have a minimum guest number which is quite...a lot.'

'Oh. Well, when you said small, I didn't think you meant that small. How small do you mean? We have to invite your Uncle Mark and Aunt Lizzie and their families, and Sharon and Bert. And then there's your cousins and their families.'

'But why, Mum? I haven't seen Sharon and Bert since I was...I don't know, fifteen? And I haven't spoken to any of my cousins for about ten years, and—'

'Well, whose fault is that?'

Jess hesitated.

'I don't know. Mine, I guess.'

'Exactly. They'll be hurt if they're not invited to the wedding.'

Jess gave a deep and loud sigh.

'Paul's wedding was huge, Mum. All his family's family and friends, and all of Katy's too. And it was horrendous. It was loud and too much. Ruby hated it. Marshall hated it. I really hated it. We just want something small. Intimate. Just the people who care about us, and who we love. You know?'

Ginny shook her head.

'Is Marshall the One?'

'I...yes.'

'Are you planning on getting married again?'

'I don't think anyone actually plans on divorce, Mum. So, no.'

'And we'll be paying for a lot of it, won't we.'

Jess slowly turned to meet her mother's eyes.

'Really? Because if you want to play that game, Marshall and I can afford the type of wedding we want, no problem. We don't need you to pay for anything.'

The two women stared at one another for a long minute, until something dark moved behind Ginny, catching Jess's eye.

She was about to mention it when her father's voice carried up the stairs.

'Girls? Are we going? I'm starving!'

Bubbles gave a bark in solidarity.

'We'll talk about this later,' said Ginny, her voice softening. 'Let's go get something to eat and see Erica.' She stood. 'I haven't seen Erica in so long. And her new partner is coming? What's his name again?'

'Alfie,' said Jess, following her mother out of the room. 'And he's a bit...' Jess still hadn't decided whether to tell her mother about Alfie's true origins.

'A bit what?'

'Different,' said Jess.

Ginny looked back to her.

'In what way?'

'In a shadows moving of their own accord type of way,' Jess murmured.

Ginny stopped on the stairs.

'Oh.'

'It's fine, Mum. He's lovely, although a bit... No, he's lovely. And Erica loves him. It won't be a problem. Come on. Let's go.'

Erica was approaching the front of the pub, on the high street past the half-finished fair, when Jess and her family arrived. They waited for her and Jess held out an arm to ask where Alfie was. Erica gave a small shrug and then, as if hearing their silent conversation, Alfie appeared from the shadows behind her.

Erica gave a small jump as he caught up and then grinned as he wrapped an arm around her waist. Jess glanced at her mother to see if she was watching.

'Erica!' Ginny stepped forward and gave Jess's friend a hug. 'It's so good to see you again.'

'And you, Ginny. I've been hearing all about your house. It sounds amazing.'

'Oh, it is, it is. Are you excited about the wedding? Jess hasn't told me much about her decisions yet but I assume you'll play a role?'

Jess stiffened and watched Erica carefully.

Her friend smiled warmly.

'Yes, maid of honour, I think.' Erica flashed Jess a grin. 'So I'm hoping it'll be a small do? I don't fancy standing up in front of so many people. I don't think Jess does, either.'

'But that's the day when it's all about the bride. All eyes will be on Jess, don't you worry about that,' said Ginny.

'Yes, but, I'm not sure she—'

'Erica!'

Jess's father wrapped Erica in a bear hug, cutting her off, and then studied Alfie.

'You must be Ric's new fella,' he said, holding out a hand. 'Eddie.'

Alfie shook his hand as Erica introduced him to Ginny.

'So lovely to meet you, Alfie. Wonderful. If you're

anything like Jess and Marshall here, maybe we could do a double wedding?' Ginny laughed and Jess tried not to smirk at the look on Erica's face.

'Oh, I don't think—'

'We wouldn't want to step on their toes,' Alfie cut in. 'And I'm hoping that Erica will agree to marry me when the flowers are just blooming. A late spring wedding, I think.'

There was a short pause as Ginny did an awkward giggle, looking to Erica.

'Not for a good while yet,' Erica told her gently.

'Shall we go eat?' said Ginny, giving Jess a sideways look.

'Yes! I'm starving!' Ruby cried.

Jess gave her a look.

'Can't have that. You wasting away,' she told her daughter. 'Come on.'

They walked into the pub, Jess's parents taking the lead. Marshall held Ruby's hand and Jess held Bubbles's lead. The dog immediately sniffed the floor and then the air, before looking up at Jess and wagging her tail.

Jess stroked her head, falling back in step with Erica and Alfie.

'Everything okay?' she asked quietly.

Erica nodded.

'Lovely. The hotel's really nice. There's a piano playing spirit in the basement.'

Jess blinked. Of course there was.

'Okay.'

'I might have a chat with the manager about it.' Jess nodded.

'Good idea.'

'And you, Alfie? Any news?' Erica asked, which Jess thought strange. She looked back to Alfie who walked with his hands in his pockets.

'No. It's a lovely evening. We could go for a walk after this.' He flashed Erica that charming smile of his, the one that left Jess's stomach churning. It didn't have the same effect on Erica. She smiled and leaned into him.

They sat at a large table that had been reserved for them and Jess took a moment to settle the dog on a blanket she'd brought.

'So, Ric, how much do you know about what happened at our new house?' Eddie asked with a shine to his eyes.

'Not here.' Ginny glanced around the pub.

'Why not? No one's listening.'

'Jess told me everything. And then my mum and gran told me it all again from their point of view.'

'It was all very exciting,' said Eddie.

Erica smiled.

'It sounds like it. I've never seen an imp before. I've barely heard of them, if I'm honest.'

'Well, I'm so glad we got to experience something rare,' Jess mumbled, making her mother smile.

'And how about you, Alfie? What do you do?' Eddie asked.

Erica, Jess and Marshall turned to Alfie, each one forcing themselves to remain silent.

Alfie looked up at Jess's father and gave an honest, innocent smile.

'Things that make me happy,' he said.

There was a pause across the table.

'Oh. I mean, for work,' said Eddie.

'I don't work,' said Alfie. 'I guess you could say that I live off inheritance.'

Jess blew out her cheeks as a wave of confusion swept over her parents.

'And he lives off grid, which keeps the costs down,' Erica added, making Jess's parents turn to her.

Eddie opened his mouth, thought better of it, and sat back thoughtfully.

Ginny, on the other hand, leaned forward.

'So what do you do with your days?'

'I read,' said Alfie. 'I used to work with wood, but these days I will read and see friends and wait for Erica.' He smiled at Erica and in the dim pub light, her cheeks flushed.

'He helps out with the business too,' said Jess quickly. 'Oh, did I tell you about the theatre we went to?'

That caught her parents' attention.

'Was there a ghost?' Eddie asked with a playful grin.

'There was. Standing on the stage. She was a singer,' said Jess.

Eddie and Ginny stared at her.

'You actually saw the ghost?' Ginny asked.

'We never saw our ghost,' said Eddie.

Ginny and Jess glanced down at Ruby, playing with a cloth napkin.

'Ruby did,' Jess murmured.

'Fascinating. So now you can see ghosts too? So, it's something you can learn?'

Jess looked to Erica to answer that one.

'It is,' Erica confirmed. 'You have to be open to it. But I'd advise not being too open.'

'Because of the imps?' Eddie asked.

Erica laughed and nodded.

'Among other things. But me and Jess are always here. Anything strange happens, just give us a call.'

'Hey. Ginny. Who're we gonna call?' Eddie elbowed his wife and laughed.

Ginny rolled her eyes, but ended up laughing too.

'Right, what are we all ordering?' Eddie picked up the menus that had been left for them and they fell into a comfortable silence as they browsed.

16

Rick

Rick stumbled through the park and landed on a bench. He couldn't breathe. Sitting back, he tried to open his lungs, but his throat was so constricted, his chest so tight, that inhaling was painful. Leaning forward, he put his head to his knees and gave a muffled scream.

He never should have left. He could see it now. All he'd had to do was stay in the new timeline, stay with her, stop her from meeting Alfie. They'd be together now, and sure, he'd still have broken the law, there would be two of him in one time, but they'd have figured it out.

When he straightened, his cheeks were wet with tears. Placing a hand on his chest, he closed his eyes and tried to meet the wave of panic building inside him. Then his gaze drifted down to the time travel device on his wrist. The stolen device.

He wasn't at rock bottom quite yet, no matter

how it felt. There were options. Minerva had told him that, as he'd waited for Erica to arrive and inevitably break his heart. Minerva's voice sounded in his head as he went through what he could do next. He could follow her advice. Or he could go back in time to when he'd left Erica, making her promise to find him so they could meet how they were supposed to. So she could meet her present day Rick and fall in love, and everything would be how it was supposed to be. He could go back to then, to just after he'd left her, and stay with her. Take her hand and talk with her, until the sun came up. They could fall in love again, and she'd refuse Alfie's advances.

Rick stared at the device on his wrist until his eyes were dry and aching.

It wouldn't take much. Just a twist of the dial, a push of a button.

He could change his life again.

A flash of bright light made him blink, but he remained on the bench. He wasn't going to jump back to her. He wasn't going to meddle any further.

He'd messed up enough.

'How did it go?' Burns asked, sitting on the bench beside him.

Rick didn't respond, he continued to stare at the device on his wrist.

'I'm guessing badly, seeing as how you're here alone looking very sorry for yourself.' Burns sighed. 'I'm sorry, Cavanagh. For what it's worth. Now that you know her answer, will you come back? I'll have to file a disciplinary for the theft of the device, but your job is still waiting for you. And no more mess ups and the disciplinary will go away.'

Rick frowned, still staring down.

'No,' he whispered eventually.

'What was that?'

Rick looked his boss in the eye.

'No. Thank you, sir. No. I don't want to go back. In fact, I think I'm done.' He stood and began walking away, his coat billowing behind him. With his back to Burns, he quickly fiddled with the device on his wrist.

'Cavanagh! Come back right now. This won't end well for you. What are you going to do? There's nowhere to go.'

And then Rick was gone, flashing out of that time.

17

Erica

Considering the issue of Alfie meeting family who weren't aware that the fae existed, the evening with Jess's parents had gone surprisingly well. They stepped out of the warm pub to be hit by the chilled, almost-November air and darkness.

'Thank you so much,' said Erica for the second time. 'That was such a lovely evening. Are you sure you won't let me give you some money towards it?'

'Of course not. It's our treat.' Ginny gave Erica a hug. 'And you'll stop by tomorrow for a tour of the house?'

'Absolutely. I can't wait to meet these shadows you've told me about,' said Erica, looking down at Ruby's sleepy expression. 'You'll have to introduce me.'

Ruby nodded and smiled, leaning against Marshall's leg. He bent to scoop up her and her eyes closed as soon as her head hit his shoulder.

Warmth spread throughout Erica at the sight. She could only imagine what it was doing to Jess.

Alfie took Erica's hand, and she wondered briefly if he'd heard her thoughts. Glancing at him, she found him watching her, a hint of a secret smile turning up the corners of his lips. Yes, he'd heard her thoughts.

Erica looked away hurriedly.

She hugged Jess's family one by one, kissing Ruby's cheek and leaving Jess to last. As Eddie, Ginny and Marshall took Bubbles's lead and led the way back to the Victorian house, Jess hung back with Erica and Alfie.

'I'll come over tomorrow afternoon?' Erica reminded when Jess appeared preoccupied. She was staring into the shadows further down the pavement. Erica followed her gaze. 'Everything okay?' she murmured.

Alfie was also staring into the shadows. He gave Erica a wink.

'I'll meet you back at the hotel,' he said, brushing a kiss against her cheek and awakening something deep inside her. His gaze lingered on hers as he pulled away, and then he turned, shoved his hands into his pockets and walked back up the high street towards the hotel.

Erica sighed wistfully, but Jess wasn't paying attention. Erica's expression fell and returned to where Jess was staring.

'What is it?' she whispered.

'You remember I thought I saw something at my parents' house? After the imp took James – the spirit – and everything went quiet. At the window.'

'Little, brown and big eyes? I remember,' said Erica, searching the shadows for something matching that description.

'It's over there,' Jess whispered.

'Can you still see it?' asked Erica. Jess nodded. 'What's it doing?'

'Watching us,' said Jess, keeping her voice low. She flinched.

'What? What happened?'

'It made eye contact with me.' Jess's voice cracked. 'I think...I think it wants us to follow it.'

Erica gave Jess a look.

'Really? You sure?'

Jess glanced at Erica.

'Should we get Alfie back?' she whispered.

Erica puffed out air in reply.

'No. We can handle this. Come on.' Erica moved past Jess, but she still couldn't see what Jess had seen. She looked back and gestured for Jess to hurry up.

They half-walked, half-jogged down the high street, turning left half way down and meandering through a car park and then a children's playground. Still oblivious to what they were chasing, Erica stayed just behind Jess. Through a residential area, to the edge of the town. They took a sharp right and kept going.

Now there was nowhere for the creature to hide and still Erica couldn't see anything. They were chasing nothing.

'You're sure about this?' she huffed to Jess as they went, frowning a little at her sudden lack of ability.

'You can't see it?' Jess asked, slowing a little.

'No.'

Jess looked over her shoulder and Erica gave her a small, awkward shrug.

They wandered quickly up a footpath and found themselves on the edge of the woods, the tarmac path turning to dirt. On the right stood the small cottage, picture perfect, as if a child had drawn it. Since Erica had last seen it, the flowers had wilted and died, and the trees had turned from green to golden. Leaves had been swept into piles and there was a glow in one of the downstairs windows.

Jess stopped and breathed deep.

'It's gone. We've lost it.' She turned a full circle, searching for the creature.

A shiver ran over Erica as she studied the cottage.

Jess turned to her. 'Why couldn't you see it?'

'Maybe it didn't want me to,' Erica murmured, stepping past Jess, towards the woods. 'I wonder why it disappeared here. It obviously wanted us – you – to follow it.'

Jess hugged herself, glancing over to the cottage.

'That's the witch's cottage,' she hissed, catching up to Erica. 'Apparently there are stories about it.'

'Why is it called that?'

'A witch lives there. Or lived there. I don't know. Everyone around here calls it that and they must have done for a while because that's what the spirit in my parents' house called it.'

Erica sighed, finding the spot she wanted and kicking some leaves away.

'There's a crossroads here,' she murmured. 'I found it when we left these woods in the spring, from the fae world.' She looked back up to the cottage. 'I didn't tell you, because for some reason it didn't connect in my head, but back then, when I found these crossroads, I looked up and I could have sworn someone was watching me from that window.' She nodded to the nearest downstairs window of the cottage. 'Might have just been some-one sitting down and wondering what we were doing. Might have been a short person or a child... with large, dark eyes.' Erica met Jess's gaze. 'What if it was what you saw?'

Jess turned to the cottage.

'You think it lives here?'

'I have no idea.'

Jess looked down at Erica's feet.

'How do you know it's a crossroads? Is that important?'

'Crossroads,' said Erica, bending to sweep away the leaves and pull at the grass to reveal where the stone paths crossed, 'are generally thought of as gateways in many different folklore.'

'I know it's where prisoners were hanged, wasn't it? To stop them finding rest, or something. And isn't it where musicians summon the Devil to get their record deals? James summoned the Devil, that's why the imp was there. To collect his soul. I wonder if he did the summoning here.'

Erica straightened and blinked.

'I imagine so.' Hands on her hips, her eyes followed the lines of the crossed pathways, hidden beneath the undergrowth and advancing woodland. 'The crossroads probably aren't important, right?' She turned back to the cottage. 'Someone's home, though.'

'You're not suggesting we knock, are you? You are, aren't you. You're going to suggest we knock. Well, I'm not knocking.' Jess hugged herself, narrowing her eyes against the cold wind. 'Is that what you're going to suggest?'

Erica smiled and stepped across the pathways, heading towards the cottage's pretty front door.

'What else is there to do?'

'Go home?' Jess hissed. 'Alfie will be worried about you. If we leave now, I can still say goodnight to Ruby without waking her up too much.'

'Alfie knows I'm here.'

'What? How?'

'Because he always knows. I just have to think it, and he knows. Sometimes not even that. When I had to tell Rick the truth and he zapped away, Alfie was right there. He must have been waiting outside the door for Rick to go. Waiting for just the right moment when I needed him the most.'

'What? Wait,' Jess said, her voice back up to normal volume. She stopped. 'You saw Rick? You told him the truth? What truth?'

Erica froze.

'Shit. I didn't tell you, did I? I guess I thought I'd tell you when I saw you.'

'What happened?' Jess asked.

Erica sighed and turned back to Jess.

'Rick showed up. I told him I wanted to be with Alfie, and how sorry I was, and all that. And he left. As soon as he'd gone, Alfie was at the front door. I think I cried in his arms sat on the floor for a good fifteen minutes.' Erica stopped as her throat began to constrict at the memory.

'Oh, Ric. I'm so sorry.'

'It's okay.'

Jess stepped forward and wrapped her arms around Erica.

'So, what happens now? Is that all over?' Jess asked, gently rubbing Erica's back.

'I think so,' Erica said into her shoulder. 'Although I think he took Alfie's pocket watch, so maybe he has other ideas. I don't know.'

Jess let Erica go.

'You think he's still waiting for you to change your mind?'

Erica shrugged.

'I hope not.' She smiled, wiping the wetness from her eyes.

Jess gave her another tight squeeze.

'We can come back tomorrow,' she whispered hopefully.

Erica shook her head.

'We're paranormal investigators, Jess,' she said playfully, sniffing as her throat began to relax. 'When others scream and run, we get curious and ask who's there. Remember?'

Jess sighed.

'But this isn't a spirit. For all we know, we just followed a very angry person home and they're going to call the police or something.'

Erica pulled a face.

'Does your gut say it was just an angry person?'

Jess shook her head, rubbing at the space between her eyes.

'No.'

'Well, then. Come on.' Erica turned back to the front door and took a deep breath. Approaching, she gave the door a quick, short knock and stepped back to wait.

Jess was right behind her, breathing too fast. Erica reached back and found her friend's hand.

There was nothing to be scared of; it wasn't as if an imp or demon was about to open the door. Unless the Devil himself lived opposite an old crossroads, which, now that she thought about it, would be very poetic and potentially plausible.

There was no taking back the knock, however, as they heard the sound of a lock shifting and the front door opened a crack.

A woman with white hair piled on top of her head and a thick cardigan wrapped around her shoulders looked up at Erica with watery blue eyes.

'Yes?'

'Oh, hello. I'm so sorry to bother you. We were looking for someone and wondered if they lived here. A short man or child, perhaps?' Erica glanced back to Jess for confirmation. Jess, who had returned to hugging herself, nodded. 'Does anyone like that live here?' Erica asked the woman.

She frowned and shook her head.

'No. Thank you.'

She shut the door.

Erica, mouth already open to ask another question, stared at the shut door. Turning on her heel, she walked back to the path.

'Well, there you go.'

'That was it?' Jess rubbed her arms through her thick winter coat, looking back to the cottage. 'Do you think she's lying? Or maybe she lives there alone. It must be scary living here on your own, especially at that age.'

'Unless she's like my gran. Can you imagine?' Erica gave Jess a grin.

'In that case, I imagine she has all the help from the woodland creatures whenever she needs it,'

Jess laughed.

'Like a Disney princess? I can't see my gran as Disney princess.'

'A new breed,' said Jess. 'Approaching a hundred, more powerful than all the villains combined and has squirrels to tidy her house every time she sings.'

Erica laughed and reached out a hand to Jess.

'Come on. Let's get back.'

'Pfft. Ye give up too easy.'

Both women stopped, frozen, eyes widening. Slowly, Erica turned back to Jess.

'Did you hear that?'

Jess, lips shut tight, nodded.

Erica glanced around, peering into the shadows, checking the windows of the cottage.

'Doon here.'

She looked down, following the raspy, male Scottish accent, but saw only the small hedge that marked the edge of the cottage's garden.

As she continued to peer into the leaves and shadows, a short, hairy man appeared. Heart pounding, Erica jumped back and then put a hand on her chest and swore under her breath. The little man gave her a stern, disapproving look.

Erica, eyes still on the man, waved her hand behind her to Jess.

'Is he...who you saw?' she whispered.

She didn't see Jess nodding, but the man gave a self-satisfied twitch of the lips which suggested she had nodded.

His head reached up to Erica's hips and his body was covered in a light brown hair, or fur, with large black eyes, a wide mouth full of small sharp, white teeth, and, weirdly, a bowler hat on his head. He was looking Erica up and down. Finally, he dismissed her and turned his attention to Jess.

'Witches, daughters of witches.' He gave a deep and slow bow, and then frowned in annoyance when he straightened and both women continued to stare at him in silence.

He huffed, jolting Erica into taking a breath.

'Sorry,' she murmured, a notable tremble in her voice. 'This is Jess. I'm Erica. And you are?'

The man looked from Jess to Erica and back again.

'My name is Mullarky,' he said.

Jess

It was him. The creature she'd seen at the window of her parents' house, moments after the imp had taken the spirit of James. She'd only caught a glimpse of him, mostly of his large black eyes, and her brain had pieced together the rest of him on the car ride home. She thought it couldn't be right, the hair and the height and the teeth. She'd even done an online search when she'd gotten home, but nothing had come up. Nothing had come close to the description of Mullarky.

When he once again became annoyed at their lack of response, Jess willed her tongue to unstick itself from the roof of her mouth and for words to be formed.

'Hi,' she breathed. 'Sorry, it's just...' She glanced at the back of Erica's head in front of her. 'It's just we don't...'

Mullarky crossed his arms and somehow

managed to look down his nose at them.

'You'se never met a brownie before?'

Jess's eyes widened a little and she glanced again at Erica, wishing she could see her friend's face.

'No,' said Erica. 'But I've heard of brownies.'

'I haven't,' said Jess in a small voice.

Mullarky's gaze flicked to hers for a moment and then his full attention was on Erica.

'If ye've heard of my kind then how come ye dinnae ken what I am?' he demanded.

Erica shifted her weight.

'I...I've never met a brownie. Until now. It's lovely to meet you, Mullarky. I'm—'

'Ye said,' Mullarky interrupted. 'Erica. Daughter of a witch. Granddaughter of a witch. You.' He snapped his attention to Jess. 'Daughter of a reluctant witch. Granddaughter of a witch who dinnae ken just what she was capable of.' He snapped back to Erica. 'Knocker of doors that shuidnae be knocked.'

Erica physically reeled; Jess watched her lean back.

'Excuse me?'

Mullarky pointed with one long arm to the front door of the cottage.

'We were following you,' said Erica, glancing at the cottage. 'We didn't know where you'd gone.'

Mullarky barked a spiteful laugh.

'Some witches, cannae even find a brownie in the shadows.' Again, his gaze lingered on Jess. She did her best not to squirm. 'And yet,' he continued, softer, 'one of you'se has conversed with an imp.'

Finally, Erica looked over her shoulder to Jess, who gave a weak smile.

'Guess that would be me.'

'Hmm.' Mullarky pursed his lips thoughtfully, cocking his head to the side to study her. 'Daughter of a reluctant witch and granddaughter of a powerful witch.' His eyes dropped to the ground and he sighed. 'It's been a long time since there was a true witch in this town, and I'm in need of help.'

Jess stepped forward to stand beside Erica.

'What do you need help with?'

Mullarky looked up and pointed behind them. Erica and Jess swivelled to look back to the woods.

'Something in the woods?' Jess tried.

'The crossroads,' Erica murmured.

Mullarky nodded.

'The crossroads,' he confirmed. 'On All Hallows' Eve, I've reason to believe a young lad will try tae summon Satan and trade away his soul. He must be stopped. He must be saved. I cannae do it, nae alone. I'm only one brownie. We're nae made for such things. But you'se... A witch can withstand Satan. Two witches can save a man's soul. That is what you'se must do. Save the man's soul.'

Mouth dry, Jess stared at the brownie.

'I'm sorry. What? What are you talking about?' She glanced at Erica and then did a double take at Erica's expression. 'The Devil?' Her voice was too high pitched. She tried to lower it, but somehow it came out in a higher squeak. 'Sunday night? Someone's going to summon the actual Devil on Sunday night and try and sell his soul? How—? Why—? What?' She couldn't breathe. Taking a step back, she crouched, placing a hand on the damp dirt to steady herself.

There was pressure as Erica placed a hand on her back.

'It's okay. Breathe.'

Jess tried to breathe. If it was that simple she wouldn't be crouched in the dirt feeling like her chest was about to explode. Tears pricked at her eyes.

'Just when I think I've got a handle on this, you throw me something new,' she growled. 'Demons and then imps and now this?' She stood, opening up her chest, and looked up at the cloudy night sky. Visions of the tarot cards she'd pulled in her parents' house that spring flittered before her eyes.

In nearly each and every pull, the Devil had stared back at her.

'Who's in trouble?' Erica was asking.

Always the level-headed one, how was she calmly asking who was about to sell their soul? How was she not reeling from the mention of the actual Devil? Jess stared at her, breathing hard.

'A young lad,' said Mullarky with a shrug of his small, scrawny shoulders.

'Do you know his name? Or where he lives? Or

works?'

'Nae. I saw him just the once, at that very spot, talking to himself about summonings and wishes and deals. He's in a great deal of pain.'

Erica sighed.

'That's not particularly helpful. Lots of people are in pain.' She gestured to Jess who gave something of a hysterical laugh. 'What does he look like?'

'Tall,' said Mullarky. 'Brown hair. White skin. Younger than ye.'

'That doesn't really narrow it down much,' Erica murmured thoughtfully. 'How tall?'

Mullarky narrowed his eyes.

'Because I'm shorter than you'se? I am in fact very tall for my kind, I'll have ye ken.'

For some reason, that calmed something in Jess. She still stood apart from them, but she watched Mullarky as he concentrated on Erica, taking in the way his limbs hung, the expression in his eyes.

'Taller than me?' Erica asked.

Mullarky peered up at her.

'Hard to say.'

Erica sighed and turned to stare down the path, back towards the town.

'It's Friday night. All Hallows' Eve is on Sunday. That doesn't leave us much time. And you've given us practically nothing to go on.'

'The town is nae that big,' said Mullarky.

'There's a few thousand people here,' Erica argued. 'And the majority are white, roughly half or so will be male. Brown hair is the most common colour. There must be something else. Any features? Scars? A certain hair style? Coat colour? Anything?'

Mullarky shrugged.

'It was dark and I wasnae close tae him.'

Jess ran her hands over her face, gathering her thoughts.

'We could just wait until Sunday, catch him when he comes back here? Because, he will, won't he? Come back here, I mean. To the crossroads.'

Mullarky and Erica considered her, a small smile spreading on Mullarky's lips.

'Unless we find another way of figuring out who he is, I think that's probably our only option,' Erica agreed.

'And Alfie!' Jess cried. 'He can do it, can't he? Talk the man out of it. No Devil summoning. Job done. Right?'

Erica put an arm around Jess.

'I don't think Alfie will be bothered, to be honest.'

Jess sighed. These damn fae.

'He'll be bothered if you're there,' said Jess matter-of-factly. 'So if he doesn't handle it, then you will, right? Which means he'll be there. Which means he can handle it.'

Erica's brow creased a little, but instead of responding to Jess, she turned back to Mullarky.

'Okay. We'll do our best. And we'll come back

here Sunday. Except we don't know when he'll be trying this summoning. Or even if you're right about all this. So' – she turned back to Jess – 'I'll come here on Sunday. You should spend Halloween with Ruby.'

Jess exhaled with a tremble.

'I can't let you do this alone.'

'I won't be alone. Like you said, when Alfie gets wind of it, he probably won't let me out of his sight.' Erica turned back to the brownie. 'This is where you live? In case we need to get back in touch with you?'

A shadow passed over Mullarky's expression and he pointed a finger up at Erica.

'Never,' he hissed, 'ever knock on that door again. My Mauve is never to ken about you'se, me or what's happening. She's innocent and she's tae be left out of this. D'ye understand?'

'Even though someone supposedly wants to summon the Devil right outside her house?' asked Erica with a sigh.

Mullarky pressed his lips together and gave a shudder of anger.

'It's okay,' said Jess quickly, stepping between them. 'We'll never knock on the cottage door again. We won't involve the woman who lives there. We promise. But how can we contact you?'

Mullarky softened a little.

'I'm around,' he said, as if that answered everything. 'I'll ken. Now, it's time for you'se tae go.'

'Great. Okay. Thanks. Nice to meet you.' Erica gave Mullarky a nod and began walking down the path, back towards the town.

Mullarky caught Jess's eye as she went to follow.

'I often visit yer mother's house, daughter of the reluctant witch,' he told her softly. 'If ye need me, ever, I'll be there. Find the lad. Save his soul.' He glanced back to the cottage behind him. 'Save the soul,' he murmured as if to himself. Then he waved to Jess and wandered back to the cottage without looking back. The downstairs light was off and a bedroom light upstairs had come on. Mullarky let himself in through the front door, closing it silently behind him.

Shivering, Jess caught up with Erica.

'What in the hell?' she hissed.

'Quite literally,' Erica agreed.

Jess said goodbye to Erica on the high street, having made plans for the next day. Nothing much had been discussed about what the brownie had told them, which concerned Jess, but an exhaustion had overwhelmed her the moment the brownie had closed the front door.

She let herself into her parents' house with her spare key and found the adults in the living room, slumped on the sofas, watching the television above the fireplace. As always, Jess's gaze was drawn to the hatch in the floor beneath the coffee table.

Bubbles, who had been curled up on the sofa beside Marshall, stepped down, stretching as she went, and sleepily brushed her head against Jess's legs, tail wagging. Jess gave her a cuddle.

'Everything okay?' Marshall asked, sitting up.

'I have no idea,' said Jess, perching on the sofa next to him, rubbing Bubbles's ears. Slowly, she slid into him until they were entangled in a hug. She breathed in his warmth and musk, forcing her eyes back open so she didn't drift off to sleep there and then.

'Where did you go? Was it ghost business?' asked her father, moving forward in his seat and setting his cup of tea on the coffee table.

Jess smiled as Bubbles curled up on the floor by her feet.

'Well, sort of. I met a brownie.' Jess pulled out her phone as her parents frowned.

'What's a brownie?' asked Ginny.

'A little girl who makes cups of tea for a badge,' said Eddie. 'Remember, Jess? You were a brownie for a while. Until that owl woman asked you to clean her house for a badge and you cottoned on.' He grinned.

Marshall snorted.

'A brownie, or brounie, is a type of hobgoblin from Scottish folklore,' Jess read from the search on her phone. 'They come out at night and perform chores around the house and farm, and are particularly good at milking cows and churning butter.' She sat back, thoughtfully staring at the words.

'You met a brownie from Scottish folklore in our South West England town, in the high street after a meal down the pub?' Ginny questioned. 'You realise how that sounds, Jess.'

Jess smiled.

'Oh, I wish it was because I'd had too much to drink,' she mumbled. 'Did Ruby go to bed okay?' she asked Marshall, slipping her phone back into her pocket.

He nodded.

'Brushed her teeth and then was out like a light.'

'Good. I'll pop in before I go to bed. Check on her.'

'What did the brownie have to say?' asked Eddie.

Jess shook her head.

'Oh, nothing.' She glanced at her mother who looked away a little too quickly. Too tired to think, Jess stored that away for later. 'I'm going to bed, if no one minds. I'll check on Ruby.' She kissed Marshall's cheek and stepped over the dog. 'Night.'

'Night, love,' said Eddie, his eyes concerned as he watched his daughter go.

'Sweet dreams,' murmured Ginny.

Jess climbed the stairs, ignored the fleeting shadow that passed on the landing, and slowly opened the door to her daughter's room. Ruby was breathing softly in the bed, fast asleep. Smiling, Jess got ready for bed and lay there, staring at the ceiling, her thoughts spinning, until Marshall joined her.

She must have slept, because she was woken. It was still dark but her phone told her it was three in the morning. Gently sliding Marshall's arm from around her waist, Jess slipped out of bed, stepped over Bubbles and pulled on some clothes. Bubbles lifted her head but Jess gestured for her to stay. The dog completely ignored her, jumping up and padding over to the door, stretching and blocking Jess's escape. Rolling her eyes, Jess let the dog out and Bubbles padded across the landing and down the stairs. Jess followed, tiptoeing through the quiet house, praying she wouldn't wake Ruby.

There came noise from the kitchen and Bubbles shook, her collar rattling.

'Shh!'

Jess rushed into the kitchen. She knew exactly who she would find, but it still came as a surprise to find her mother by the back door instead of by the kettle.

Ginny froze, eyes wide.

'What are you doing, Mum?'

19

Connor

'What the hell, Connor? Dad says you turned down his job offer. Again!'

Connor could see where this was going. He saved his game and turned the PlayStation off as quickly as it would allow him. Maggie walked through the small living room and carefully sat on the chair near him, leaning back and kicking her shoes off. He sat back and watched her.

Finally, she threw up her arms at him.

'Well? Why?'

'Because something else is coming,' said Connor quietly.

'What?'

'Something else is coming,' he said a little louder, avoiding her gaze. 'Everything'll be all right on Monday.'

'Someone else offered you a job?'

Connor shook his head.

'No, but—'

'Connor, I swear to God, if you don't take this job with my dad, I'm leaving you.' She stroked her large baby bump as if for emphasis.

Connor met her eyes.

'Please. Please, just trust me.'

'I've been trusting you. Ever since those bastards made you redundant and you said you'd have a new job within a month, I've been trusting you. And look at where we are. I'm working full time, my back is killing me, I can't feel my feet – hell, I can't *see* my feet anymore. And every evening when I come home you're playing stupid games. You haven't even tidied the flat.' She looked around at the state of the room. 'I'm not doing everything, Connor. Not with you around. If I have to do everything myself, then I might as well just be a single parent. Okay? So, do you want to take that job with my dad or not?'

Connor ground his teeth.

'I promise you, by Monday—'

'You're not listening to me, Connor!'

'I'm not working for your dad!' Connor blurted. 'He treats me like shit.'

'Yeah, because you're the arsehole who got his daughter pregnant and then spent every day playing computer games instead of looking for a job.'

'It's not like I didn't have a job when you got pregnant. This isn't my fault.'

Maggie closed her eyes and took a deep,

steadying breath. Just the sight made anger bloom in Connor's gut; he was so sick of her feeling the need to do that around him.

'I know it's not your fault that you lost your job,' she said gently. 'But it is your fault that you're not looking for a new one.'

'You don't know that I'm not,' Connor snapped. 'For all you know, I've spent all day applying for jobs and I only just stopped.'

His girlfriend raised an eyebrow.

'Have you? Is that how you've spent your day? How many jobs have you applied for?'

Connor turned back to the television, fiddling with the PlayStation controller.

Maggie gave a grim smile and shook her head.

'If you take this job and work hard, my dad will start treating you better. And you'll feel better about yourself. It's not healthy to be stuck at home playing games all day.'

Connor bit back tears burning at the back of his eyes and concentrated on the black television screen.

'I know you, Connor,' came her soft voice. 'You're capable of so many great things. I just want you to see that.' There was pity in her tone and Connor couldn't stand it.

He stood, throwing the controller down.

'I'm going out.'

'What? Where?'

'To get a job,' he snapped mockingly, pulling on

his shoes and grabbing his coat and keys, slamming the door behind him.

The tears were falling as soon as the door was closed. Knees and fingers trembling, he made his way down the road, yanking on his coat against the bitter chill of the evening air, oblivious to the dark eyes following him from behind the neighbour's hedge.

20

Erica

'Where were you last night?' Erica asked quietly as Alfie opened his eyes. They lay next to each other, naked, the sheets resting over their shoulders. It would be cosy and an invitation for something more if Erica hadn't spent most of the night lying awake, worrying, and watching as Alfie snuck out after midnight and back in before dawn.

He frowned, blinking awake, and then reached out for her.

She resisted, waiting patiently for an answer.

Alfie sighed and rolled onto his back, lifting an arm. She took this invitation, snuggling up and resting her head against his chest. The comfort from his warmth and smell was immediate and she had to quickly force her eyes back open to stay awake.

'I'm not happy about tomorrow night,' he said,

stroking her hair and staring up at the ceiling.

That night, Erica had found Alfie in their hotel room waiting for her, and had explained everything the brownie had told her and Jess. Alfie had not been pleased. Rather than ban her from going out on Halloween or demand that he accompany her, however, he'd remained silent.

They'd made love on the hotel bed and Erica, body tingling pleasurably, had fallen asleep. It was probably the only sleep she'd had that night. She woke as Alfie slipped out of bed and had watched him from over the edge of the covers as he'd left the room.

'I don't think any of us are happy about tomorrow night,' she told him. 'Where did you go, though?'

'To the crossroads.' He pressed a kiss against her hair. 'To the witch's cottage.' His hand slipped down her arm and over her waist to land on her hip.

'And?'

'I didn't see the brownie. Mullarky, was it? I found the crossroads.'

'So, it's a real threat? This bloke could actually summon the Devil?'

When Alfie didn't respond, Erica propped herself up and looked at him. 'It's real?'

He met her eyes and some of the worry dissipated.

'It's real. But that doesn't mean we have to be involved.' He smiled. 'Why do you always have to be involved in everything?'

Erica placed a kiss on his chest.

'Because someone's going to get hurt. And not just hurt a little. That spirit in Jess's parents' house, he sold his soul to the Devil, didn't he? And an imp waited who knows how long to drag his soul to hell.'

Alfie sighed and then lifted himself to brush a kiss over her lips. Wrapping his arms around her, he pushed her back and over, until he was lying on top of her.

'Isn't that his choice?' he asked, placing kisses down her neck. He lifted Erica's arms above her head and she left them there as he lowered himself to kiss her collarbone.

'Yes. But what if he doesn't understand what he's doing? What if he doesn't really think it'll work? What if he's so desperate that he's not thought it through properly? Because you'd have to be desperate, right? To summon the Devil.'

'Not always,' came Alfie's muffled voice as his lips found her breasts.

Erica didn't reply. She couldn't. Every time a thought occurred to her, Alfie's tongue stopped it from being said. Soon she couldn't remember what they were talking about. Not until he dipped down to her stomach. Erica stared up at the ceiling, trying to reorganise her thoughts as her body throbbed for him.

'So if you found out that some poor bastard was about to try and sell his soul to the Devil, you'd just let it happen?'

Alfie paused and lifted his head to look at her.

'It happens more often than you think,' he told her. 'It happens regularly, and you have no idea. What makes this one so special?'

Erica went to respond, but Alfie slipped lower and the words left her mouth in a rushed exhale instead.

Erica and Alfie left their room at the same time, making their way downstairs and didn't see another soul. It gave Erica some comfort that perhaps no one had overheard the noises she'd worked so hard to cover up. They walked into the breakfast room, still busy with late risers, and her cheeks flushed, giving her away.

Alfie gave her a smirk and then wandered over to the buffet while Erica found a table.

They were just settling with fruit, croissants, coffee and juice, when they were politely interrupted.

'Mrs Murray?'

Erica looked up to find a man in a suit standing over their table.

'Miss. Yes?'

'Sorry, Ms Murray. Adam Drescott, I'm the manager. You asked to see me?'

Erica smiled warmly, hoping to ease some of the concern etched into the man's face.

'Hmm.' She wiped her mouth on a napkin. 'Yes. I wanted to talk to you about the history of this place and some noises I heard.'

'Oh, I do hope you weren't disturbed.'

'Oh, no, no. Nothing like that.'

Alfie gave a soft snort and Erica ignored him. 'I heard piano music coming from the basement,' she explained, and watched as the manager paled. He struggled for words for a moment. 'Does anyone here play the piano?' she asked.

'No. I mean...'

'I'm a paranormal investigator,' she told him, and watched his pale worry turn to wariness. 'I believe you have a pianist spirit in your basement. Your receptionist mentioned something about you wanting to turn the basement into a restaurant – it would certainly create a good atmosphere with music like that.'

The manager glanced around and then dragged a chair over from a neighbouring table.

'What is it that you're asking, Ms Murray?'

'If you're aware of any paranormal activity in your basement.'

Adam sighed.

'Yes,' he admitted. 'We often hear the piano down there being played when there's no one down there to play it. But it's an old piano. And I keep meaning to get it checked.'

'Do you know who it is?'

Adam gave her a strange look.

'No. Like I said, it happens when no one's down there. It's the piano. Something must be sticking.'

'For the music I heard, that's one hell of a talented, sticky piano.'

Alfie attempted to hide a laugh by gulping some coffee.

'Is that all, Ms Murray? I do hope everything else is satisfactory.' Adam glanced down at their breakfast.

'Very. It's a gorgeous hotel,' Erica told him. 'But I'd get someone in to check the basement before you start any renovations to turn it into a restaurant. Spirits generally don't like renovations. And if you'd like to make some money out of it, there's a possibility of ghost tours. Especially in a town like this. I imagine it's crawling with stories. I've already heard something about a witch's cottage.'

Adam started, and Erica and Alfie watched him curiously.

'This town has a good history,' he said.

'You know about the witch's cottage?' Alfie asked.

Adam turned to him, as if seeing him for the first time.

'It's just a story. There's a cottage on the edge of the woods, really old. It's said that a witch once lived there, that's all. These days an old lady lives there, but she's no witch. She's very kind and gentle, keeps to herself these days. Sometimes her daughter comes to visit. I imagine they'll rent it out as a holiday cottage one day, I know I would.'

'Witches often are kind and gentle,' Alfie said in a low voice.

Erica looked up at the manager.

'And I bet this building has some stories too. Have a think about the ghost tour possibility. It doesn't have to be a ghost tour. It could be a history tour. Or you could do both, they have different audiences, attract different people. You could hold them during your slow months, create a little package deal out of it.' That caught Adam's attention. 'And if you'd like a survey done, to see if you really do have a spirit and look at the potential for ghost tours, let me know. My friend and I run a paranormal investigation agency, although my friend loves the history side of it too. I imagine she'd love to put together a history tour for you. We can even run them for you, we don't live far away. A bit closer to the city. There are references on our website.' Erica passed a business card to Adam. He glanced at it and then slid it into his pocket.

'Please let me know if I can assist with anything else,' he said, going back to his script, before turning and leaving them alone.

'Nice pitch,' said Alfie, finishing off an apple.

'Worth a try.' Erica sipped her coffee, her gaze shifting from Adam's back to the door by the bar that led down to the basement. She sighed thoughtfully. 'How do we figure out who this Devil summoning man is when we only have a vague description and no name? If we could find him today and talk him out of it, we could relax,' she murmured.

'You're still on this?' Alfie's gaze flicked up to her. 'It's got nothing to do with us.'

'Like Bethany vanishing into your world didn't have anything to do with us?'

'Exactly.' Alfie leaned back. 'But you still made me take you to rescue her.'

'And did she need rescuing?' Erica pointed out.

Alfie smiled.

'Depends on who you ask.'

Erica rolled her eyes.

'Fine. Then what about the demon in the woods? You didn't complain about helping then. And that bastard scarred your face.'

Alfie's fingers absent-mindedly moved to the silver scar below his eye, quickly fading into memory.

'That was different. The demon was killing people and you were adamant about going into those woods. It could have killed you.'

'Well, the Devil will ultimately kill this guy,' Erica hissed, leaning forward in order to be heard while keeping her voice down.

Smiling, Alfie mirrored her, leaning forward on the table.

'He will die when his time has come. As do we all. And it is his choice if he wishes to send his soul to hell. There's a difference, Erica. The walkers in the woods had no choice about whether the demon took their lives, this man is making a choice about where his soul ends up.'

Erica leaned back, staring at Alfie hard.

'You know, Bethany followed Fen into your world because she felt desperate. Let's ignore all the magic flowers that helped along the way. She wanted to escape, and he gave her that opportunity. But she regretted it. Deep in that forest, when she realised what she'd done, she regretted it.'

'No, she didn't,' said Alfie. 'Did you know that Fen and Bethany are still together? She spent a whole month in our world over the summer, leaving to go to work and then returning every evening to be with him. He's moved to a village closer to London so they can carry on in the same way while she's at university.' Alfie sipped his coffee. 'It worked for her. It could work for you.'

Erica blinked. How had he turned the conversation that quickly?

'Bethany doesn't have a ninety-year-old grandmother to worry about.'

Alfie puffed out air.

'As if Minerva doesn't spend most of her evenings in my world these days.'

Erica stopped.

'What?'

Alfie's eyes widened a fraction and then he shook his head, returning to his breakfast.

'Nothing. My point is that Bethany didn't regret anything. And maybe this man won't either.'

Erica frowned.

'Fine. A, if Bethany didn't regret it, then why did you show her versions of her future to help her realise what she was letting herself in for? And B, I wouldn't compare falling in love with a fae with selling your soul to the Devil. Two very different things.'

'You're the one comparing them,' Alfie pointed out. 'And I showed her versions of the future because I wanted the whole thing to be over.'

Erica studied the fae sitting opposite her, calmly drinking, watching the other patrons over the rim of his mug. Beneath that gentle exterior he was angry. She could feel it coming off him. Frustrated, annoyed, but hidden well. The couple at the next table would have no idea.

She wondered briefly what Alfie could show her to make this conversation be over.

'I brought her up because she was desperate,' she said carefully. 'I imagine this man is too. You'd have to be, right?'

For a brief moment, Alfie met her gaze.

It was enough for her.

'Come on, drink up. Let's go meet Jess.'

21

Jess

Eddie and Ginny were awake and up early for a Saturday. Jess was dragged from bed by Ruby and was surprised to find her parents already in the kitchen preparing a breakfast of bacon rolls for everyone. Jess told Ruby to go wake Marshall, and the five-year-old ran up the stairs shouting Marshall's name, Bubbles bouncing along behind her.

Jess cringed; she'd pay for that later. Although surely the bacon roll would make the rude awakening worth it.

'You're up early.' Jess wandered over to the brand new coffee machine Ginny had treated herself to.

'Lots to be doing,' said Eddie as Ginny jumped up to make Jess a coffee, gently pushing her daughter out of the way and gesturing to a seat at the kitchen table.

Jess sat and a memory of sitting there as an imp wandered the house trying to rip a soul to hell flashed before her.

'Hmm,' she murmured. 'Do you remember what the imp wanted?' she asked quietly.

Her father stared at her and then leaned forward, his eyes far too bright and wide for her liking.

'Yes. To drag a man's soul to hell.' He tapped his fingertips eagerly on the table.

Jess glanced at her mother, but she was focusing on the coffee machine.

'And there was a witch bottle under the floor,' Jess murmured.

Eddie nodded.

'And the saucer. Which we've still got,' he added.

Jess watched her mother's shoulders flinch.

'The brownie Erica and I met last night said that he believes a man is planning on summoning the Devil tomorrow night and selling his soul,' Jess said in a rush, eyes on the door to the hallway to make sure Ruby wouldn't hear her.

Ginny turned and both of Jess's parents stared at her.

'Don't be ridiculous,' said her mother after a moment's pause. She placed a cup of coffee in front of Jess. 'The Devil isn't real.'

'Then how do you explain the imp, Mum? And the spirit that the imp dragged down to hell?'

'And the massive crack in our window,' Eddie

muttered.

'We don't know the imp took the spirit to hell,' Ginny pointed out. 'And I just assumed that the Devil thing was...I don't know, code.'

'Code for what?' Jess asked as Ginny turned back to make another coffee ready for Marshall.

'I don't know. Drugs or something.'

Jess and her father exchanged a look.

'You know, I did some research on that spirit. James,' said Jess, running her fingers over the hot ceramic of her coffee cup. 'He lived here in the nineteen hundreds and died here. That means the imp must have been here, hanging around and waiting, for over a hundred years.'

'Well, that explains it,' said Eddie.

Jess looked up.

'Explains what?'

'We received all the house records when we were buying this place. This placed changed hands a lot at one point. Someone would buy it, live here for maybe a year or so, and then sell it again. Over and over. Until the last owners bought the place. They stayed here a good twenty years until presumably one of them passed away or left, and the other died in a nursing home. Even then, their children couldn't sell it, could they. That's why it ended up at auction and how we managed to get it for such a good price.' Eddie grinned and leaned across the table. 'Because all those people could feel the darkness that surrounded this place.'

'If that's true then why did we buy it?' scoffed Ginny.

'Because, darling, you're a witch. And a witch is more than capable of handling an imp and a spirit.'

'And shadow people,' Jess added.

'And them as well.'

'I'm not a witch,' said Ginny.

Jess smiled to herself.

'The brownie called you a reluctant witch.'

Eddie laughed and clapped his hands.

'Perfect!'

Ginny turned to pull a face at her husband and daughter.

'What does any of this have to do with anything?'

Jess sobered.

'Because a man is going to try and sell his soul to the Devil tomorrow night,' she whispered.

'It's Halloween, Jess,' said Ginny slowly. 'The town is spreading stories. It's nothing. I doubt the brownie was even real. Probably someone dressed up, or one of those automated things.'

Jess frowned. Mullarky had seemed very real to her, but now in the cold morning light with a steaming coffee in front of her, it would be so easy to brush the memory off as wrong.

There was a thudding and then Ruby appeared at the bottom of the stairs with Bubbles.

'Walk down the stairs, don't run,' said Jess automatically.

'Marshall's in the bathroom,' Ruby declared,

climbing into her seat at the table and taking a gulp of the orange juice Ginny had prepared for her.

The adults watched her in silence for long enough that Ruby looked at each of them in turn before landing on her mother with wide eyes.

'What do you want to do today, Ruby?' Jess asked, breaking the spell.

'Go to the fair!' Ruby shouted.

Jess laughed as her parents cringed.

'The fair isn't open until this evening. How about we go explore the playground?'

Ruby nodded enthusiastically and then gave a shrill, albeit slightly muted, shriek when her grandmother placed a bacon roll on a plate in front of her.

'What do you say, Rubes?' Jess asked as Ruby went to take a bite.

Ruby took the bite and then looked up at her grandmother.

'Thank you,' she said around the food.

'Ruby!'

'It's okay. Good enough,' said Ginny, holding back a laugh. 'Don't do that with your mouth full to anyone outside of this family, though. It's rude,' she warned Ruby.

Ruby nodded and took another bite.

Jess stood to feed Bubbles her breakfast, placing the bowl on the floor near the back door.

'What's Marshall helping you with today?' she asked her father.

'Today we are pulling up the old patio and preparing the ground for a new one,' Eddie declared. 'Thank you, my sweetheart,' he told Ginny as a bacon roll was placed in front of him.

'What about you, Mum? Do you have plans? Or do you want to come to the playground with me and Ruby?'

'No, no,' said Ginny, turning back to the kitchen worktop. 'I have some errands to run. Will you be meeting with Erica and her boyfriend?'

'Yeah, if they're up yet.'

'He seemed nice,' said Ginny.

'Alfie's great.'

'He's a fae,' said Ruby.

Eddie and Ginny stared at her.

'A what?' asked Eddie.

'A fae!' Ruby shouted.

'Ruby. Keep your voice down. And don't shout with your mouth full, for the love of everything not disgusting,' Jess admonished before flashing Marshall a smile as he entered the kitchen and took in the scene.

As they ate breakfast, they talked about what Eddie and Marshall were going to do with the patio and what time they were going to the fair. As soon as it was polite to do so, Jess excused herself and went back up the stairs to the spare bedroom she shared with Marshall.

As she reached the landing, something moved to her right. She automatically looked and saw a shadow drift across into her parents' bedroom. With a shiver, Jess entered her own bedroom and closed the door softly behind her.

She wasn't sure how her parents were doing it. She couldn't live with shadow people in her house, even if they were friendly enough and didn't complain when you changed your mind about a wall colour.

Jess made the bed and then sat on it, pulling her box of tarot cards from her bag. Idly shuffling the cards, she began to form a question in her mind. Should she ask about the identity of the man they were looking for? She wasn't sure how the cards could help with that. No, there was a more obvious question.

'How do we stop this man from selling his soul?' Jess asked the cards, stopping the shuffling when a tingle shot through her. She pulled the card.

The Devil stared back at her.

'Yeah, no shit,' she muttered, placing the card to one side and returning to shuffling the pack.

'How do we stop this man from selling his soul to the Devil?' she repeated.

She waited until her intuition told her to stop and then she pulled the card.

The Ten of Wands.

Jess sighed and flicked through her little book to double check that she'd remembered its meaning correctly.

Jess's mouth went dry and she snapped the cards together, pushing them back into their box. Her phone beeped and she pulled it from her pocket as she made her way back down the stairs, ignoring the drifting shadow by the front door.

'Rubes? You ready to go meet Erica and Alfie?' she asked as she entered the kitchen.

Marshall was already pulling on his boots and her father was standing outside on the patio, giving it an appraising look with his hands on his hips.

'You will be careful, won't you,' Jess murmured as Marshall leaned over to kiss her.

'Of course. I'll take care of your dad, don't worry.'

Jess smiled and stole another kiss before Marshall could escape. He wandered outside smiling to himself.

'Ready, Mummy. Can Bubbles come too?'

'Of course.' Jess moved to fetch Bubbles's harness and lead. 'Mum? You sure you don't want to come?'

'Hmm? Oh, yes, no, I'm sure. Thank you.'

Jess studied her mother, but relented as Ruby began talking to something in the hallway. Jess looked down at the dog beside her and then counted everyone around her.

'Rubes? Who are you talking to?'

'The shadow—'

'Well, please don't,' said Jess quickly. 'Come on. Let's get your shoes on.'

The playground wasn't far from Jess's parents' house and it was empty when Jess, Ruby and Bubbles arrived. Ruby ran off to the climbing frame while Jess made herself comfortable on a bench. Bubbles barked after Ruby until Jess told her to lie down. The dog got a treat for her troubles, although she continued to whine as she watched Ruby play. Then she was back on her feet, letting out an excited bark.

Jess looked up to see Erica and Alfie approaching. Erica smiled and opened her arms to the dog and, as there was no one else around, Jess released the lead and let Bubbles bound over to the couple.

Alfie bent to greet the dog and Bubbles sat, offering the fae her paw. Erica left them behind to join Jess on the bench.

'Good morning.'

'Is it?' Jess asked, watching Alfie and Bubbles. 'I'm never sure if I like how good he is with her,' she murmured.

Erica followed her gaze.

'He loves dogs,' she said by way of explanation. 'They don't have dogs in his world. I'm planning on

using it as a bargaining chip if I do decide to stay
here.'

Jess looked at her.

'You haven't decided yet?'

Erica seemed just as surprised.

'Apparently not. How would you feel? If I moved
in with Alfie?'

Jess sighed, watching Alfie and Bubbles slowly
approach while Ruby went down the slide and
started her climbing game again.

'Honestly? A little worried about you. About us.
About how to reach you. But we'd make it work, you
know. It'd be okay.' She tried not to notice Erica
studying her.

'When I first met Alfie, you told me to steer clear
of him,' Erica murmured.

Jess met her friend's eyes.

'Yeah. I did. And I was wrong. I trust him now.
And I trust him with you. And Bubbles, and Ruby.
Move in with him if you want to. Hell, marry him if
you want to! I just don't want to lose you, or what
we have.'

Erica smiled and slipped her hand into Jess's to
give it a squeeze.

'Never.'

Jess smiled, warmth spreading through her
chest.

'Did you tell Alfie about Mullarky?'

Erica's smile fell.

'I did. He's never met a brownie and he doesn't

want us involved in the whole thing.'

'Wow. You surprise me,' said Jess, giving Erica a look.

Erica smirked and looked up as Alfie reached them. Bubbles pushed her head into Erica's lap until she began rubbing the dog's ears.

'Don't want Erica saving a man from the Devil, huh?' Jess asked bluntly. 'What about me? Am I allowed?'

Her smile fell as Alfie turned a dark expression on her, the warmth from Erica's hand replaced with a flash of cold dread.

'No,' said Alfie. 'It's nothing to do with either of you, and you don't seem to understand how dangerous it all is. You can't save everyone. You'd be wise to just leave it alone.' He turned to face the playground and watch Ruby make her way to the top of the slide.

'What about Mullarky?' Jess asked quietly.

Alfie shrugged.

'No harm in the brownie. But neither of you should help him with this particular task,' said Alfie, keeping his back to them.

Erica and Jess exchanged a look, Erica raising an eyebrow ever so slightly.

'Fair enough,' Jess murmured. 'Fine. So,' she said brightly, 'what do you guys want to do today? There's only so long you can watch Ruby on the climbing frame and slide before you start to need vodka. I speak from experience.'

Alfie's shoulders moved as he laughed silently.

'What about the swing?' he asked, scanning the playground.

'Same, except you have to be involved,' Jess told him, gesturing that he was free to give it a try. 'Ruby? Want Alfie to push you on the swing?'

'Yay!' Ruby flew down the slide and ran over to the swings.

Alfie checked with Jess over his shoulder.

'Not too hard and not too high,' Jess told him.

Alfie gave a solemn nod and wandered over to the swings and Ruby as Jess grabbed onto Bubbles to keep her at a safe distance.

'What do you think about the Mullarky situation?' Jess whispered to Erica.

'What if we can stop this today?' Erica whispered back, keeping her eyes on Alfie pushing the laughing child on the swing. 'We just need to find out who this guy is. I think we need more information.'

Rick

Bristol, two months ago

The cemetery was quiet, probably due to the fine August mist of rain drenching everything in sight. The café might be busy, but outside the air was fresh, the cemetery was green and Rick was alone. For now.

He wandered slowly along the path, past gravestones covered with ivy, beneath tall self-sown ash trees, and then paused at a bench. He couldn't sit, the wood was too wet, so he pulled his coat tighter around him, blinked through the rain and waited.

Sure enough, soon he had company.

Alfie wandered up, hands deep in his denim pockets, his white shirt almost see through in the rain, showing off a body that made Rick's stomach clench. He wrenched his gaze up to meet Alfie's eyes and tried hard not to think about Erica.

'Hello, Rick.' Alfie blinked water droplets from his eyelashes.

'Really? No coat?' Rick mumbled.

'I don't own a coat. I like the rain,' Alfie explained. 'It's good to be close to nature.'

Rick harrumphed and Alfie cocked his head to the side, smiling an annoying smile.

'Can I help you?'

Rick sighed.

'Yes. Please.'

Alfie narrowed his eyes.

'What time have you come from? Or do you not know anymore? This is the first time you've managed to call out to me like this, for a meeting. Or at least, it's my first time. Is it yours?'

'Yes.'

Alfie grinned.

'Who taught you that, I wonder.'

Rick shook water from his hair and sighed.

'Minerva.'

Alfie nodded.

'And why did she teach you that?'

'Because I need your help,' said Rick through gritted teeth.

Alfie glanced around the empty cemetery.

'Go on.'

Rick flashed the time travel device on his wrist before covering it back up with his coat sleeve, not wanting to get it too wet.

'I need this changed. Minerva said you knew someone who could help.'

Alfie gazed over Rick thoughtfully.

'Changed how?'

Rick sighed.

'You win,' he told the fae. 'All right? You win. I messed up. I messed up my whole life and my timeline, all in one fell swoop. And if I stay in this timeline, I'm doomed to stay in an unethical job that I hate, alone.'

Alfie watched him.

'You want to change your timeline,' he murmured.

'I want to change the timeline I'm in,' Rick corrected. 'I want a new start. There's got to be a better place than this. A place away from my boss and his stupid job. A place away from...' Rick sighed and Alfie's smile fell away.

'I'm sorry. For the pain I've caused you.'

Rick shook his head again, sending more rain flying.

'It's not you. I mean, it is you. Completely. But it's me too. I'm an idiot. The answer was there all along and I didn't see it. And it's Ricci's fault. She still could have chosen me, but...' Rick's gaze accidentally slipped back to Alfie's chest through his sodden shirt. 'I just want this pain to stop,' he finished in a whisper.

Alfie flinched.

'I can help,' he said gently. 'I will help. Come on.

Come with me.'

Alfie held out an arm and, strangely, it gave Rick a sense of comfort as he let the fae lead him away, through the cemetery and out the other side.

Erica

It was approaching midday when Ruby led them to her grandparents' house. Erica and Alfie paused to take in the double-fronted Victorian building. Without looking, Alfie took Erica's hand. She glanced up at him and then back to the house.

'What is it?' she whispered.

'Nothing,' he lied.

Jess opened the front door and they walked through into a beautifully, newly decorated hallway.

'The floor tiles are original,' said Jess proudly.

'Wow.' Erica looked around the room in awe. 'And your dad and Marshall did all this themselves?'

'And Mum. Isn't it amazing?' Jess beamed and led them through to the kitchen.

The room was empty, but through the back door

they could see Marshall and Eddie working on the patio. Bubbles bounded through and gave a small bark, making Eddie give a short yell.

'Scared the life out of me! Don't do that, pooch.' He ruffled Bubbles's fur as she investigated what he'd been doing, sniffing the pulled up patio slabs and then leaping over to Marshall to push her face into his dirty hands.

'Erica!' Eddie brushed off his hands and gestured to the work he and Marshall had done. All of the patio slabs had been pulled up and some had been stacked over to the side.

'How's it going? You have a beautiful house,' said Erica, stepping out into the dirt. Given the low cloud, she had no doubt that it could soon be turned into mud. 'Wrong time of year to be doing this, though, isn't it?'

'No time like the present.' Eddie beamed. 'Have you met our resident shadow people?'

'Dad! Give her a chance,' said Jess, standing next to Marshall and hugging herself as she surveyed the work done. 'Is Mum home yet?'

'Not yet.' Eddie, still beaming, turned to Alfie. 'You look like a strong one, fancy joining us?'

Alfie glanced over the patio and then turned a charming smile on Eddie.

'Looks like you've already done all the heavy lifting.'

Eddie looked down at the patio slabs near his feet.

'True.'

'I'd much rather meet these shadow people, to be honest,' Alfie continued.

Jess sighed.

'I can show you!' shouted Ruby, jumping back into the house and pushing past Alfie. She went to take his hand and then seemed to think better of it, skipping through the kitchen into the hallway instead.

'I'll come too,' said Erica.

'No.' Erica reeled at Alfie's tone. He softened a little and smiled, but she wasn't convinced. 'No. You stay here.'

Erica frowned, watching him follow Ruby through the house.

'Please don't take this the wrong way, but I think I'll join them,' said Jess quietly, pushing past Erica to get back into the kitchen.

There was a silence as Erica, cheeks burning, stared down at where the patio slabs had been pulled up.

'That was weird,' said Marshall. 'You okay?'

Erica nodded and then pulled herself together. This was meant to be a weekend away, something fun, and she had been the one to ruin it with talk of brownies and the Devil. Maybe Alfie was right. It was time to get back on track.

'Can I help?' she offered, lifting her head up and plastering a smile on her lips. 'I can make tea, if nothing else?'

'Oh, a brew would be great. Thanks,' said Eddie. 'And if you want to grab a shovel, you can help us out here.'

The idea of throwing her emotions behind a shovel had a certain appeal. Erica nodded.

'Absolutely love to. And then you have to give us a tour.'

'Oh, yes! I know Jess has told you all about the imp waiting to collect the ghost's soul, but I bet I can tell it better and show you where it actually happened.'

Erica laughed and then stopped as her voice cracked.

'Here. I'll help you make the tea,' came Marshall's concerned voice. 'Let's take a break, Eddie.'

Jess's father placed down his shovel and wiped his hands on his paint splattered jeans.

'Good idea.' He gave the area a tidy as Marshall and Erica busied themselves in the kitchen. Erica filled the kettle and clicked it on while Marshall found the cups and tea bags.

'Wanna talk about it?' he asked eventually.

Erica gave him a sideways look.

'Did Jess tell you about last night?'

'About the brownie? Yeah.'

Erica smiled to herself.

'What do you think? Do you think we should help this guy?'

Marshall sighed and turned to lean back against

the worktop, crossing this thick arms against his chest.

'Yes. But, you know, also no. I don't want Jess in danger. Or you, for that matter. And this sounds so dangerous it's on the verge of ridiculous. You know, like going to war. Or working for a mob or cartel. So ridiculously dangerous that you just wouldn't do it and it seems unreal.'

Erica pondered this.

'That's the kind of stuff people do when they're desperate,' she murmured, looking up at Marshall. 'What if this guy is just desperate.'

As they both gave this some thought, the kettle clicked off and Erica began pouring boiling water into the cups, over the tea bags.

'I guess any logical person would have to be desperate to want to make a deal with the Devil, but not everyone is logical,' said Marshall slowly. 'Some people want the adrenaline. Some people just want to see if it's real.' He looked at Erica. 'What about people who do seances and Ouija boards?'

Erica hesitated.

'That's true,' she murmured.

'What does Alfie think?' Marshall asked, his eyes narrowing.

Erica smiled.

'He's completely against the idea of us helping.' When she looked up at Marshall, his expression was stone. She turned back to the cups of tea and then floundered, searching for the fridge and the milk.

'Because it's dangerous?'

Erica found the fridge and opened it.

'Because it's dangerous. And people do dangerous, stupid things every day. What makes this one so special that we should save him,' she explained. 'What about the spirit who was here? Jess told me what she's found out about him, but she still doesn't really know what he did. Sounds like he was desperate,' she continued as she pulled out the milk and closed the fridge door.

Marshall's expression had somehow hardened further, his eyes dull.

'Ruby knows,' he said bluntly. 'She shouldn't have to know.'

Erica didn't move from the fridge.

'Do you know?' she asked quietly.

Marshall met her eyes and then gave a single nod.

'Was he desperate?'

Marshall's arms flexed as he sighed.

'He'd murdered someone... A woman or a girl... So yes, he was desperate to not get caught and punished.'

'Oh.'

Marshall gave a sad smile.

'It's one thing calling someone desperate, but you need context.'

Erica nodded.

'We don't even know this guy's name, never

mind the context.' She removed the tea bags and poured milk into each cup. 'Sugar?'

'Ah, I think it's starting to rain,' said Eddie, stepping into the kitchen and closing the back door against the late October chill. 'Spitting.'

Marshall took over finishing off the tea and handed a cup to Eddie.

'Hopefully it won't pour down just yet.'

'I hope you don't mind me asking, Erica, but how come you're not allowed to meet the shadow people? They're not dangerous, are they? They've always seemed very friendly to me,' said Eddie, sipping his drink.

Erica flinched inwardly.

'Alfie's a bit...weird like that sometimes, I guess. I don't know. Have you managed to speak to them? The shadow people?'

'I try to, but they don't talk back. But Ruby has full blown conversations with them. It's nice listening to her, although a bit odd. Seems like she already knows them so well, it's a bit like they're just part of the family.'

Erica sighed and looked down into her tea.

Marshall called out through the house to let Jess and Alfie know there were drinks waiting for them.

24

Jess

Ruby and Alfie were on the landing when Jess caught up with them, Ruby streaming sentences in an attempt to explain the shadow people to Alfie. Judging by the look on Alfie's face, the fae didn't need any explanation, but he listened to Ruby nevertheless, nodding and smiling at her. Jess hung back at first, to see what would happen.

'Hello!' cried Ruby, and then a darkness fell over the landing. It wasn't ominous, there was nothing malicious. It formed the vague outline of a person which then crouched beside Ruby. Jess thought she caught the glimpse of a smile, but immediately shook the thought away.

There was something about these shadow people. They weren't just figures created by an unnatural absence of light, they were something else. Barely visible on the edge of her vision, a movement in her periphery, a shape that faded at the edges and was gone by the time she turned her head to look properly. She'd never truly seen the shadow figures and the fact that Ruby could obviously see them, and could talk to them, sent shivers of unease through her.

Bubbles lay down near Ruby and gave a soft whine, placing her head on the plush carpet, waiting patiently but unhappy about the situation, as she always was when Ruby talked to the shadows.

Alfie crouched beside Ruby and whispered something. He was talking to the shadow, Jess realised with a jolt, watching Ruby look between the fae and the figure.

After a few moments, when Ruby was talking and Alfie was watching, Jess plucked up the courage to speak.

'Why didn't you want Erica here?' she asked quietly.

Alfie stood and joined her by the stairs, watching the child talking to something that wasn't quite thin air.

'I can't say just yet.' As if that explained any-thing, as if that was okay.

'I hate it when you're secretive. Makes me think my first impressions of you were right.'

Alfie turned sharply to Jess.

'Your first impressions?' He smiled. 'I thought you liked me now.'

'I do. But then you go and say something like

that.' Jess looked up at him. 'Why can't you tell me?'

Alfie went back to watching Ruby.

'Because it isn't time yet.'

'When will it be time?'

Alfie shifted his weight uneasily.

'Soon.'

There was a pause as they watched Ruby drawing patterns on the new carpet with her finger while she talked.

'You don't think we should help this man tomorrow,' Jess said.

'No.'

'Why?'

'Because—'

'—No, I know what you told Erica.' Jess looked up at Alfie again as he watched her daughter. 'But why really?'

Slowly, Alfie turned to meet her gaze and then smiled.

'It's dangerous, Jess. This is the Devil we're talking about. It isn't some fae leading teenage girls astray. It isn't an imp sent to collect a soul, unable to return to its master without it. It isn't some demon, hungry because its master has starved it. It *is* the master. The Devil is worse than the angry poltergeist and the demon and the imp and the murdering spirit. The Devil is worse than war and famine and disease. The Devil is worse than death. He is a fallen angel, cursed and kicked out. He is rotten and intelligent and calculating and older than any of you seem to realise. He will turn up knowing that he can buy a soul, but also well aware that there are witches present. And a fae. And a brownie, presumably. Unless this Mullarky fella has any sense about him and stays away. Unless we all come to our senses and stay away.'

Jess was hugging herself by the time Alfie was finished, rubbing her arms through her thick jumper.

'What would he want with witches and a fae?'

Alfie sighed.

'What does the powerful want with those with power,' he said.

There was a pause as Jess fought the tightness in her chest.

'We shouldn't go there tomorrow night.'

'No,' said Alfie. 'And yet...'

Jess looked up at him.

'Is there a version of our future where we don't go?'

'Of course,' said Alfie after a thoughtful moment.

'And that could be our future.'

Alfie gave a soft, sad laugh.

'I'm not so sure.'

Jess turned back to her daughter and bit on her lower lip to stop any emotion seeping through.

'Jess! Alfie! Tea!' came Marshall's voice.

Glad to have the excuse to move, Jess reached out to Ruby.

'Come on, Rubes. Time to say goodbye.'

Ruby whispered some more to the figure and then stood. As she did, whatever she had been talking to faded away. Ruby skipped happily over to Jess and Alfie, and they followed her down the stairs, Jess lost in her own thoughts as Bubbles raced to get to the bottom first.

They reached the kitchen just as the front door opened and Ginny arrived home.

'I'll make another cuppa!' Eddie cried, moving to the kettle.

Jess settled Ruby at the table, and Bubbles lay protectively beneath Ruby's feet, wagging her tail furiously as Ginny walked in.

'Have I missed lunch?' she asked, placing a bag of shopping on the worktop.

'Just in time,' said Eddie, reaching for the bag to unpack.

Ginny left again to remove her coat and shoes, and then sat beside Ruby at the table as Marshall passed her a cup of tea.

'Everything okay, Mum?' asked Jess, finding Ruby's bag of things to do and offering it to her. She happily rifled through the contents.

'Of course. It's started raining, though. How far have you got with the patio?'

'It's all up. Ready for the next stage.' Eddie beamed. 'What does everyone want for lunch? Shall we go down the pub for chips?'

'Yes!' Ruby screeched.

Marshall chuckled.

'Sounds good to me. Might have stopped raining by the time we're done.'

'A good hearty lunch to give us the strength to lay a new patio. Or to have a good kip if it's still raining,' said Eddie, closing cupboard doors and turning on his daughter and Erica. 'What do you think?'

'Chips do sound good,' said Erica.

'Think we're going to the pub. I'll go get Ruby's shoes.' Jess got to the kitchen doorway when she realised Alfie hadn't said anything. She turned back to him. 'Alfie? Pub?'

He was staring at her mother, and the sight made Jess stop altogether and try to catch his eye. 'Alfie?'

'Hmm? Yeah, pub sounds good,' he murmured, wrenching his eyes from Ginny.

Jess's mother kept her head down, but as soon as the heat from his gaze had lifted, she looked up and studied him.

'Everything okay?' Jess murmured.

Alfie gave her a smile and then herded her out of the kitchen. She relented and went to fetch Ruby's shoes from near the front door. When they were a safe distance from the kitchen, Jess turned back to Alfie.

'What the hell?'

Erica had taken up a position leaning against the worktop, facing the others but next to the kitchen doorway. For a moment, she caught Jess's eye and then looked away.

'Your mother. The reluctant witch,' murmured Alfie, smiling to himself as if he'd told a vaguely funny joke.

'Yeah? And?' Jess hissed.

Alfie shrugged.

'Don't you wonder why the brownie called your mother a reluctant witch?'

Jess hesitated in reaching for Ruby's shoes.

'Because she is a reluctant witch. She doesn't want to be one, but there's obviously something in her that I have, that Erica has, and Esther, and Minerva. So what?'

'It's almost as if the brownie has met your mother,' said Alfie, letting the words drift into the space between them.

Jess stared at him, and then bustled past and back into the kitchen.

'Mum?'

'Hmm?' Ginny was sipping her tea.

Jess crouched to put on Ruby's shoes.

'What were you really doing this morning so early?'

The room fell quiet. Eddie looked at his wife while Marshall frowned, watching Jess. Alfie had followed Jess and stood close to Erica, their arms brushing against one another.

'Excuse me?'

'You were up before dawn, Mum. In the kitchen.

Why?'

Ginny looked from Jess, to her husband and then glanced briefly at Alfie.

'Nothing. I wanted a glass of water. Is that a problem?'

'No. Of course not,' said Jess, her mind whirring.

'What are you doing?' Marshall whispered.

'Oh, I told Alfie about that saucer we found with the witch bottle. Do you have it handy? He'd like a look at it.'

Ginny and Jess stared at each other. Ginny's eyes narrowed ever so slightly.

What do you know?

Jess kept up the stare. She wasn't sure what she knew, but she knew that there was definitely something to know.

'Gin? What's going on?' Eddie asked gently.

'Nothing's going on. The saucer's in there.' Ginny nodded in the direction of a drawer.

Eddie moved to retrieve the saucer and went to pass it to Alfie when he stopped.

'It's damp,' he proclaimed, moving back to the drawer. 'Why is it damp? Do we have a leak?'

Jess looked back to her mother.

'You've been using it,' she said quietly.

Ginny sighed.

'Fine. Yes. I've been using it. It's damp because I washed it and I guess I didn't dry it well enough.'

'What have you been using it for? Why didn't you put it with the other plates?' Eddie asked, examining the saucer.

'Because I've been putting it outside. With milk in.'

The whole room stared at Ginny. She fidgeted with the hem of her top and sighed again.

'There's nothing wrong with feeding the wildlife in my own garden,' she told them. 'It's for the hedgehogs. Or foxes. Or whatever we have.'

'Next door's cats, more like,' Eddie grumbled, looking out onto the rain soaked garden. Big, dark clouds had rolled across the sky and the rain was getting heavier, pattering against the windows.

'Or a brownie,' came Alfie's voice.

Ginny laughed before she could stop herself.

'Don't be ridiculous.'

Jess's eyes widened a little and Marshall moved closer to her. Subconsciously, they had both created a barrier between Alfie and Ginny.

Alfie blinked slowly. It didn't escape Jess's attention that Erica gently moved her hand to take his.

'Your house is beautiful,' said Alfie after a tense moment. 'You must spend a lot of time cleaning it.'

Ginny opened and then closed her mouth.

'Yes. Thank you,' she finally said, although unsure.

'Your garden, as well. Everything seems neatly trimmed and the leaves swept. It must keep you both very busy.'

'Well, Marshall helps,' said Eddie, although he

frowned and looked out of the window again. 'Saying that, we haven't swept the leaves in a while. There just haven't been many to sweep.'

'But I bet other trees around the town have still been dropping leaves,' said Alfie in a level voice. 'I bet your pile of leaves has been growing, too.'

Eddie moved to the window and studied the garden. He turned to his wife.

'Gin...?'

Ginny shook her head.

'It's not a brownie, or whatever.'

'Mum, it's okay if it is. There's nothing wrong with giving a brownie a milk offering. Is there?' Jess checked with Erica, who shook her head.

'Absolutely not. People have been doing it for centuries. I did some research on it last night. I believe it's how a lot of farmers and homesteaders in Scotland managed to keep on top of everything.'

Ginny, cheeks reddening, shook her head.

'I should never have started doing it. It's insane. It's just...I saw a hedgehog one evening and thought it could do with some water. But instead of water, I put milk out. And in that saucer. I don't even know why. Well, I won't do it anymore.'

'There really is no harm in it,' said Alfie.

Ginny looked up at him.

'Then why are you all staring at me?'

Alfie grinned.

'Because Mullarky was right about you.'

A rapping at the back door made them all jump.

Jess gave a little squeal, jumping and turning, and Bubbles jumped up, barking loud and deep at the door. They all stared at it as Marshall told the dog to be quiet.

As soon as Bubbles stopped, it came again. A sharp, short rapping at the lower part of the door, where there was no glass and no way of seeing who or what was there.

Bubbles growled, and just before she could bark again, there came a voice.

'Hello? Excuse me? Can you'se please open the door. It's a wee bit wet out here.'

25

Mullarky

Everything was better with a steaming cup of tea and some shortbread biscuits. Even if there was a whole room of humans and one large, furry canine staring at you.

Mullarky appreciated that the dog had stopped barking at him, although he wasn't keen on being sniffed and licked. Thankfully, the largest of the humans had pulled her away and made her lie down. Still, she watched him with big, curious eyes and perked up ears in such a manner that made him overly protective of his biscuits.

The smallest human, on the other hand, was wary, staying back and hiding behind her mother but never taking her eyes from him. That was fine with Mullarky. He'd rather young humans stayed away from him, he'd found they often had sticky fingers.

'So...you're a brownie.'

Mullarky nodded, sipping his tea and looking over to the oldest of the male humans, although he certainly wasn't the oldest in the room. From the corner, the fae stood protectively over the strongest of the witches. Mullarky kept his eye on them. It wouldn't do to let the fae out of his sight for too long.

'Mullarky,' said Mullarky. 'And I'm very pleased tae finally meet you'se all in person. I've been watching for some time. Although, I met you'se two last night. Erica and Jess.' He gestured to Jess and Erica.

'Other way around,' said the strongest witch. 'I'm Erica, she's Jess.'

Mullarky bowed his head.

'My apologies.'

'And these are Jess's parents, Ginny and Eddie. This is their home.'

'The reluctant witch and her husband.' Mullarky attempted a bow, which was difficult considering he was sitting so far back on the sofa that his short legs stuck out directly in front of him.

'Marshall, Jess's fiancé.'

Mullarky gave the big man an appraising look, wondering if he would come in handy.

'Ruby, their daughter.'

From behind Jess, the little girl waved.

Mullarky waved back.

'And Alfie.'

Ah yes, the fae. Alfie and Mullarky considered

one another. Alfie lowered his head.

'It's an honour,' he said. 'I've never had the pleasure of meeting a brownie before.'

'Really? Good. Because I've had the displeasure of meeting fae before.'

Alfie bristled, but glanced at Erica and remained quiet. Which, from Mullarky's point of view, was incredibly interesting. He stored that vital piece of information away.

'What about the canine?' he asked, giving the dog a dirty look.

'This is Bubbles,' said Jess, stroking the dog's ears. 'She won't hurt you.'

'Hmm.'

'Fascinating,' said Eddie in a low voice. 'So lovely to have you here. Can I ask what brought you to our back door? Were you looking for milk?' He glanced at his wife.

Ginny looked down at the floor and Mullarky followed her gaze.

'That was where they kept the saucer after they stopped giving me offerings,' he said gently, gesturing to the hatch in the floor. 'Along with the bottle my mistress made for them.'

He was suddenly aware of the silence that filled the room and looked up to find Jess staring at him with wide eyes.

'Your mistress?' asked Erica.

'Why did they stop?' asked Ginny.

'Who were "they"?' asked Jess.

Mullarky noted that none of the males asked questions. But then, that was witches for you. He looked at the smallest witch and waited. Her little brow was creased as she peered around Jess.

'James?' she whispered.

Mullarky nodded.

'That was the name of the lad who lived here. Vile man he was n'all.'

There was another pause before Eddie muttered, 'We're not going to the pub, are we.' He sighed. 'I'll go make some sandwiches. Cheese? Ham? Mullarky, would you like a cheese and ham sandwich?'

That was the moment that Eddie became one of Mullarky's favourite humans.

26

Erica

While the day had grown dark with the rain clouds, Jess's parents had done a good job of ensuring that their living room was filled with light. When she'd first met Mullarky it had been dark and he'd been in the shadows. Now Erica could get a good look at the brownie.

His skin was dark and covered in a light brown hair – she wasn't sure it could be called fur, especially when compared to Bubbles's thick coat – and while she'd thought his large eyes were black, they were in fact a deep brown with a strong flicker of intelligence behind them. Yet, there was nothing malicious about him. He was out of the ordinary, yes, and her eyes were taking delight in studying him in order to process what was sitting on Eddie and Ginny's sofa, drinking from one of their cups, but there was also something fairly calming about his presence. When she was finally able to take her eyes from him, she surreptitiously studied Ginny from the corner of her eye. Did Jess's mum know what she was doing when she left out that saucer of milk?

'Don't discuss anything without me!' Eddie cried as he escaped to the kitchen to make sandwiches.

'I'll give you a hand. Me and Bubbles. And… Ruby,' said Marshall, offering Jess a questioning look.

'Do you want to go into the kitchen or do you want to stay?' Jess asked Ruby softly.

Ruby, without taking her eyes from the brownie on the sofa, said, 'Stay, please.'

Jess gave Marshall something of a reassuring smile, not that he looked convinced. He bribed Bubbles into following him with the promise of a treat and they heard the click of the kitchen door as it closed behind him.

The women watched the brownie, and the brownie curiously watched the women.

Mullarky sighed.

'What an awkward ten minutes it'll be if we cannae discuss anything until those sandwiches are made.' He looked out of the window to his right and pulled a face. 'Rotten weather, but I do enjoy the rain. It keeps the humans in their houses and out of trouble. I cannae stay too long, you'se ken. Mauve needs me.'

Erica twisted her lips, desperately trying to keep

the question in until Eddie returned.

'Mauve? Is she... Are there more of you?' Ginny asked.

'She is my mistress,' said Mullarky sadly. 'And nae, there are not more of me. I'm the only one. At least, the only one around here and that I'm aware of.'

'Your mistress. The woman who lives in the cottage by the woods?' Jess ventured.

Ruby had crept forward to sit beside her mother and Jess wrapped a protective arm around her.

Mullarky nodded.

'Alas, she is nearing the end. I'm nae sure what will happen when she's gone.'

'Hey! You said you wouldn't discuss anything! Now you have to catch me up,' said Eddie, bursting into the room with a tray of sandwiches and plates. Marshall followed with another tray of cups of tea, Bubbles trotting along beside him, happy to be involved. She returned to her spot beside Ruby and the little girl dug her fingers into the dog's thick fur.

'Mullarky's mistress is the woman who lives in the cottage by the woods,' said Jess. 'You haven't missed much. That's the quickest anyone has ever made sandwiches and tea.'

'Well, no one said they had to be neat sandwiches.' Eddie offered around the plates and the group gathered closer together, taking sandwiches from the coffee table in the middle of the room. Marshall pointed out which tea cup to take, and

soon they were happily sitting around the room – Ginny and Eddie on end of the sofa Mullarky sat on, Erica and Alfie on the floor, Marshall on the other side of Ruby with Jess on the second sofa – munching on their sandwiches. At least, Mullarky was taking big bites. The others were nibbling and watching him, waiting for more.

'We need more seats,' Eddie mumbled to his wife. She nodded, eyes on Mullarky.

'Has your mistress always been the owner of that cottage?' Erica asked when it became apparent that the brownie was so involved in his sandwich that he'd forgotten where he was.

'She has,' said Mullarky proudly, before popping the last of his sandwich into his mouth. 'I moved down tae England two centuries ago, give or take. Back then, I used tae help the farmers, but then in one particular village, I met a witch. She was kind and never held back on the offerings. She asked me tae stay with her, and so I did, following her down the country until she bought that cottage where she lived out the rest of her years. Her daughter inherited it, moved in and took over. When she passed, her son sold the cottage and another witch bought it. Sadly, the line of witches died a long time ago. Mauve is nae witch and I've overheard her children arguing over what'll become of the cottage when she's gone. They even threaten to take the cottage from her before she passes. Putting her into a different home of some sort.' The brownie visibly

shook with rage.

'A retirement home, perhaps,' Ginny offered. 'Is she ill?'

'She's nae what she was.' Mullarky looked down at his lap. 'She's nae in the best of health, I s'ppose. Her coughing wakes me sometimes, and I've saved her from more falls than I can remember.' He lifted his eyes to the plate of sandwiches on the table, then scooted forward and helped himself to three more.

'I'm sorry to hear that,' said Ginny quietly.

'What about your mistress who created the witch bottle for this house?' Erica asked. 'Why did she do that?'

'The lady of this house requested protection. Ah, but that is nae the bottle yer referring to.' Mullarky cleared his throat and gave his sandwich a sad look. 'The bottle you'se found?' He turned to Jess, then Marshall, then turned his gaze to Eddie and Ginny. 'That was made for the man o' the house. James, as the wee witch correctly guessed. Tae protect him from Satan's servant who would come tae collect what was owed.'

Erica's stomach turned.

'The imp,' said Jess quietly.

Mullarky nodded.

'It did its job well, too. When that crook of a man finally died, that imp cuidnae get near him. Poor creature was waiting a hundred years or so. I wonder sometimes if my mistress would have been proud of that accomplishment. I dinnae think so.'

Erica frowned.

'Why did she help him?'

Mullarky shuffled in his seat to get more comfortable and finished another sandwich.

'I asked her that often. The man was a villain. She only ever remarked that sometimes when someone is desperate, they'll do something stupid. And sometimes they will do something evil. And in their moment of desperation, can they be truly blamed? She certainly dinnae think he deserved an eternity in hell. But I did,' said Mullarky, holding his head high. 'I thought he deserved that and more.' He turned to Marshall. 'You did the reit thing, sir. Exactly the reit thing. I only wish it cuid have been done sooner.'

'He killed someone,' Ruby whispered.

The adults all turned to her and Erica's chest tightened, her gaze flicking to Jess, wondering if she would stop the brownie answering. Her friend lowered her head, lifting her shoulders and shifting closer to her daughter, as if trying to shield them both from the answer.

'He did.' Mullarky nodded. 'He killed his wife and his wee daughter.'

A silence fell over the room, and Marshall and Jess exchanged a look.

'Why?' asked Ruby.

Mullarky looked up at the little girl and his eyes softened. It was an incredible sight and something inside Erica softened with them.

'I dinnae ken, little one,' he said gently. 'My mistress claimed he was desperate. But, in my experience, some humans just dinnae deserve the wonders they're given, for whatever reason.'

'He was probably ill,' murmured Jess, squeezing her daughter.

Marshall made a noise and, inexplicably, exchanged a look with the brownie.

'Either way, James did the deed and then realised the trouble he'd caused. This was his wife's house, built by her pa who was a wealthy trader. Now the authorities were after James and if they caught him, her pa would make sure he hanged for his crimes. So James went tae the crossroads by the cottage one night and summoned Satan. I saw it. I saw it all. They made a deal and by the next morning, the authorities were nae longer looking for James. His wife's pa, full of sorrow, shared his grief with James and allowed him tae stay here.

'But then James became scared of what he'd done. Not the murders, nae, but the pact with Satan. Soon they would come for him, and his fate wuid be worse than being hanged. Which is why soon after he made the deal, he turned up at my mistress's front door asking for protection. He wanted a witch bottle, the same that she had made for his wife. That he had found beneath the floorboards and had smashed.' Mullarky sniffed and hesitated.

Erica thought that perhaps the emotion was too much, but then Mullarky shifted forward again and placed the last two sandwiches on his plate before scooting back and continuing.

'My mistress obliged, although I begged her not tae. And, ye ken the rest.'

'He put the witch bottle under the floorboards with the saucer. Why the saucer?' Eddie asked, staring at the hatch in the floor.

'That saucer was his wife's. She had a way of witches about her. My mistress suggested she leave offerings, which were for me, o'course. I was tasked with helping her once she became with child, with chores around the house and soothing the bairn when she was born. I dinnae ken why James would put his witch bottle with the saucer. I s'ppose there's a possibility he saw his wife's bottle with the saucer and the idiot thought that's how the bottles worked.' Mullarky barked a cynical laugh.

'And now someone else is going to try and summon the Devil,' came Alfie's soft voice.

Erica had almost forgotten he was there. She gave him a weak smile and he took her hand, brushing his thumb over her soft skin.

'Indeed. And we *must* stop him. I nae longer have a witch for a mistress, so I cuidnae call upon her. But here you'se are, witches arriving in my town, making yerself known, tidying up the mess left behind by others. Aye, you'se'll be good for this. I have faith that you'se'll do the reit thing.'

It was difficult not to take that as a compliment, even though Mullarky's tone suggested otherwise in places.

'Well, if we don't know who this man is, the only choice we have is to wait at the crossroads for him tomorrow night,' Erica suggested.

Alfie made a scoffing noise.

'That's not your only choice. The preferred choice here is you let this man do whatever he wants and don't get involved.'

Mullarky's eyes widened.

'But you'se must help! The young lad'll suffer a terrible fate otherwise.'

'But you wanted that fate for James,' Marshall pointed out.

'Because James deserved it. Connor, on the other hand, does not.'

Erica's eyes snapped up, connecting with Jess across the room.

'Connor?' she asked.

'You know his name?' Jess checked.

'I ken his name and I ken his worries.' Mullarky nodded. 'He's a truly desperate lad who is about tae make a stupid, reckless decision that'll be his downfall.' He turned his attention solely onto Alfie. 'And he *must* be stopped.'

Brownie and fae glared at one another for longer than was comfortable. Erica looked between them, wondering whether to break them up.

'Has he killed someone?' came Ruby's little

voice, slicing through the tension.

Mullarky pulled his gaze from Alfie and turned – brightly, softly – to Ruby.

'Nae, little one.'

'Has he hurt someone?'

'Only himself, little one.'

Ruby looked up at her mother.

'Will you be hurt?' she asked.

Jess opened her mouth and then shook her head.

'I won't let anything happen to your mum,' Erica offered. 'We won't. Will we, Alfie?'

Alfie pursed his lips and then shook his head.

'No harm will befall your mother, Ruby.'

Ruby, satisfied, sat back and said, 'Then you should help him.'

Jess looked up at Marshall who gave a subtle shake of his head.

'I'd like to help, if I can,' said Eddie, standing and brushing the crumbs from his lap. 'Shall I make more sandwiches?'

Mullarky's eyes brightened further as he smiled, showing off little sharp, white teeth. 'Oh, yes, please. Thank ye.'

Jess

By five o'clock Mullarky had long since left to return to his mistress, Mauve. The rain had stopped, but it was too dark to continue the garden work outside. Eddie and Marshall had agreed to start again in the morning, whether it was raining or not, and then Ginny had shooed them out of her house. What with a large dog, a young grandchild, a fae and a brownie, it was all becoming a bit much.

It wasn't until Jess, Marshall and Ruby made it to the edge of the fair on the high street that Jess realised her mother had stopped talking about the wedding.

'What are you grinning about?'

Jess shrugged.

'Just, turned into a nice evening, didn't it.'

Marshall narrowed his eyes at her, but then smiled and agreed. The rain had stopped and the clouds had parted, leaving the early evening dark and cold but fresh and full of the delights of the fair.

Ruby, sitting on Marshall's shoulders, pointed to the largest ride on the high street. Jess didn't know what they were called. This one swung people around, lifting higher and higher, spinning, before slowing and lowering. She had nicknamed it The Nope.

'Can we go on that one?' asked Ruby.

'Absolutely not,' said Jess immediately.

Marshall laughed.

'Maybe when you're older, Rubes.'

'Nope. She's never allowed on there.'

'Not even when I'm old?' asked Ruby.

Jess looked up into her daughter's eyes.

'Not if I have anything to do with it.'

Marshall laughed again.

'Let's find something a little more your mum's speed, huh? How about the teacups? They're gentle.' He pointed to the little ride, undercover, going round and round. Each teacup was empty, spinning every now and then, likely to try and entice people to have a go.

Jess pulled a face.

'Yes!' cried Ruby, clapping her hands.

'I'll go with you,' said Erica, appearing behind them with Alfie in tow. The fae had both hands deep in his pockets and he was gazing around with a soft smile on his lips.

'Come on, Rubes. You, me and Erica.'

Ruby clapped again and Marshall took her to the front of the queue, Erica following closely.

'You okay?' Jess asked Alfie quietly.

He nodded.

'My cousin worked at a fair like this.'

Jess gave him a curious look.

'A fae chose to stay in this world to work at a fair?'

'Oh, no. He was human. My father's sister's son.'

Jess smiled to herself, looking back to the ride to watch her fiancé, friend and daughter climb into a teacup. A queue was forming behind them.

'I would have thought the fair would be a good place for fae to meet impressionable teenagers looking for an escape,' she murmured.

She kept her eyes ahead as Alfie turned to look at her.

'That doesn't mean they have to work at the fair.'

Jess laughed.

'Good point.' The ride started and Ruby called out to her to make sure she was watching. Jess waved and then pulled out her phone. After recording a short video, she lowered the phone and turned back to Alfie. 'You're still not happy about tomorrow night.'

Alfie sighed.

'I will never be happy about Erica meeting the Devil. Or you, for that matter. I'm surprised Marshall isn't putting up more of a fight.'

'Me too,' she said quietly, watching the big man in the teacup. Maybe he'd given up on fighting her about these things. Maybe he agreed that Connor needed saving. 'Best thing, of course, would be to find Connor now so we never get to the Devil bit,' she added. She looked up at Alfie. 'Mullarky told us where he lives. Why don't we go see if we can find him and talk him out of it?'

'You're doing that tomorrow morning, remember,' Alfie huffed. 'That was a whole other argument.'

'Because what if he's out. What if he's here.' Jess looked around the fair, slowly filling up with families and groups of friends. She shuddered when she wondered if among them was a man waiting to sell his soul. 'But I guess if we're all going to die tomorrow night, we should have some fun today.'

Alfie smiled and elbowed her gently.

'You won't die.'

'How do you know?'

'Because you've survived this far,' said Alfie. 'Plus, I can see the future, remember?'

Jess looked back to him.

'We're all going to make it through this, right? So, there's nothing to worry about, is there?'

Alfie's smile fell, if only for a moment. He quickly tried to replace it, but the damage had been done. Jess turned back to the teacup ride, her mouth dry, heart pounding, and watched her family laughing as they span and span.

Once the teacup ride was over, they bought burgers and chips at one of the stalls and found a table to stop and eat. Jess was wiping tomato sauce from Ruby's face when Erica asked, 'Has your mum been going on about the wedding?'

Jess grinned.

'Not since Mullarky came into the picture. Great, isn't it.'

'I feel like I'm not holding up my end of the bargain.' Erica took a bite from her burger.

'Mummy?'

'Of course you are! It's lovely having you here. Do you want to do the haunted house next?'

Jess and Erica both snorted and laughed, forcing smiles onto Alfie and Marshall's faces as the men exchanged a look.

'Mummy?'

A ball of something akin to fear dropped into Jess's stomach. She plastered a smile over it and turned to her daughter.

'Yes, sweetheart?'

She waited for Ruby to point somewhere, or to ask what that scary shadow was, or why the imp had returned and was watching them.

'Can we get candy floss?'

Everyone at the table jumped as Jess laughed.

'Oh, yes! Absolutely, we can.' Jess kissed her daughter's head a little too hard and then ignored Marshall's questioning raised eyebrow.

Once they'd eaten, Ruby led them over to the candy floss stall and Erica treated them all, despite Jess arguing that if she couldn't afford her rent increase, she shouldn't be buying candy floss.

*

Marshall and Alfie stood to the side, watching.

'There's no stopping them, is there,' Marshall said quietly. It wasn't a question, even though he was becoming desperate for Alfie to correct him.

'No.'

Marshall sighed.

'That wasn't the response I was looking for.'

'I know. I'm sorry.'

'There never will be any stopping them,' Marshall added in a whisper, mostly to himself. 'Just gotta live with this stress.'

Alfie patted the big man on the back.

'You'll get used to it, I'm sure. Are you excited about the wedding?'

Marshall brightened.

'Very. If Ginny would just back off a bit. All this brownie and Devil stuff is a distraction, but it won't last long.'

Their attentions were caught by a passing man turning sharply to look at them, fear in his eyes.

Marshall glanced at Alfie.

'What was that about?'

'I do believe that was a man who became scared when he overheard you mentioning the Devil,' Alfie murmured thoughtfully. He cocked his head to the side. 'How much do you want to bet that's Connor.'

Marshall started.

'Should we go after him? We should go after him, right?'

Alfie nodded.

'Worth a try.'

'This isn't something you've foreseen?' Marshall asked, leading the way as they pushed through the crowds after the man.

'No. I don't always see everything.'

Marshall hesitated.

'So, Jess isn't necessarily safe, is she.'

'None of us are.' Alfie urged Marshall on.

'Comforting,' Marshall mumbled, pushing past a large family.

They reached another burger stall and turned on the spot.

'Where did he go?' Marshall searched through the growing crowds of people.

Alfie stayed still and took a deep breath.

'This way.' He led Marshall past the burger stall and a cake and toffee apple stall – Marshall would have to tell Jess about that one – where he broke into a run. Marshall did his best to keep up but quickly lost Alfie among the people.

Finally, he rounded a ride and there, on the edge of the fair, was Alfie talking to a young man in his twenties. His blond hair was ruffled, his eyes wide, his chest heaving with the deep breaths he was taking. Alfie, on the other hand, looked as though he'd barely moved. His hand, however, was hovering close the man's wrist, ready to grab him if he tried to run again.

Marshall approached carefully, wondering for the first time if this was such a good idea.

'Everything okay?' he asked.

The young man looked at him sideways and seemed to relax a little.

'No! No. This man was chasing me!'

'All I want to know is if your name is Connor,' said Alfie evenly. The fae looked into the man's eyes and Marshall watched in horror as the young man blinked, relaxed and nodded.

'Yes, it is,' he said, but the fight and worry was gone from his voice.

Marshall stared at Alfie.

'What did you do?'

Alfie waved him away.

'Connor, my name is Alfie and this is Marshall. We need to talk.'

'I don't owe you any money. Do I?' The worry was creeping back into Connor's voice.

Marshall's chest tightened.

'You don't owe us anything, Connor,' he said gently. 'We want to help. We're friends.'

Connor looked from Marshall to Alfie, then gave Marshall a disbelieving look. Having seen Alfie working his magic, Marshall could hardly blame him.

'Please. Can we talk?' He held out his hands in the universal sign of not being a threat.

Connor considered this and then relented.

'Come over here for a moment.' Alfie led them off to the side of the road, putting the noise of the fair to their backs, hiding in the shadows.

'Do you have plans tomorrow night, Connor?' asked Alfie.

'Right. Because that doesn't sound threatening,' Marshall mumbled. 'Connor, we know what you're planning to do tomorrow night.'

Alfie smirked.

'Much less threatening.'

Marshall took a deep breath. Did Jess and Erica have this much trouble?

'I don't know what you're talking about,' said Connor, still trying to catch his breath.

He was a bad liar.

'You're planning on summoning the Devil,' said Alfie.

'By the witch's cottage,' Marshall added.

'And we can't let that happen.'

Marshall gave Alfie a sideways look.

'Because it's all very real and very dangerous,' he said pointedly.

'How do you—' Connor breathed. He shook his head. 'I have no idea what you're talking about. You're talking crazy.'

'Look, maybe if you tell us why you want to do this, we can help,' said Marshall, aware that his tone was becoming more high pitched. He took a quick breath to calm himself. 'Please. We just don't want anyone to come to harm.'

'What do you care about me? You don't even know me,' Connor growled.

Alfie smiled.

'No, but the women we love are going to stop you tomorrow, and in doing so they will be putting themselves in harm's way. And that's putting it lightly. Honestly, I don't give a fuck about you. But I will not have the woman I love meeting the Devil.' Alfie closed the small gap between him and Connor, and somehow the fae was suddenly towering over the young man, the shadows around them deepening and darkening.

'Alfie!' Marshall shouted, trying to make his voice audible over the darkness.

Alfie flinched and backed away, but only a little.

Connor looked to Marshall, eyes wide with fear.

'If you do this,' Marshall said gently, 'you're going to put a lot of people in danger. The women we love, the people you love. Even if you don't care about yourself and spending eternity in hell, which, trust me, is what will happen, then think about whoever is in your life. Your parents, family, a partner, friends. Whoever.'

Connor sagged.

'How do you know?'

'Because I've seen it,' said Marshall. 'Because I've seen what comes for you.'

Rick

Bristol, two months ago

Alfie didn't lead Rick far from the cemetery. They wandered up a row of Victorian terraces a few roads away from where Alfie lived. When they reached a house with a dark green front door and window boxes filled with beautiful flowers, Alfie stepped up the short front path to knock.

Rick waited cautiously on the pavement, his feet turning him around, ready to run back to the cemetery if need be. Likewise, his fingers twitched, ready to reach for the device on his wrist and get him out of there.

The door opened and an elderly man narrowed his eyes at Alfie.

'Aelfraed,' he murmured bitterly.

Alfie bowed his head and then gestured back to Rick.

'I apologise for disturbing you, but I come in search of aid for a friend.'

Friend! Rick almost scoffed out loud, but he stopped himself in time for the old man to look past Alfie and meet his eyes.

'Aid?' the man asked gently.

Alfie turned and gestured for Rick to approach. He wandered up the path to just behind Alfie. The fae took Rick's arm, lifted it and pulled up the sleeve.

They stood there in the rain, water bouncing from the device on Rick's wrist as the elderly man pulled down the glasses from the top of his head and inspected it.

He gave a sharp nod.

'You'd best come in.'

Rick took a deep breath before he entered the stranger's home, following Alfie and staying close. A narrow hallway led through to the small, cosy living room on the left and a galley kitchen up ahead. Between them, where Rick had expected a dining room – where most estate agents would expect a dining room – was a workshop.

Around the period brick fireplace were wooden worktops and benches, lined with drawers and shelves. In the middle of the room was a large wooden workbench, half-carved wood and tools and scraps lying around where a tall stool had been pulled up to work from. A large magnifying glass on a metal arm attached to the table was sitting beside a lamp. The light from the window was dimmed by the curtains being half-pulled shut.

The whole place smelt of wood, grease and freshly baked bread.

Rick breathed it all in as the elderly man reached for his workbench.

'So, who do we have here?' he asked, replacing his small reading glasses with a much larger pair and blinking at Rick.

'Rick Cavanagh,' said Alfie. 'A time traveller and policeman by trade.'

The man sniffed hard.

'I don't like policemen.'

'He wants to leave the force,' Alfie explained. 'But to do so, he needs a new timeline. Can you change his time travel device so that he can jump timelines?'

The man screwed his face up in thought and then nodded.

'Maybe. Maybe. Give it here.' He reached out a hand, and Rick froze.

Alfie looked Rick up and down, and raised his eyebrows. *Go on then.*

Placing a hand over the device on his wrist, Rick willed himself to remove it and hand it over. Instead, he stood there, staring at the old man.

'What's the matter with it?' the man asked Alfie.

'It?' Rick murmured.

Alfie sighed and rubbed the space between his eyes.

'Rick, this is Percivale. He is a fae who has chosen to live in your world. And he is the most talented engineer from my world. He will be able to alter the device on your wrist and allow you to seek out the life you're looking for.' Alfie turned to the older man. 'Percivale, this man has lost the woman he loves and the life he thought was his. Have kindness.'

Percivale gave Alfie an appraising look, a smile slowly spreading across his face.

'You took the woman he loves. And now – what? – guilt, is it, Aelfraed?' He tutted, chuckling to himself. 'Come on, then. Rick, was it? Hand it over, let's see what we can do.'

Rick chewed on his lower lip.

'It's my only chance of escape,' he murmured.

'Then best hand it over quick, boy.'

Rick released the clasp on the device and it popped from his wrist. With trembling fingers, he handed it to the elderly fae.

Percivale turned it over in his hands, pulling out extensions to his glasses that allowed him to see further, magnifying the device. He reached for a small screwdriver on his worktop and deftly unscrewed the latch that revealed the inner mechanism.

Turning his full attention to it, Percivale perched himself up on the stool, flicked on the lamp and got to work.

Alfie and Rick waited beside him, Rick watching

his every move as Alfie's gaze wandered around the room.

'Interesting,' the old fae murmured, reaching blindly for a tool and picking up another screwdriver.

'Has he done stuff like this before?' Rick whispered to Alfie.

'More or less,' said Alfie. 'I told you, he's the best there is. If anyone can do it, he can.'

Rick nodded, wishing he could truly believe him.

'Do you think this is the right thing?' he asked, although he realised he wasn't necessarily asking Alfie.

The fae studied him.

'Your gut is telling you this is the right thing. Your head is telling you it's the only thing. What does your heart tell you?'

Rick shot Alfie a disgusted look.

'A yes or no,' he told him. 'That's all I was looking for.'

Alfie grinned.

'Yes,' he whispered to Rick. Their eyes met for one meaningful moment and then Rick jumped as Percivale cried, 'Aha!'

The old fae sat back, grinning.

'Beautiful machinery,' he said. 'I could have made it better, of course, but there we are. Aelfraed, go put on a pot of tea. And bring me the biscuits. The shortbread, in the back of the cupboard. The good biscuits. I will need about half an hour,' he added to Rick. 'So go help in the kitchen and then make yourself comfortable. Do you have an idea of the timeline you wish to go to?'

Rick hesitated and shook his head.

'I don't have a clue.'

'Not a problem, not a problem,' said Percivale, waving them away to the kitchen.

Alfie gestured for Rick to take the lead and when Rick turned back, not sure where the tea or the biscuits were, Alfie was gone. Frowning, Rick wandered back and caught sight of Alfie whispering something to Percivale. The old fae nodded and smiled, patting Alfie's arm.

Rick hurriedly turned back into the kitchen as Alfie joined him, clapped his hands and said, 'Right. Good biscuits. Where are you.'

'What did you say to him?' Rick asked.

They were sitting on a battered old sofa against the wall facing into the workshop, beside the kitchen. There was barely room for it, but Rick was glad of it. It had been forty minutes since he and Alfie had made the tea and found the biscuits.

'When?'

'When I went into the kitchen and you went back to him. You said something to him. And he patted your arm. What did you say?' Rick whispered, watching Percivale work.

Alfie sat back.

'You understand that I can see versions of the future?'

'Yeah.'

'I know which timeline you should be heading for.'

Rick turned to Alfie.

'Oh?'

'I was letting Percivale know. Don't worry. If I'm wrong and you hate it there, you'll be able to jump around.'

Rick sat back.

'Oh. Well, thank you.'

'I don't think you need to thank me, Rick. Not when you're of the mind that I have stolen the woman you love away from you.'

Rick smiled to himself.

'Fair enough.'

'There!'

Alfie and Rick both jumped as Percivale held the device in the air. 'Finished!'

Rick jumped up and approached the old fae.

'See, I've had to add a button. Now, you do as you would normally. Turn this dial, choose where you would like to go, twist this, and then push this new button to travel between timelines. You must take extra care. More care than travelling through time, but otherwise the same rules apply. You may have to leap a few times before you find a timeline where you can fit in.' Percivale flashed a quick look to Alfie. 'Or you may hit on it first time. Now, hold out your wrist.'

Rick pushed up his sleeve and offered his wrist to Percivale. He hesitated when a strange noise sounded. A chiming. Rick glanced around the room, searching for an elusive clock. Then he realised the chiming was coming from the pocket watch in his coat. The pocket watch he thought he'd left on Erica's parents' kitchen table.

Flinching, he forced himself to hold still for Percivale. Noise behind Alfie made Rick half turn. Alfie moved to stand in the way as the front door was forced opened.

'Quick!' cried Alfie.

'Shit,' Rick murmured, pulling away at just the wrong moment.

The device fell from his wrist and there was a sickening crunch as it hit the tiled floor.

Percivale's eyes widened and he slowly stooped to collect it, but Rick was quicker. He bent and retrieved the device just as Burns pushed past Alfie and appeared in the workshop doorway.

29

Erica

For once, Erica woke before Alfie. She wasn't entirely convinced that she'd slept at all. Alfie, on the other hand, never seemed to have trouble sleeping once he'd had sex. On such an anxious-ridden night, the intimacy was helpful, more intense, and usually also helped her to sleep. It was a good distraction, but this time she had remembered what lay before them the following evening all too soon and had lain awake, staring at the ceiling, listening to Alfie's deep breathing and willing herself to drift off.

After five o'clock, she gave up.

Slipping out of bed, she dressed as quietly as possible, used the bathroom and then poked her head through the curtains to see what was happening outside. The morning was dark, as if it was still night, but there was something in the air.

A stillness and magic that only came about when most people were asleep and dawn was approaching.

Checking that Alfie was still breathing deep, Erica crept from the room and found herself in the silence of the sleeping hotel.

She tiptoed through the hallway to the stairs, cringing at the creaking door, and wandered through to the foyer and reception. It was empty. As was the bar and breakfast area, although she was certain it wouldn't be for long. Outside the hotel, through the front doors, she could see the fair, sitting still and silent in the dark, waiting.

Shivering, she turned her back on it.

An empty fair in that magic space before dawn was not a place she wanted to look at, never mind wander through. What a stupid place to hold a fair. Putting huge, shuddering rides right next to medieval period properties. Just watching how close people were swung to the buildings lining the high street made Erica's pulse quicken, and not in a good way.

Erica made her way to the door that led down the basement and stopped to listen. There was no piano music, no sound whatsoever. Trying the handle, she found the door unlocked and when she opened it, she stopped. Heart pounding, she gazed down at the wooden stairs. She couldn't see anyone, but the light was on.

Had someone accidentally left it on?

Taking a deep breath, grasping for the pre-dawn magic in the air and reminding herself who her grandmother was, Erica stepped out onto the stairs.

'Hello?' she whispered. Clearing her throat, she tried again, aiming for louder and more confident. 'Hello?'

A face appeared at the bottom of the stairs and, after the initial heart wrenching shock, Erica relaxed, turning slightly, hand on her chest as she coaxed her heart down from her throat.

'Mr Drescott, you scared me.'

Adam, the hotel's manager, stared up at her with wide eyes.

'Ms Murray? You scared me! Hotel guests are not allowed down here.' He glanced into the room and Erica made her way slowly down the steps. Adam looked back to her, frowning deeply. 'Is everything okay? Can I get you anything?' He moved to block her way, to herd her back up the stairs.

When she reached him, Erica scanned the basement and found the piano still in the middle of the room, waiting for someone to play it.

'Sorry,' she murmured. 'I couldn't sleep. And then I remembered your resident spirit and wondered if they fancied a chat.'

Adam hesitated and Erica took full advantage, slipping past him. She wandered slowly over to the piano.

'They play the piano so beautifully,' she said,

looking around the room at the boxes piled high, the stacked tables and chairs, the Christmas decorations that didn't have much longer to wait.

'Please, Ms Murray—'

'Maybe if we give them some space,' said Erica, gesturing for Adam to sit on the bottom step with her.

He relented and sat beside her.

'How long have you worked here?' she asked quietly after a few moments of silence.

'Since I was sixteen, on and off,' said Adam, sighing. 'My family own the hotel, and now I'm a part owner. My parents retired last year.'

'That must be fun. Did they want to do stuff to this basement?'

Adam shook his head.

'No. They always said enough had happened down here. It should be used as storage and nothing else.' He smiled. 'But, in all honesty, the hotel isn't doing what it could be doing.'

'Business isn't great?'

Adam's smile fell.

'The economy isn't great,' he mumbled.

'Tell me about it. Our business is doing all right, considering, but not enough that I can afford the rent increase my landlord's just lumbered me with. I'm going to have to move back in with my parents at this rate.'

Adam glanced at her.

'What about your husband?'

Erica sat back and smiled.

'We're not married. Not yet. He wants me to move in with him but I'm not sure it's for the best.'

Adam watched the piano.

'If business doesn't pick up here soon, I'll either need another job or we'll have to cut expenses. I can't bear to let anyone go. I've been talking to my wife about downsizing our home instead.'

'Do you want to downsize?' Erica asked.

'No. I want to grow this business,' said Adam. 'But my parents are adamant about this basement not being developed. We're full but just for the weekend, thanks to the fair. What are we going to do next week?' He glanced at her out of the corner of his eye. 'Sorry. I shouldn't be telling you this.'

Erica shook her head.

'I'm glad you are. Look, my business works with hotels in the city. We've seen what a well put together ghost tour can do for a hotel like this. And it doesn't have to cost much. Honestly. We don't want to run you into the ground, we'd just be running ourselves into the ground with you. We want to help you.'

'And help yourselves,' said Adam.

'Isn't that life?'

Adam's lips twisted in acknowledgment.

'There's no ghosts here,' he murmured.

'There are,' said Erica. 'Trust me. I grew up surrounded by spirits. I know that sounds ridiculous and you don't have to believe me. Even if you don't believe in spirits, this hotel has such a great history. You could run history tours.'

'We wouldn't need you for that,' said Adam. 'Actually, we wouldn't need you for some silly ghost tours, either.'

Erica bristled.

'Well, that's up to you.' She turned her attention back to the piano. Then she stood and approached until she was a few paces away. 'Hello,' she called out. 'Remember me? My name is Erica. I know you're here, but it's all right if you don't want to talk. This man, Adam, doesn't believe you're here and wants to redevelop this whole basement without talking to you first. So, perhaps you could make yourself known. Perhaps by playing us some music.'

There was a long pause and, just as Adam was opening his mouth to scoff, a key on the piano pressed down, letting a single note ring out.

Adam's mouth fell open.

Another note played, and then another.

Erica smiled and turned back to Adam, gesturing to the piano.

'I think your resident spirit would like you to explain any renovation plans to them beforehand.'

Adam stood, shaking his head.

'It's a trick. You rigged something up.'

'You're more than welcome to check,' said Erica, stepping back. She thanked the spirit and then returned to sitting at the bottom of the stairs.

Adam checked all over the piano, looking for hidden wires, standing where Erica had and stamping his feet, checking the keys that had been pressed.

'How did you do this?' he asked, his breath coming out in a cloud. Jumping back, Adam huffed out more air and watched it cloud in front of him. 'How—?'

'There's a spirit next to you, you can feel it in the sudden chill,' Erica explained calmly. 'As for how I did it, I didn't. I wouldn't know the first thing about rigging up a piano. And if you want more evidence, perhaps we can ask the spirit to do something else.'

'Like what?'

Erica shrugged.

'What would make you believe?'

There came a loud crash and bang deeper into the basement. Erica jumped to her feet, heart pounding.

'Is someone else here?' she asked, hand on the banister, ready to leg it back up the stairs.

'Shouldn't be,' said Adam, pulling out his phone and putting on the torch. He led the way, around the piled boxes and a stack of tables. 'That shouldn't be shut,' he breathed.

Lit by his meagre torchlight was what Erica assumed was the old bank safe, the large, heavy round door closed.

In the dancing shadows there were shades of blue to the thick metal. Erica, head tilted as she studied it, stepped forward as Adam swung the torch around, looking for someone who shouldn't be there. Forced to take out her own phone and turn on the torch, Erica studied the door.

'This is gorgeous,' she murmured. And terrifying. But she didn't say that. Reaching up to touch the long handle of the safe door, she made contact with the metal and waited for a moment. A small shock went through her fingertips as she brushed the handle.

Erica smiled.

'Was that you?' she asked. 'Did you close the door?'

'Close the door? Slammed it is more like. I've never heard that thing close that loud,' said Adam behind her. 'There's no one here. How did this happen?'

Erica forced Adam to take a few steps back with her.

'Thank you,' she called out. 'For slamming this door. Could you please open it? If it's not too heavy.'

There came a creak and then, slowly, the heavy door of the safe inched open all on its own.

Behind her, Adam shifted, his breath catching.

'It's not possible,' he murmured.

'If I was you,' said Erica, 'I'd have a chat with your parents about who this might be, and just why they want you to leave the basement alone.' She glanced back to him and he nodded, not taking his eyes from the safe. 'And if you're still interested, you have my card,' said Erica, turning back to the open safe. 'Thank you!' she called out to the spirit. 'I hope to hear your beautiful piano playing again soon.'

When Adam and Erica reappeared from the basement, the hotel staff were setting up for the start of breakfast. Erica left the visibly shaken Adam and made her way back up to her room. Alfie was awake, sitting up in bed, naked, although the sheet covered his lower half, drinking a cup of tea.

'Couldn't sleep?' he asked.

Erica sat on the bed beside him.

'Nope. How did you sleep?'

'I dreamt,' said Alfie. 'Memories and voices and...' He sighed. 'You're still adamant about helping this Connor?'

'I am.'

'There's nothing I can say that will dissuade you?'

Erica studied him and then smiled, leaning over to kiss his cheek.

'We're going to visit him this morning and see if we can talk him out of it. Maybe we won't need to do anything tonight. Maybe we can just go for dinner, watch the kids all dressed up, come back here, enjoy our last night in this hotel bed and then wake up tomorrow morning, refreshed and ready to go home.' Erica's smiled faltered.

Alfie put his tea onto the bedside table and wrapped his arms around her, scooping her closer until her cheek rested against his bare chest.

'Move in with me,' he whispered into her hair. 'We don't have to marry. I will do everything I can to make it smooth. Just give it a go. A week. Maybe two. Then, if you don't like it, you can move back in with your parents.'

Erica closed her eyes and breathed Alfie in.

'Okay,' she murmured. 'I'll think about it. And don't you worry about tonight. It'll be all right. Won't it.'

Alfie kissed her hair again as her thoughts began to untangle, wandering away from her, the darkness creeping in.

'I would never let anything bad happen to you,' came Alfie's voice as Erica drifted off to sleep.

Jess

The family were up and each doing their own things after eating breakfast together. Ginny and Ruby were putting some finishing touches to Ruby's Halloween costume, while Eddie and Marshall attempted to finish the muddy patio. Jess sat on the bed she was sharing with Marshall and looked down at the tarot card she'd just pulled.

The Devil.

Swearing under her breath, she reshuffled the cards and tried again, altering the question slightly.

'What should I do about tonight?'

She went through the cards until all the instincts Alfie had taught her to hone screamed at her to stop. Pulling the card, she turned it to find the Devil staring back at her.

'Oh, for f—'

Jess placed the Devil card over to one side, reshuffled the cards without it and tried again, asking the same question this time.

'What should I do about tonight?'

She pulled a card and yelped as the Devil looked up at her. The card she'd placed to the side was gone.

'Fuck. Fuck, fuck, fuck.'

Stomach churning, she shuffled the cards and then, thinking better of it, placed them back in their box and returned the box to her bag. Lying back on the bed, she tried to make sense of it all.

What were they going to do?

They were going to go speak to Connor. That would fix it. Just as soon as Erica arrived, they'd leave. Mullarky had given them the address, more or less. He'd given them a rough description of where Connor lived, which no one had understood, but he'd been able to point to the building when Jess had shown him a map on her phone.

It was worth a try.

It was all they had.

Although, there was always the chance that Alfie was right. He was right about so many things. Perhaps they should be leaving this well alone.

Heaving an exasperated sigh, Jess rolled off the bed and made her way downstairs, shielding her eyes from any shadows that fancied forming on the landing as she passed. In the kitchen, she watched through the window as her father and fiancé wrestled with the new patio slabs. Beyond them, Bubbles lay in the wet grass, no doubt getting a muddy belly.

Jess opened the door and called the dog in, brandishing a towel her father kept near the door, just in case of muddy paws.

Bubbles tiptoed around Marshall and Eddie, then leapt over a patio slab waiting to be put in the right place. Once inside, Jess wiped her down and rubbed her belly without closing the door.

'It's looking good,' she told the men.

'It'll all be worth it,' Eddie agreed. 'Glad I have a strong man to help me out, though. This would take forever if it was just me.'

Marshall chuckled.

'I love this sort of work. Especially when it's all done.' He winked at Jess and then stopped to study her. 'You all right?'

Jess nodded.

'I keep pulling the Devil card.'

The man went back to work.

'I guess that's to be expected,' said Marshall.

Jess sighed, sitting on the floor. Bubbles sat beside her, pushing her big head into Jess's lap for a cuddle.

'What if Alfie's right and we should let whatever's going to happen, happen?'

Marshall stopped working and stretched his arms over his head. Jess did her best not to stare, especially considering her father was right next to Marshall.

'What if I told you that I'd already spoken to

Connor? Would that help?'

Jess stopped breathing.

'What?' she squeaked. 'You spoke to him? When? How? What happened?' she asked in a rush.

Marshall looked down at the patio uncomfortably.

'Me and Alfie spotted him at the fair last night and followed him. We...explained. Asked him not to do it.'

Jess's eyes widened.

'And? Did he believe you?'

Marshall shook his head.

'What would you think? Two men come running after you through the fair and when they catch you, they know your plans and tell you to absolutely not do it.'

'I'd wonder how they knew my plans, reckon they knew more than me and absolutely not do it,' said Jess.

Marshall stared at her, slowly raising his eyebrows.

She sighed and then groaned into Bubbles's fur.

'If you can't talk him out of it, what luck are Erica and I going to have?'

Marshall shrugged.

'You might have some. Alfie mentioned you both to Connor. If Connor actually meets you and hears the warning again, maybe it'll have more of an impact.'

Jess nodded defiantly.

'Worth a try.'

'Worth a try,' Marshall echoed.

'I don't suppose anyone cares what I think?' asked Eddie.

They both turned to him.

'Of course, Dad. What do you think?'

'I don't think you should be going anywhere near this fella. Especially if Marshall and Alfie have already talked to him. Leave well alone, love.'

Jess frowned.

'But the imp. What happened to James.'

'You heard Mullarky; James was a bad man.'

'That doesn't automatically mean Connor is too. These are two different situations, Dad. What if Connor is just...desperate.'

'How can anyone be that desperate? He has a home, doesn't he? Mullarky gave you his address.'

'What if he's about to lose it?' Jess pondered. 'The same way Erica's being forced out of hers by the rent going up.'

Eddie hesitated.

'I suppose.'

'If he doesn't have any family to turn to... Or friends...' said Jess.

Eddie sighed.

'But this is the Devil, Jess.'

'I know, Dad. But, hey, that imp was all right. I actually managed to speak to it and everything.'

'It broke our window.'

Jess tried to hold back a laugh when her father

gave her a stern look.

'You tell the Devil he owes me window money. Except, don't, because that's terrifying. The imp was fascinating, the spirit too, but the Devil? I don't like this. Your mother doesn't like this. Just come trick or treating with us tonight and let that be it.'

Jess chewed her bottom lip and then started as there was a knock on the front door.

'That'll be Erica. Look, I'll chat with her about it and we'll see if we can find Connor and talk to him. Maybe that's all we'll need to do anyway.'

Eddie nodded but it was disgruntled.

'Fine. You know more about this than I do.'

Jess went to let Erica in, sick to her stomach; if her father, usually excited and open-minded, was worried, then things might be worse than she'd thought.

'Did Alfie tell you that he and Marshall had already tried this?' Jess asked as she and Erica walked through the town towards Connor's.

'No.' Erica frowned. 'Did they? When?'

'At the fair last night. They saw Connor and went after him, tried to explain everything. Marshall isn't convinced it's helped. I got another talking to this morning about how we shouldn't be getting involved...' Jess let her words trail off slowly, watching Erica's reaction from the corner of her eye.

'I would have thought Alfie would mention it,' Erica murmured.

'Is everything okay between you two?' Jess asked when Erica didn't say more.

'Yeah, why?'

'It's just...you don't seem to be...talking properly. About all this.'

Erica sighed.

'No. I think that's my fault.'

Jess waited patiently for Erica to find the words as they skirted the edge of the fair, its workers getting ready to open for the afternoon.

'I've been getting frustrated when he brings up us moving in together in his world,' Erica told her eventually. 'I've been getting frustrated by a lot of things lately. Where to live, the business, Rick... I thought coming here would take my mind off it all. But here we are, another thing we disagree on. We had one argument about this whole Devil thing and now it's like Alfie's purposefully not bringing it up.'

'So, you haven't talked about it at all?'

'Not really.'

'Oh.'

'Why?'

Jess turned to find Erica watching her. She quickly looked back to her feet and where she was walking.

'It's just...Alfie and I talked.'

'When we went to your parents' and you both disappeared upstairs with Ruby?'

'Yeah.'

'When Alfie said I wasn't allowed to go with you.'

'He didn't say that. Not exactly.'

Erica huffed.

'So, what did you talk about?'

'I asked him what he saw in the future, about tonight. I think the reason he's not picking a fight with you about it is because he only sees one outcome. We're going and that's it. He can't change your mind.'

Erica relaxed a little as they left the high street and found a footpath that would lead them to Connor's road. Jess glanced sideways at her friend. 'You know,' she murmured, 'if this weekend was supposed to be different, then let's make it different. You and me seem to be the only ones who think this is a good idea, Ric. And maybe that's out of some misplaced duty instead of logic or what's actually right. What if this Connor is like James?'

Erica sighed and caught Jess's eye.

'What if he's not? Do you want that on your conscience?'

'But Alfie's right. We can't help everyone. What about the posh woman in Bristol not selling us the Ouija board. You know that's going to come back to bite her. Maybe literally. We could have been more forceful. But you said it was her decision.'

'A Ouija board is different to summoning the Devil.'

'Is it?' questioned Jess. 'Surely it depends on

what comes through the door the Ouija board opens.' She turned back to the look up at the houses on either side of the road they were walking along. 'At least, that was my understanding. Have I got that wrong?'

Erica's pace slowed.

'No. No, you haven't.' She stopped walking.

Jess stopped and looked back to her. The conflict was obvious in Erica's eyes, so Jess gave her a smile and held out a hand.

'Come on. Let's go have a chat with this Connor and see what happens. We can make a decision when we have more information.'

Erica nodded and caught up, keeping her gaze down. Jess closed her eyes momentarily to centre herself.

The address Mullarky had sort of given them was a house split into two flats. They shared the same front door, so Mullarky wasn't certain which one was Connor's. He also didn't know Connor's surname, which was how the doorbells were labelled.

After staring at the two buttons for a while, Jess plumped and rang the top one.

They waited, Erica hugging herself, her eyes glazed in thought. Jess's mind whirred. It was enough to make her wish they'd stayed at home this Halloween. Still, she was glad Erica was there. If Erica and Alfie hadn't come, this would all still have happened but she'd be doing it alone.

'Have you spoken to your mum or gran about this?' she asked quietly.

Erica shook her head.

'I'm too scared to, to be honest. They'll tell me to just come home immediately and forget all about it.'

Erica and Jess exchanged a glance when the intercom for the doorbell kicked in.

'Hello?'

'Oh, hello. We're looking for Connor. Is this the right place? We're friends,' Jess added hastily, remembering what Marshall had told her about his meeting with Connor.

There was a pause, long enough for Jess to wonder if the person – a woman – just wasn't going to respond.

'How do you know Connor?'

Jess breathed a sigh of relief.

'My name's Jess, my friend here is Erica. We think he could be in trouble and we want to help. We just need a few minutes to talk to him.'

'In trouble with what?'

'Please, can we just talk in person? Just for a minute,' Erica asked. 'We won't take up too much of your time.'

'Fine.'

There was a buzz as the intercom turned off. They waited patiently and, finally, the front door opened to reveal a heavily pregnant young woman. Jess stared at her baby bump with widening eyes, thankfully Erica was quicker to act.

'Hi. I'm Erica. This is Jess. Thank you so much. Is Connor home?'

'No,' said the woman, crossing her arms.

'Oh. Do you know where he is?'

'Out looking for a job, I hope. What sort of trouble is he in?'

Jess couldn't breathe. She could see exactly the sort of trouble Connor was in. Her gaze travelled up to meet the eyes of the young woman.

'Are you his partner?' she asked weakly.

The woman nodded, giving Jess an appraising look.

'And my back, legs, bladder and head are all killing me. So please just tell me what sort of trouble he's in.'

Jess's breath caught.

'He's going to try and go out tonight,' said Erica shortly. 'Don't let him.'

'What? Why?'

'Because he's going to do something stupid. Do you have any ideas where he might be right now? Maybe you could call him and find out?'

The woman, eyes wide but lips twisted with mistrust, shook her head.

'Sorry,' said Jess quickly. 'Sorry. We'll let you go.' She pulled Erica away. As she dragged Erica down the road, she glanced over her shoulder. The woman watched them go and then pulled out a phone from the pocket of her dressing gown, closing the door.

Jess stopped.

'She's going to call him now. We could wait. He'll probably come home, right?' The words came out in a rush. Far too fast. Jess couldn't catch her breath.

Erica placed a hand on her back.

'Breathe,' she instructed gently. 'It's okay.'

'A baby on the way and no job. That's why he's desperate,' said Jess, gulping in air, memories of her own fraught pregnancy with Ruby flashing through her mind.

Her head became light and Erica helped to ease her into a sitting position on the pavement.

'We don't know that there's not more. Lots of people have babies on the way and no money coming in. They don't all summon the Devil to make a deal.'

'Maybe because they don't know it's an option,' said Jess, putting her head between her knees. 'I think we need to do some proper research into this.'

31

Connor

Maggie was watching from the living room window. Connor spotted her as he walked up the road, arguing silently with himself about whether he should be returning home or not. The problem being that the stuff he needed for that night was at home. He'd have to go back eventually. Apparently the spell could be done another night, but All Hallows' Eve would make it easier, and he'd come this far.

No, Connor was determined. Even if it meant he had to go through another row with his girlfriend to do it. It would all be worth it in the end. She'd see that. Maybe as early as the next day.

He could but hope.

Connor let himself in through the front door and climbed the stairs to their first floor flat, letting himself in again through their personal front door.

'Are you in trouble?'

Connor heard her and the quiver in her voice

before he saw her. She'd called out to him before she made it to the hallway, hand on her belly, skin pale with a sheen of sweat.

'Have you been throwing up again?' he asked. 'Sit down. Please.' He herded her back into the living room and waited until she was as comfortable as she could be on the sofa.

'Please, Connor. Some women came to the door and told me you were in trouble. They were looking for you. Are you in trouble?'

'What? No. Of course not. Who were these women?'

'I don't know. Jess and something. Erin, or something.' She shook her head, rubbing at her temples. 'Why are they saying you're in trouble?'

Connor's mind whirred. They must have been the women the weird men from the fair had mentioned.

'I don't know. I don't know who they are. I'm not in trouble. I promise.'

'Have you borrowed money or something?'

'No. No loans, no dealing with scary people. I've been job hunting. And down the job centre. I swear.'

His girlfriend searched his eyes and then sighed, her lower lip quivering.

'I can't do this, Connor.'

'I know.'

'I'm about to give birth, which is terrifying enough. And then we're going to be raising this baby on just my salary and my career has been set back, which is bad enough. And now you're throwing in people knocking on my door telling me you're in trouble?'

'I'm not in trouble. I promise.'

When she looked at him again, her eyes were burning.

'Are you planning on going out tonight?'

'What...?' Connor realised his error immediately. He shouldn't have hesitated, he shouldn't have let the question trail away.

Maggie's eyes widened and Connor ran a hand down his face.

'No,' he said forcefully. 'I'm not going out tonight. Why?'

'You're *not* going out tonight. We might have kids knocking on the door – I'm not traipsing up and down those stairs. You can do it. You can stay here tonight. I want you on this sofa with me. Okay?'

Connor nodded, swallowing against his dry mouth.

'Okay. Of course.'

She gave a defiant nod.

'Good.'

'I'll go make you a cup of tea, shall I?' Connor offered, turning to leave.

'Thank you.'

Connor looked out of the kitchen window as he waited for the kettle to boil. The road was empty.

Slowly, a plan formed in his mind, slotting together. She would be furious with him, but it would be worth it. She'd see. She'd see it would all be worth it in the end.

He gave her the cup of tea and some of her favourite biscuits, making sure she was comfortable. Once she had the television on and was quietly sipping her drink, Connor escaped to the bedroom. Beside the small double bed was a cot, ready and waiting for the baby. It was a tight squeeze to get to the bag he'd stashed under the bed. Once he had it, he crept through the flat, carefully lifting up his keys and slipping out of the door. Jogging down the stairs, he opened and closed the main front door just as carefully and quietly, and then he went to run down the road.

Erica

Hearing the heavy footsteps of someone running, Erica stepped out and blocked their way.

The young blond man she'd intercepted gave a screech of shock and skidded to a stop. Breathing hard, he went to go around her, but she sidestepped to stop him. Looking at her as if she was mad, he turned away and found Jess blocking his way back.

'What the hell. Are you the two crazy bitches who scared my girlfriend? What the hell is your problem? Get out of my way!'

'Where are you going, Connor?' Erica asked calmly. 'It's too early to go to the crossroads.'

'We just want to talk, Connor,' said Jess. 'We're so sorry about scaring your girlfriend. We just wanted to talk to you, that's all. Please.'

When Connor looked like he might run again, Erica continued. 'We know exactly what you're going to try and do tonight. Six months ago, Jess had to deal with the Devil coming to collect a soul living in her parents' new house. We *know* about this, Connor. Talk to us.'

That got his attention.

He stopped, lowering his arms and the bag he was carrying to his side. He turned to Jess with a querying look.

'You did?'

Jess nodded.

'It wasn't pretty,' she told him. 'An imp came to collect him.'

Connor raised an eyebrow and then scoffed.

'Rubbish.'

'I know they sound small and maybe cute. This thing was not small or cute, I assure you,' said Jess. 'It was big and scary and all it wanted was this man's soul because this man had sold it to the Devil in a trade.'

'That's what you want to do, isn't it, Connor,' said Erica. 'That man had it coming. He was a murderer. But you don't.' She watched his reaction carefully, the fear touching his eyes. 'Please, just stop for a moment and talk to us.'

'We just want to help,' Jess added gently.

Connor pressed his lips together to create a thin line, blinking hard, presumably to hold back tears. Eventually he sighed and nodded.

They sat together on the pavement, Connor between them, gripping his bag close. Erica tried to study it subtly, wondering what was in there. What did one need to summon the Devil? She hadn't taken the time to find out. It wasn't something she thought she needed to know, but now it dawned on her that the spell in question might be of importance. That there could be a way of breaking it, if need be.

Not that they would need to do that, because they were going to talk Connor out of it, right now.

'When is your girlfriend due?' Jess asked gently. 'She looks like it's any day now.'

Connor nodded.

'It is. Two weeks.'

Jess smiled.

'I remember the last weeks before my due date. I hated them. I could barely move, nothing was comfortable. Does she work? Your girlfriend? Is she on maternity leave?'

Again, Connor nodded.

'She's off sick today. Maternity leave starts next week, but she didn't sleep much.'

'No. I always thought that was cruel of nature. To not let you get good sleep before the baby comes,' murmured Jess.

'And you're looking for work?' Erica added. 'That must be rough, looking for a job with a baby on the way.'

'I got made redundant,' Connor said in a small voice. His head dropped, his voice breaking. 'She deserves better.'

'So do you,' Erica pointed out.

'And you don't get better this way,' said Jess. 'I know it doesn't seem like it now, but things will work out. You'll find a job and you'll have a gorgeous baby and everything will be great. You have to trust and keep doing the work.'

Connor lifted his chin, pulling a face, and turned on Jess.

'What do you know about it?'

Erica smiled to herself.

'Quite a lot, actually,' she murmured, although Connor ignored her.

'When I was at your girlfriend's stage I was in a job I hated, living with a man I didn't love and absolutely terrified. Okay, so I had money, but I was going to become a single mother and I had no idea how that would work. Now I have the most amazing five-year-old, I run my own business and love it, I own my own house and I'm getting married to a man I love. See? If I'd told me back then where I am now, she'd have laughed in my face. And I didn't need to do anything drastic to get there. I worked hard and I did what felt right to me and I got very lucky. Lucky in the sense of being able to buy a house and meeting the man of my dreams, but I worked hard to bring up my daughter and I stayed in that horrible job to make it all happen.'

Connor rubbed his hands over his face.

'What's your business?' he asked, his voice muffled.

'We're paranormal investigators,' said Jess.

'Which is why we know a lot about what you're planning to do tonight.'

'But...how?' Connor dropped his hands and looked between them.

'Because a brownie overheard you and came to tell us,' said Jess with a smile.

Connor's eyes widened in horror.

'I was right. You're both crazy.'

'We're not crazy,' said Jess quickly, exchanging a panicked look with Erica.

'Look, Connor. We have experience with this type of thing. A brownie is a creature from Scottish folklore. He lives in the witch's cottage, by the crossroads where you're planning on summoning the Devil. The same spot where he watched James summon the Devil a hundred years ago. James is the person who Jess watched having his soul collected by an imp, a servant of the Devil. And it doesn't matter that James was a murderer and a vile human and deserved what he got, because none of that matters. If you make a deal with the Devil, the same fate will be yours. And that's what we're trying to stop.'

'We want to help,' soothed Jess. 'Maybe we can help you find a job,' she murmured, her brow creasing.

'My girlfriend's dad offered me a job,' said Connor quietly. 'But I can't take it.'

'Why not?' asked Erica.

'He hates me.' Connor shook his head. 'He'll treat me like shit. I can't do it. I can't.' He covered his face again. 'I need to find something else. And I can't. I've looked. I've applied for everything. Most places don't even get back to me. The Job Centre is useless. I'm maxed out on all the benefits we're entitled to. We're going to lose our flat. My girlfriend doesn't even know the half of it. Because if she knows, then she'll leave me and she'll take the baby. She'll go home to her parents and her dad won't let me see her or the baby. I know it. I just know it. I can't let that happen. I can't.' Connor's eyes brimmed with tears as his shoulders shuddered. He shielded his face as best he could, enough that when he lowered his head, Erica glanced at Jess over his back.

'We won't let that happen,' said Jess softly, placing a hand on his back. 'We'll help however we can.'

Erica sighed. She had to admit, there was a chance that Alfie was right. Connor's predicament was no different to hundreds, if not thousands, of people's across the country. Why should they get involved?

'How did you find out about summoning the Devil?' she asked. 'How do you know how to do it?'

Connor sniffed and wiped his eyes on his sleeve.

'Everyone knows the story. The crossroads by the witch's house is where the Devil lives. I Googled a summoning spell.'

Erica sat back. There was a good chance that the spell wouldn't work. Was that a chance they could take at this point?

'But you don't have to do it now, do you,' Jess soothed. 'Because we're going to help you. Yeah?'

Connor shook his head.

'I don't have a choice.'

'You always have a choice, Connor,' said Erica, her mind still working hard, trying to fit different pieces together. 'The spell might not work. What's your plan then?'

Connor's lower lip quivered again and Jess shook her head.

'No. No, no. We're going to help you, Connor. You don't have to do any of this.'

'She's right.'

'But tonight is my last chance. The website I found said the spell works best on Halloween. I can't wait another year or chance it on another night. It's now or never.'

'Then it's never,' Erica told him.

'Because you don't need to,' Jess added. 'We'll help you. Come on. Let's go get a drink or something and chat it over.' She went to stand but Connor shook his head.

'Thank you. I think I'm going to go back to my girlfriend. She'll be furious when she finds out I've left again.'

Erica nodded.

'Okay. Fair enough. But promise us you won't try

and summon the Devil tonight, okay? And we'll figure out the job thing for you.'

Connor managed a weak smile and nodded.

'Promise.'

'Poor man,' Jess murmured as they wandered back to her parents' house.

'Hmm.'

'I wish I knew more people around here and could find him a job. I bet that would fix everything.'

'Hmm.'

Jess stopped and Erica stopped with her on autopilot.

'Ric!'

Erica focused on her friend.

'What?'

'Where are you? What are you thinking?'

'I don't know. Just about what Alfie said. How many people in this country right now are struggling for work with a baby on the way and their rent going up? I wonder how many of those are turning to drastic measures.'

'So?'

'So, we can't help all of them.'

'But we can help this one. Without getting anywhere near the Devil. Helping one person is better than none,' Jess pointed out.

'Another free job,' said Erica. 'Not like we can get

paid for this one.'

Jess sighed.

'Well, there's getting paid and there's principles. This one falls under the principles category.'

'Yeah.'

'Look, I understand that you're not happy right now and you're struggling. But you have a man – fae – who loves you and wants to live with you, and parents who are happy to support you. Okay. So stop being miserable about it and let's just help this man. The rest will sort itself out,' Jess blurted, stomping off ahead.

Erica watched her go, heart pounding. Instead of following, she diverted, slowly ambling back to the hotel. A headache was blooming at her temples and she felt the sudden need to be alone and have a lie down.

The lie down didn't happen. Erica found herself at the hotel bar, staring out of the window, replaying Jess's words over and over, wondering what her problem was.

'Everything okay?' Alfie asked, taking the stool beside her and ordering a beer.

'Not really,' said Erica, not bothering to turn to look at him. 'Why didn't you tell me you talked to Connor last night?'

'Because there wasn't any point.'

'Why?' She slowly looked up at him.

He shrugged and thanked the barman for the pint placed in front of him.

'Because it didn't change anything. How did your talk with him today go?'

'I have no idea. But at least we know why he wants to do it.' She sighed. 'I'm sorry that I've been so down lately.'

'It's understandable. Money is of great importance to humans.'

'But not to fae. Not in your world.'

'No.'

Erica lifted her gaze to his and found him watching her with soft, blue eyes.

'I think we should live together. In your world,' she murmured.

A slow grin spread across Alfie's lips.

'Permanently?'

Erica tapped her fingernail against the glass of her drink.

'We'll see how it goes.'

Alfie leaned across and kissed her cheek.

'Thank you.'

Erica gave a short laugh.

'Thank you! For giving me somewhere free to live.'

'Well, you say free. The house requires maintaining. It won't cost money, but it will cost time and labour.'

'That's fine,' said Erica, sipping her drink. 'We can make that work.' She leaned closer to him, slipping her hand onto his thigh. 'I think we did get through to Connor. Maybe we can just relax tonight? What do your spider senses tell you?'

Alfie gave her a strange look and then entangled the fingers of his free hand with her fingers resting on his thigh.

'I think we should relax. Enjoy our last evening in this town.' He sipped his pint. 'It's a pretty place. We'll enjoy the fair and the children dressed up, then we'll come back here and enjoy our hotel bed.' He gave her a wink and then lifted his pint back to his lips.

Erica smiled, but still, something tugged at her insides, demanding attention. She forced it to be quiet, sipping her drink and stroking Alfie's fingers to keep the feelings at bay.

Jess

'What's wrong?'

Jess jumped as Marshall appeared behind her. She was sitting at the bottom of her parents' stairs, Bubbles at her feet rolled onto her back, four legs in the air as Jess rubbed her belly. Jess shifted over so Marshall could pass, but he didn't go far. He crouched to give Bubbles's belly a rougher rub and the dog's tail wagged furiously.

'I think I had an argument with Ric and I said something stupid. I don't even know why.'

Marshall gave a small smile.

'Maybe because for some reason you both think you have to stop a man from summoning the Devil tonight? That's quite stressful. You know, it's a lot. And I still don't think you have to do it. You've warned this bloke, right? So have me and Alfie. So, just leave him to it. If he decides to go ahead, you can't say he wasn't warned. And I have a feeling about this. If you go and he's there, you won't stop him. People are crazy, Jess. He'll summon the actual Devil, because that's how these things go, isn't it. And then what? I don't want you anywhere near that. Ruby doesn't need you anywhere near that. We both need you here, safe, with us.'

Tears burned the back of Jess's eyes and she gritted her teeth to keep them there, nodding.

'Okay.'

Marshall caught sight of her reddening eyes.

'Oh, honey. I'm sorry. I didn't meant to upset you.' He collapsed to the floor and wrapped his arms around her, dragging her off the stairs and into his embrace. She allowed him to, unable to stop a laugh as he pulled her in close and Bubbles rolled over, jumped up and tried to push her head between them.

'All right. Okay. I'm okay,' said Jess, tears forgotten as she pushed Bubbles away. 'I know you're right,' she added quietly, stroking the dog's ears as Marshall's arm settled around her waist. 'It's just... What's the point of our business if we're not really helping people?'

'You do help people, Jess.'

'Yeah, but, this is a big one, isn't it. We help people say goodbye to people they love, or reclaim their home, or build their business. But this is literally saving a soul.' She met Marshall's eyes. 'He's got a baby on the way, Marsh. He's scared. That's all this is. Fear and desperation. He's stuck.

We need to stop him, and then...'

Marshall raised his eyebrows.

'What then? He'll still have no job and a baby on the way.'

'Yeah.' Jess sighed. 'I don't know.'

'Is there a way of breaking the crossroads? So no one can summon the Devil?' Marshall asked thoughtfully.

'I...don't know. We should ask, right? Surely it's just about lifting up the path.' Jess frowned.

'Probably need permission from the council for that.' Marshall tutted. 'Don't think they'd believe our reasoning somehow. A pathway like that probably has heritage they want to conserve, right?'

'Especially as its tied to folklore in the town.' Jess nodded.

They both sat back quietly.

'I get why you feel you have to do this,' Marshall murmured, kissing her shoulder through her jumper. 'I'm just telling you that you don't. Have to, that is.'

'I wish my conscience felt the same,' Jess whispered, brushing her lips over his.

There was a moment of heat between them as their eyes met, noses touching, and then she kissed him hard. They broke away, aware that someone might have seen, but there was only Bubbles, sitting and watching them with her head cocked to the side. She gave a whine and then pounced into them, knocking them both back.

Laughing, they pushed the dog back and Jess's phone beeped. She pulled it from her pocket as she found her feet. It was a message from Erica. Butterflies bounced around her stomach as she opened it.

Hey. I'm sorry. I don't know what's wrong with me lately. This is such an easy fix. I'm moving in with Alfie when my rent contract is up. Let's just relax tonight? Have fun. Let's assume our chat with Connor worked. How is Ruby's costume looking?

Jess smiled and hugged the phone to her chest.

'Everything all right?' Marshall pulled himself up, hindered slightly by the dog under his feet. Jess showed him Erica's message. He read it and smiled. 'There you go! See. Maybe Alfie saw a change in things.'

Jess nodded.

'I hope so.'

She paused to respond to Erica.

That's ok. Please don't apologise. I'm glad you're moving in with Alfie. Just don't forget about us! Happy to help in any way we can. And yes, let's relax tonight. Ruby's so excited about her costume. You'll have to wait until she can show you herself!

Jess hit send and then followed Marshall and

Bubbles into the living room where Ginny was putting the finishing touches to Ruby's costume.

'Oh, Rubes! You look amazing,' said Jess, sliding her phone back into her pocket.

'When are we going out?' Ruby asked, beaming.

'Not until tonight,' said Marshall.

Ruby pulled a face.

'Don't worry, Rubes. Plenty to do before then. We can go to the playground and walk Bubbles and—'

'Can we play hide and seek with the shadows?'

Jess stopped.

'Erm, no? I'd rather not.'

Ruby pulled another face.

'Can I wear this all day?' she tried.

Jess looked at her mother, who sat back and admired her work.

'I don't see why not.' Ginny released Ruby. 'Go show your grampy.'

They watched as Ruby skipped out of the room to the garden where Eddie was contemplating the new patio. Bubbles ran out after her.

'Are you sure, Mum?' Jess murmured. 'She might rip it before tonight.'

'Of course. When else is she going to wear it? It's like a wedding dress, isn't it. Speaking of which...'

Marshall jumped up.

'Think I'll go help Eddie with the patio,' he muttered, leaving the room.

Jess watched him go. Coward.

'It's okay if you want a small wedding.'

Jess snapped round to look at her mother and then narrowed her eyes suspiciously.

'Really?'

Ginny nodded.

'It's just...I know some people who will be upset if they're not invited.'

'But why? Why would they be upset? They're mostly people who I haven't seen since I was tiny. They have no idea who I am now.'

'Because,' said Ginny. 'Weddings are often the only time they get to see the wider family. Weddings and funerals. And weddings are obviously much preferred.'

Jess bit her lip.

'Oh. Yeah, I can see that.'

'But of course I want you to be happy. And if you want a small, intimate wedding instead of a big party, then that's up to you.'

Jess exhaled heavily through her nose.

'I suppose it would be different if we know the people, if they're our own families.'

Ginny gave her a questioning look.

'Well, because, you know, Paul's wedding was so...awful.'

'Your ex-boyfriend's wedding was awful for you to attend? What a shock,' said Ginny.

Jess laughed.

'Yeah, okay. Fair enough.'

'Is he invited to your wedding?'

Jess pulled a disgusted face.

'I don't know. I guess I have to, right? He's Ruby's father.'

'Ruby isn't the one getting married,' Ginny pointed out.

'But he invited us to his.'

'Knowing Paul and his new wife, that was so that they could show off and make you feel small.'

'Paul doesn't want to make me feel small,' said Jess quietly. 'His wife does.'

Ginny gave an *I told you so* gesture.

'Think about it,' she said.

Jess nodded.

'Thanks, Mum.'

Ginny wandered over and hugged her daughter. Jess hugged her back tight.

The rest of the day went by too quickly. Ruby ate lunch, went to the playground and played with Bubbles in the garden while wearing her Halloween costume. By the time they were preparing to leave for the fair, she had a spot of mayonnaise down the front and part of the lace of the skirt had been ripped by an overexcited Bubbles.

Still, she was enjoying it.

That was what Jess kept telling herself.

They met Erica and Alfie on the edge of the fair, Ginny proudly showing off her sewing work.

'What are you meant to be?' Alfie asked as Ruby

twirled for him.

'She's a pirate princess riding a dinosaur, of course,' said Jess. 'Isn't it obvious? What did you think she was?'

Alfie smirked.

'The mayonnaise stain is model's own,' Ginny informed them. 'From lunch.'

'I love it,' Erica declared. 'You look incredible, Rubes.'

'I know,' said Ruby, looking down at herself. 'Can we go on rides now and eat candy floss?'

'I'm not sure those two things go together,' said Marshall.

'Let's go get a burger so you can add a tomato sauce stain to match the mayonnaise one,' Eddie offered, taking Ruby's hand.

The five-year-old skipped ahead of her grandfather, towing him along towards the nearest burger stall that thankfully didn't have much of a line yet. The others followed at a more sedate pace.

Erica and Jess fell into step with one another.

'I'm really glad you're here,' Jess told her, purposefully knocking shoulders with her friend.

'I'm glad too.' Erica grinned and took a deep breath. 'Do I wish that horrible ride was at least two metres further into the road and away from that building so it doesn't look like it's going to crash into it every time it goes up? Sure. But I'm glad I came.'

Jess laughed.

'Yeah. I never understand how this place gets permission to be right here on the high street every year.'

'I'm glad I don't live in that house,' Erica murmured. 'Or any of these houses. Your parents did the right thing, buying one off the main thoroughfare.'

'Even though it came with a spirit, an imp and some shadow people.'

Erica chuckled.

'At least the shadow people mean no harm.'

'I did some research. Just on the internet. About summoning the Devil,' Jess whispered.

'And?'

'Lots of videos and posts about how to do it, not so much about what to do next or if it goes wrong or how to unsummon him. It's like they think you can summon him, but when you ask about unsummoning him, then you're crazy for believing in it all. What's that about?'

'People think it's cool to do occult stuff these days, but deep down they probably don't believe in it. Or know what they're talking about,' Erica murmured.

Jess gave her a look.

'Cool?'

Erica smiled.

'Yeah, you know. Hip. Groovy.'

Jess snorted a laugh.

'My point is, I'm still none the wiser what to do if

Connor summons the Devil. The internet seems to think it won't actually work, but what if it does? There must be a way of breaking the spell, but I don't know how. There must be a way of sending him back, right?'

Erica sighed.

'I honestly don't know. I rang Gran at lunch-time.'

'Oh?'

'Told her about Connor.'

'What did she say?' All of the tension immediately returned to Jess's shoulders, her stomach flipping and tying itself into a knot.

'She wasn't happy about it. She doesn't know much about it all either. She reckons the Devil might come from the same dimension as the demon that was in the woods, so technically the same magic and banishing spell should work. Except the Devil isn't a demon, so chances are it won't work. Maybe what we need is an angel banishment spell.'

Jess shook her head.

'I checked that. Same thing. Lots of summoning information but nothing about how to get rid of them.'

'Great. Well, Gran said we did the right thing. Reckons we should stay away. Basically, she agrees with Alfie on this one.'

'Really?' Jess genuinely hadn't expected that. 'I would have thought Minerva would want us to help save a soul.'

Erica gave her a curious sideways look.

'We do help people, you know. And there are safer ways of helping people. Ways of helping people that don't involve the Devil.'

'I know.'

'Like, we could do volunteering. Or charity donations as part of the business, or something.'

Jess smiled.

'I think we need to sort out our own profit first.'

Erica shrugged.

'I don't know. I don't need the rent money anymore. And if that's what's bothering you, then let's do something about it.'

Jess nodded and Erica slowly moved away, finding Alfie in the queue with Eddie and Ruby. Was that what was bothering her, or was it something else? There was a difference between supporting a charity and saving a man from selling his soul. Wasn't there?

They ate their burgers at a table, chatting happily. Ruby managed to spill some tomato sauce and they gave a cheer when it landed next to the mayonnaise stain. Jess took a photo to commemorate the moment.

The strain was gone. The tension had lifted once more. Alfie was laughing with her family, as if he'd always been there, holding Erica's hand.

Jess watched it all and breathed in deep, letting the contentment overwhelm her for a second.

Something pulled at the hem of her coat. She

turned, expecting to see a small child or that someone had brushed past. She held her breath, freezing, when she found Mullarky staring up at her.

'I've been looking everywhere for you'se,' he chided. 'Where've you'se been?'

Jess gestured to the fair.

'Never mind, never mind. We dinnae have time. Come on.'

'What?'

'It's happening,' Mullarky hissed.

Jess glanced back to her family to find that they had quietened and were watching her and the brownie.

'What's happening?' asked Marshall, his tone deep.

Ginny put a protective arm around Ruby, holding her close.

Alfie sighed and stood.

'If the boy has decided his fate, then his fate is decided,' he told the brownie.

Mullarky opened his mouth in shock.

'O'course ye wuid say that. Filthy fae.'

'Now, hang on a moment,' said Erica.

'What's a fae?' Eddie whispered to Ginny.

'I cannae do this alone,' said Mullarky, looking imploringly up into Jess's eyes.

'They don't have to do anything,' Alfie declared. 'They've done enough.'

Jess looked back to Erica for help.

'Time is running out,' said Mullarky. 'Soon Satan will be among us.'

Jess's heart dropped into her gut as Marshall rubbed his face with both hands.

'Fine. I'll go. The rest of you will stay here,' said Alfie, standing and approaching the brownie.

'I need witches,' Mullarky hissed. 'What good is a fae.'

'I'll show you the good of a fae,' Alfie hissed back, his eyes flashing.

Jess stepped back, looking for the answer.

'You're not going without me,' came Erica's voice.

'Well, *you* can't go without me,' Jess found herself saying.

'Absolutely not.' Marshall stood with force. 'It's Halloween. We're having a lovely family evening. Everyone should just sit back down.'

'He's coming,' Mullarky whispered.

An image of Connor's pregnant girlfriend flashed before Jess and she nodded.

'Come on then. Let's stop this before it starts. We need to hurry.'

Erica nodded and rushed after Alfie, towards the witch's cottage and the crossroads, Mullarky leading the way.

'Jess.'

Jess stopped at her father's voice and turned back to her family.

'Keep Ruby safe. And I'll be back soon. I love you

all the most.' She gave each of them a meaningful look and then went to hurry after the others before her body could have second thoughts.

The further she ran from her family, the more her stomach threatened to push the burger she'd just eaten back up her throat. She swallowed hard, hoping against hope that Erica and Alfie would have the situation under control by the time she got there.

34

Connor

At first, Connor could only hear the fair as he stood near the witch's cottage, staring at the space where the crossroads lay beneath grass and fallen leaves. Screams and shouts and music drifted across to him on the wind. He pulled his coat tight around him and approached the crossroads.

He'd been worried that there would be people here. The crossroads were hardly in the middle of the woods, hidden away. They were pretty much in plain sight. He checked the windows of the cottage to his right. There was a dim light in an upstairs room, but no movement.

The closer Connor got to the crossroads, the less he could hear the fair, which didn't seem right. He'd only taken a few steps and the wind hadn't dropped. He turned, but nothing about the view behind him had changed.

Biting his lip, taking in gulps of air in an attempt to steady his heart, which he was certain was about to burst through his chest, he reached the edge of the crossroads and lowered his bag to the ground.

The trees and darkness of the woods in front of him caught his attention as goosebumps lifted painfully over his arms and the back of his neck. Connor shivered. The noise of the woods was loud; how had he not heard it before? He'd assumed it would be silent, given that there would be no bird song. But every now and then there was the sound of a twig snapping, or a strange sound that was perhaps an owl, or a bat. It sounded like wings. What else lived in the woods?

Connor emptied his bag. If he was going to do this, he should do it quickly. Just get it over with. He was setting up, laying out the salt and pestle and mortar, when he heard movement behind him. Spinning around, breathing hard, he searched the shadows.

There was nothing there.

And then the light around him dimmed further. Jumping, he turned to the house to find the upstairs light had gone out. He waited to see if another light would come on, but it didn't. Had the woman who lived there run behind him? No, she could barely walk. She wouldn't run. Yet, as the silent seconds ticked by, Connor's brain offered him an untangled memory of the sound of quiet, running footsteps behind him.

'C'mon, Connor. Get it together.' Even his hushed voice sounded too loud.

That was all it was. The darkness and silence of the evening amplified the normal sounds of life around him. Everything he was hearing was normal.

All he had to do was get this done and over with, then he could go home and curl up in bed next to the woman he loved and his beautiful unborn baby. And everything would be okay.

He repeated that to himself, in his head, over and over as he set up the summoning spell. Pricking his finger and squeezing his hand to release drops of blood was the worst part, but he'd been psyching himself up for it all week, and in the end, it wasn't as bad as he thought.

He sat back on his haunches and surveyed the scene.

He was ready, but he still went over his checklist a couple more times. If this worked, he didn't want anything to go wrong. Given the warnings from the two strange men and those two women, he couldn't afford for anything to go wrong.

Taking a deep breath and closing his eyes, Connor tried to regain control of his thumping heart and his roiling stomach.

Just do the spell.

It won't work anyway.

Just do the spell, be disappointed and go home.

Tears pricked at his eyes.

Go home and get shouted at. Screamed at. Chucked out. Become unemployed, homeless and never be allowed to see your baby.

He shook away the thoughts, stood and began the spell through gritted teeth, not wanting to give it another thought. Once he'd finished, he stepped back and waited, holding his breath.

For the longest moment, nothing happened.

Connor released a long exhale through his lips.

It hadn't worked.

He knew it wouldn't. Deep down, he'd known.

Oh well.

Turning on his heel, Connor went to jog down the path and head for home, when he remembered his bag and all of the stuff he'd brought, lying in a triangle over the crossroads. He couldn't leave anything there. Imagine the headlines in the local news that would appear the next morning.

Sighing to himself, he hurried back, landed on his knees and began shoving things back into his bag. He was just starting to blow on the salt circle, to scatter it, when a shiver ran over him. He fought through, blowing the salt, making himself slow down a little as his head started swimming.

Then he stopped.

Gone were the sounds of the woods. There came no noise from the fair.

This was what silence truly was.

Connor's heart hurt his chest tightening. Screw the salt, the wind would blow it away. He jumped to his feet, clutching the bag to his chest, and told his feet to take him home. His feet didn't move. Connor remained rooted to the spot, facing the crossroads and the woods, a cold sweat beading over his forehead and down his back. The only sound was that of his heavy breathing and pounding pulse in his ears.

And at the back of all of that, a small voice.

What have you done? Stupid. Stupid. Run! Now!

Still, his feet wouldn't move.

'It's all right, Connor, there's nothing to be afraid of.'

Mouth dry, Connor scanned the darkness of the trees, where the man's voice had come from. It didn't sound like the men from the fair, but he found himself hoping – praying – that it was them.

There came a chuckle, and then a figure emerged from the darkness. For a moment, Connor could have sworn that the figure's dark eyes glowed red, but then it became a man walking out of the woods towards him. He had short dark hair and large dark eyes. Connor wanted to say that his skin was brown, but then he watched in confusion as the man's face darkened to black and then gradually lightened to white, and it didn't stop until he was the shade of thin porcelain. The skin colour changes highlighted the dark beard on his chin and around his mouth.

He stopped on the other side of the crossroads, arms by his side. He was wearing a suit with a thin tie, and Connor found it strange that that was the fact that scared him the most. Not the glowing eyes

– he could dismiss that as a trick of the darkness – or his skin changing colour – Connor was obviously panicking. No, the suit remained the same throughout, and why would a man in the woods be wearing a suit?

Finally, Connor's feet allowed him to move and he took a step back.

The man was a little taller than Connor, and gave a smile that cut through Connor's breath.

'Are you…?' Connor breathed.

The man held up a finger.

'Hold on, Connor. Not just yet. We're not all here yet.'

Connor snapped his mouth shut.

There came noise behind him and Connor, not wanting to turn his back on the strange man, swivelled his head quickly to see who was there.

One of the men from the fair, followed by the two women, running towards him, led by… Well, that couldn't be right.

Connor stared down at the strange little furry creature that skidded to a halt beside him.

'Be gone, Satan!' it cried in a curious Scottish accent, holding an arm defensively in front of Connor. 'Ye cannae have him!'

The man on the other side of the crossroads raised a curious eyebrow at the creature and then laughed. He laughed so hard, he bent double, hands on his knees.

The man from the fair appeared on Connor's

other side, forcibly pushing him back to the women who had stopped, both trying hard to catch their breath.

'Oh. Oh, Mullarky.' The suited man straightened and wiped laughter tears from the corners of his eyes. 'You do make me laugh. As if you have ever had the power to stop me.'

Erica

It took Erica a while to take in what was happening. There was Connor facing a man, who was strangely wearing a suit while standing next to the woods on a Sunday night. Between them were the crossroads and what Erica was pretty certain was half a triangle made out of sticks and a circle of salt. She frowned. Was the salt supposed to protect Connor? It didn't seem to be doing a great job.

She looked back up and found the suited man's gaze directly on her. Just like that, the air left her lungs but she didn't reach for another breath. She simply stopped and stared back.

'I'm nae joking!' cried Mullarky, although his voice was too high and it cracked a little at the end.

Jess groped for Connor while staring at the suited man, finally finding him and pulling him further back.

'We should go,' she whispered. 'We should go.'

Alfie sidestepped, coming between the suited man and Erica, breaking his hold over her. She gasped for a breath and then, without thinking and without any control, fell to her knees.

'Ric?'

Jess's voice sounded far away, despite her standing next to Erica.

'What do we have here, then? Connor, my lad, how wonderful of you to bring some friends.'

Connor shook his head as Jess helped Erica back to her feet.

'Can we run now?' she whispered in Erica's ear. 'Please.'

Erica gripped onto her friend and shook her head.

'What if he follows,' she whispered back, still struggling to fill her lungs. When she risked glancing up again, she found the suited man watching her around Alfie, his eyes glowing a soft red.

Erica clenched her eyes shut and demanded her lungs to breathe properly. The air whooshed in and she gasped, suddenly released from whatever was stopping her.

'It's been such a long time since I conversed with witches,' said the man to Connor. 'I must thank you, Connor. Name your terms, boy.'

'He willnae be naming terms. We're nae making deals with ye,' Mullarky spat.

The man gave him a tiresome look.

'Oh, Mullarky. This act has never worked. Either shut up or I will shut you up.' He looked back to Connor, glancing at Erica and Jess in turn. 'I haven't forgotten about you, fae. I'm just not sure what the point of you is.'

Erica's breath started to come easy, although a ball of anger dropped into the pit of her stomach. She straightened, leaning closer to Alfie.

So, this was the Devil.

He was shorter than she'd been expecting. More human looking. But that probably didn't mean much. She imagined he could change his appearance at will, depending on his audience.

Hearing her thoughts, the Devil chuckled. When she shifted her gaze to him, he winked, making her stomach clench. She swallowed hard on the bile that rose up her throat.

'Speak, boy,' the Devil commanded.

Connor yelped as he fell to his knees. Shaking, his lifted his head and took rasping breaths.

'Please. I need a job. A good one. A well-paying one. I need money.'

Erica shook her head. That was too vague. Below her, Mullarky also shook his head.

'And why do you need money, boy? Do you know how many of your kind come to me each day asking for money?' The Devil smiled and the crossroads between them trembled, lifting worms and beetles out of the earth and grass.

'Please. I can't afford the rent. I have a baby coming.'

Erica clenched her eyes shut and Jess gave Connor a push.

'Shut up!' she hissed, giving Erica and Alfie a pointed look.

'A baby,' the Devil whispered thoughtfully.

'Nae! Nae. Ye cannae have him or the bairn!' cried Mullarky, holding out his arms to create a sort of protective barrier around Connor. 'Leave now, Satan!'

The Devil gave the brownie a disdainful look.

'Mullarky. When you panic, it shows in your voice. Which is now grating on me. While it is wonderful to see you again, and you haven't changed in the slightest, be quiet or I will take the soul of your mistress. With a click of my fingers.'

Mullarky gasped and stepped back. He went to talk but snapped his mouth shut, looking back to Erica and Jess for help.

Jess was clinging to Connor, easing him back, trying to pull him to his feet.

What were they supposed to do? Who was going to step up?

What would Minerva do?

Tears in her eyes, Erica stepped up beside Alfie and made herself look at the Devil.

'What're you doing? Get back,' Alfie hissed.

But he couldn't do this alone. The Devil wouldn't even look at him.

The Devil didn't want a fae. He wanted a witch.

As if to prove her point, the Devil turned his attention from Connor to her, watching her as she moved, smiling softly as she met his eyes.

This time her stomach didn't react in disgust. Instead, this time, there was something else. That twinge and twist that she recognised from the first time Alfie had smiled at her, from the first time he'd kissed her. Erica blinked and then frowned at the Devil, giving a subtle shake of her head.

The Devil threw back his head and laughed. Then he turned back to Connor.

'You will have riches beyond your wildest dreams,' he said without much conviction. 'In exchange for your soul. Upon your death, *whenever* that may be, your soul be will mine.'

Erica was pretty sure there was some small print attached to the word 'whenever'.

'No!' screamed Mullarky as Connor drew breath to respond.

Growling, the Devil lifted an arm and Mullarky was in the air, flying backwards into Jess. They tumbled together, away from the others.

Erica turned to watch, alarmed.

'Jess? You okay?'

'She's fine,' mumbled the Devil. 'Speak, boy. Do we have a deal?'

'No,' said Alfie. 'No deal. Take the kid, get him out of here,' he added to Erica.

She stared at him.

'I'm not leaving you here,' she hissed.

Alfie shrugged and then looked her in the eye.

'Please. Go.'

The air rushed out of Erica's lungs, although this time it wasn't an outside force making her breathless. Never before had she seen such fear in Alfie's eyes. Tears filled her eyes and began falling down her cheeks as she shook her head.

'I'm not leaving you,' she repeated, sterner this time, through a tight throat.

The Devil smiled.

'When a witch loves a fae,' he crooned. 'Neither one willing to let the other be hurt. That's fine. Really, it is. Take the deal, boy,' he added to Connor. 'Just a verbal agreement for now. We can sign on the dotted line later. As you can see, I have other matters to attend to.' All the while, he didn't take his eyes from Erica and Alfie.

Swallowing hard, Erica turned on Connor as he opened his mouth to speak. She caught his eye, made sure she had his attention and then gave him a look her grandmother had taught her.

'Don't you dare,' she told him. 'Go check on them and not another word from you.' She pointed back to Jess and Mullarky.

Connor, visibly trembling, went to respond when a sob overwhelmed him. The tears came next, streaming down his cheeks. He nodded, gripping his gut as he turned and stumbled back to Jess and the brownie.

Still channelling her grandmother, Erica turned back to the Devil.

'Now, I apologise for you being summoned here. But there's no deal here for you. Please leave.'

The Devil watched her curiously and then glanced at Alfie.

'But I could have so much fun here,' he murmured, appraising the fae. 'Two witches and a fae. The fae I have no use for, but your love for this witch could be fun to play with.' He grinned and this time, instead of blunt, pearly white teeth, they were sharp and tinged with blood.

Erica stood her ground, fighting the urge to be sick.

This wasn't supposed to happen. They should have gotten here earlier, they should have known that Connor wouldn't listen to them. Erica wished she'd listened to her grandmother. Why hadn't she listened?

The Devil watched her curiously, smiling in a charming way, his teeth now human. His skin darkened until he appeared less like a doll in a horror movie and more like a handsome billionaire ready to find her endearing.

'I'm asking you again,' she declared, her voice stronger than she felt. 'Leave now. You will find no deal here.'

Much to her horror, the Devil stepped towards her. It was only one step, but the sight of it made her knees tremble, threatening to buckle beneath her. She kept her position, clenching her hands into fists at her sides.

'Have you seen your world lately?' he asked in a voice so soft it was carried on the wind.

Erica swallowed hard.

'Do you know how much work, over how many centuries, it's taken to get to this point?' the Devil continued. 'I can only appear in your world when I am summoned, and once a deal has been struck, I am pulled back to my own realm. So it has taken those centuries of whispering in ears and waiting for the desperation of humans. Thankfully' – the Devil grinned – 'you humans are a desperate lot. It was so easy to twist your cultures and societies, growing petty squabbles into wars, driving up your desire for money and riches until some poor saps just can't survive any longer without calling upon me.' He glanced back to Connor. 'As I said, Erica Murray, a deal will send me back to my own world. And it doesn't have to be a deal with him.' He took another step towards her, the toes of his shoes brushing against a line of salt in the grass. 'It could be with you.'

Alfie held an arm out in front of her.

'Take Connor and the others, and go,' he growled to her.

Erica shook her head, keeping her eyes on the Devil who continued to smile, lips lowered over his teeth now, waiting for her to draw the conclusion he wanted.

'I'm not leaving you,' she repeated quietly.

'A deal, then,' said the Devil. 'If Connor no longer wishes to part with his soul in exchange for a happy relationship and enough money to provide for his baby, which is coming now, by the way—'

'What?' came Connor's hushed voice.

'—then I will take the fae. What do you say, Aelfraed? Connor's soul and the witch you love so much can go free.'

Erica glanced at Alfie, eyes wide.

'No!' she yelled before Alfie could speak. 'Absolutely not!' She wouldn't admit it there and then, but she'd rather the Devil took Connor's soul than Alfie's. Which rather rendered their being there useless. Again, Erica told herself they shouldn't have come. Next time Alfie and her grandmother agreed on something, she would remember this and listen to them.

'The baby's coming?' came Connor's voice.

A weight lifted from Erica as the Devil turned his attention away from her.

'Yes. Can you not hear your love screaming in pain?'

Connor went to run, but the Devil lifted a finger and Connor fell to the ground, yelping.

'What are you doing?' Jess screeched, reaching for Connor.

'Nothing, little witch. Such a green witch, aren't you. So new and fresh to this whole thing. I can taste it.' The Devil smacked his lips. 'You two come as a package, I think. Yes, two for the price of one.'

'Let Connor go!' shouted Erica, digging her fingernails into the palms of her hands until she was sure she'd drawn blood. 'Let him go and we'll talk a deal.'

Alfie turned to her for a second.

'What are you doing?' he hissed.

'Let Connor go,' Erica repeated.

The Devil cocked his head at her thoughtfully, shrugged and said, 'No.' He snapped his fingers and the click echoed around them, bouncing between the cottage and the woodland trees.

Jess

When the Devil had thrown Mullarky back into Jess, landing on the ground had knocked the wind from her lungs. Stunned, she gasped for breath. She hadn't felt this utter desperation for air, as if her lungs were locked shut, since she'd been winded on a bouncy castle aged nine. Jess clenched her eyes closed and shook her head, willing the air to come.

Finally, her lungs unlocked and the air seeped in. She took in big gulps and grasped around for Mullarky.

Upon arriving, her eyes had immediately found Connor. It had taken a while before she had looked at the Devil. Even then, she had looked away. Staring at the backs of her friends or the blades of grass at her feet or the fallen leaves around them was imminently better than even glancing at that...thing.

Every part of her body was screaming at her to

run.

Her fingers found Mullarky's body not far from her and she scooted over to him. How did one check a brownie was alive? Her fingertips found his little neck and she felt for a pulse.

There. It was strong, pounding beneath her touch, with fear or adrenaline, or perhaps this was just what a brownie's pulse felt like.

'Mullarky?' she whispered, taking his shoulders and giving him the smallest of shakes. 'Mullarky?'

Erica had stepped forward, beside Alfie, which wasn't what Jess had wanted. Jess wanted them to leave, now. But they couldn't just leave the Devil standing there, could they. There had to be a way of sending him back. Why had the internet been full of ways to summon him but not to send him away? Had no one successfully sent him away? Or did the internet just not know what they were talking about?

Jess suspected the latter, but she couldn't rule out the former.

The Devil was still trying to get Connor to take the deal, although she could have sworn his heart wasn't in it. His eyes were on Erica.

Jess shook Mullarky harder.

'Mullarky!'

The brownie opened his large, dark eyes and mumbled something.

'Oh, thank god. Are you all right?'

He nodded and went to sit up, holding his head.

Feeling it bare, he searched for his bowler hat and jammed it in place.

'Bastard made me fly,' he grumbled.

'Yup. Both of us, technically.'

'Are ye hurt?' The brownie's gaze flittered over her.

Jess shook her head.

'Bruised, terrified, but physically I'm okay. Might vomit. Who knows.'

Mullarky nodded.

'Fair enough.'

Erica sternly sent Connor to look after them and Jess was glad to have Connor back within reach as he stumbled, sobbing, over to them. She grabbed on to him as soon as she could reach and dragged him down to the ground with them.

Connor flinched away from Mullarky as the brownie began to recover.

'How do we fix this?' Jess hissed. 'How do we get rid of him?'

Mullarky shook his head.

'I've never seen Satan unsummoned without him getting something in return,' he mumbled, rubbing his shoulder where he'd crashed into Jess.

'He needs a deal?' Jess asked. 'No. There has to be another way.'

'Ye're the witch, ye figure it out.'

Jess glared at Mullarky until Connor's sobs distracted her.

'You didn't read anything about what to do if this

all went wrong?' she whispered to him.

He shook his head, trying to calm himself.

Jess resisted the urge to hit him.

'Why?' she growled. 'You decided to do this huge thing and you didn't have a plan B?'

'I just wanted to make the pain stop,' said Connor between the hiccupping sobs.

Jess's sigh turned into a groan.

'This is life, Connor. And you've got a baby on the way. It's just going to get more scary and more painful, trust me.' She relented and steadied herself as Connor gave her a strained look. 'Sorry. It's also wonderful. And you know what? Babies don't care if you have a lot of money. You'd have figured it out. People always do. People have been figuring it out without resorting to selling their soul for centuries. We told you we would help.'

Connor shook his head.

'I just—'

'It disnae matter nae more,' said Mullarky, finding his feet. 'It is what it is, and Satan is sizing up yer friend, witch.'

'Jess.'

'Hmm?'

'I'm Jess, she's Erica. Please, stop calling me witch.'

Mullarky gave her a strange look.

'It's a compliment, lassie. Better a witch than an ordinary human.'

Jess smiled. While part of her agreed with him,

she wasn't entirely convinced. She looked over to where Erica and Alfie were creating a barrier between them and the Devil. What could they do?

'As I said, Erica Murray,' the Devil was saying, creeping closer to Erica. 'A deal will send me back to my own world. And it doesn't have to be a deal with him.'

'Is that true?' Jess whispered to Mullarky.

The brownie gave a shrug.

'Nae, as far as I've seen and experienced,' the brownie murmured, watching the Devil with narrowed eyes. 'Hell disnae just suck him back when a deal is made and a contract signed. That vile creature walks back, chin up, laughing until yer bones rattle. He chooses when tae return tae hell.'

Jess sucked on her teeth, staring at Alfie's back, willing a solution to come to her.

'Does the signing of a contract open the door, though?' she wondered.

Mullarky glanced at her.

'Nae one's signing anything, lassie. That's why we're here.'

'But what if it wasn't signing away a soul,' she offered.

Mullarky frowned and looked back to the Devil.

'What else is there?'

'What does he value?' Jess whispered, following the Devil's gaze to Erica. 'Power,' she realised. That was why he wanted Erica. What could they give him of equal power to a granddaughter of such a strong witch?

'...His baby, which is coming now, by the way—' The Devil's voice floated through Jess's thoughts, which were shattered by Connor's quiet, 'What?'

She grabbed on to his shirt and held him down.

'He's lying,' she hissed.

'Nae, lassie,' said Mullarky. 'Satan is many things. A twister, manipulator, a slitherer and charmer, but he's nae liar.'

'The baby's coming?'

'Can you not hear your love screaming in pain?'

Connor was on his feet, wrenching his shirt from Jess's grasp, leaving her fingers throbbing. He went to run when the Devil lifted a finger and Connor collapsed back to the ground with a gut-wrenching yelp.

Jess reached for him again.

'What are you doing?' she screeched as Connor writhed in pain.

'Nothing, little witch. Such a green witch, aren't you. So new and fresh to this whole thing. I can taste it. You two come as a package, I think. Yes, two for the price of one.'

Jess's stomach twisted, bile surging up her throat. She swallowed on it hard before it got too far, urging herself to remain strong.

There had to be a way out of this.

'Let Connor go!' cried Erica, and for a moment, Jess wondered if she was talking to her. She raised her hands, freeing Connor, but the Devil was still somehow pinning him down.

There came a click of the Devil's fingers and then everything went silent.

Gasping, Jess searched for Erica and Alfie, reaching out for Mullarky.

What was happening?

The stars above their heads seemed to dim, a darkness enveloping them, and then Alfie was down on his knees, clutching his chest.

The silence of the woods was broken by Erica's scream.

'What are you doing? Let him go!'

Alfie said something in a broken voice, but Jess couldn't make out the words. She could guess, though, and her best guess was that Alfie was telling them to run.

It wasn't such a bad idea.

The Devil raised his finger and Alfie collapsed. They waited a moment, watching, hearing their own breathing and hoping to see Alfie's chest rise and fall.

Erica was immediately by his side.

'Alfie? Alfie? Are you okay?'

'Only one way to tell,' said the Devil, and Erica was pushed back by invisible forces. She landed a few steps away from Alfie and when she stood and tried to return to him, something would push her back again.

'Oh dear,' came Mullarky's voice by Jess's ear.

'What do I do,' Jess murmured. What could she

do?

Erica screamed and then turned to face the Devil. Her shoulders square, hair blowing back in the autumn wind that had now returned, just as noise from the fair and the sleeping woods returned.

Jess couldn't see what happened next, as Erica's back was to her, but she could feel it.

There was power, real power, emanating from her best friend. Her arms were by her side and then lifted a little, and Jess could have sworn that tendrils of blue fire wormed their way around her fingers.

Connor gasped as the Devil released him, and Jess was too captivated by Erica to stop him from finding his feet and running away as fast as he could.

'Go back from where you came,' came Erica's voice, except it wasn't just Erica's voice. Jess recognised Esther's and Minerva's too. There were more than three female voices there, much more.

Erica wasn't just the granddaughter of witches, she was the great-great-great-granddaughter of strong, powerful witches. More than that, likely.

'Beautiful,' said the Devil, his dark eyes shining with a deep red glow.

'Ric,' Jess murmured, wondering if she should shout but not wanting those red glowing eyes on her.

'Go back,' Erica repeated, louder this time, the

voices singing it together.

'My darling, you have so much power, but it's been dormant for too long. You could be so much more,' said the Devil, licking his teeth as if tasting the words.

He glanced back to Jess then, and she held her breath, waiting for some terrible fate to befall her. Instead, he smiled and returned his attention to Erica.

'What do you say, Jessica Tidswell?'

Jess started. The Devil wasn't looking at her, but he was talking to her in a deep, soothing voice.

'Sign the contract and send me away, before your friend does something she'll regret.'

A scroll appeared beside Jess, but Mullarky jumped on it before she could even consider picking it up. He unrolled it and read it, his eyes flashing back and forth as he scanned the words.

'Dinnae sign it, lassie,' he told her, rerolling the scroll and brandishing it at the Devil. 'He wants both of yer souls. Well, ye cannae have 'em!' He looked to Erica. 'Finish him, lassie!'

Jess looked between Mullarky and Erica, bewildered.

'Finish him? What are you expecting her to do?' Jess found her feet and moved to stand beside Mullarky while she contemplated moving to Erica.

'Send him back!' cried the brownie.

The Devil's soft gaze was on Erica.

'Only if you come with me,' he murmured gently.

This time he didn't click his fingers; he clapped.

Erica and Jess both fell to the ground and Jess dug her fingernails into the dirt in an attempt to ground herself and stop her insides from swirling. She glanced up, searching for Erica, and found her friend lying on the ground close to Alfie.

Erica groaned, shifting onto her back, and then the Devil was standing over her, gazing lovingly down with those glowing red eyes. As her vision swam, Jess could have sworn that two large, leathery wings protruded from his back. His fingernails elongated into claws as he reached down to Erica, brushing against her cheek and drawing a bead of blood.

That was when Jess tried to scream.

Rick

Bristol, two months ago

'Not yet!' cried Percival as Rick slapped the time travel device onto his wrist. The destination dial was broken and wouldn't move, but that wasn't important right now. As Burns pushed past Alfie, threatening the fae with a gun and then throwing a wooden chair from the side of the room into him, Rick pushed the button on the device and then dug his hand into his pocket, gripping the chiming watch.

The flash of light was blinding.

But it was also strange. There was a hint of blue in the light, and instead of being filled with the bright light of time travel, as his body was broken down into atoms, something inside Rick twisted.

He yelled in pain, grabbing his stomach and then his arms, hugging himself tightly.

The light dimmed a little and, as the watch in his hand chimed for the final time, there was Erica, lying on her back. Rick went to reach out for her, but something stopped him.

She was lying on her back and someone was standing over her.

Alfie?

No. No, there was Alfie. Lying a few steps away from her, his eyes closed, out cold. Or dead.

So who was standing over her?

Rick focused on Erica's features. Her large eyes were wide with fear, her mouth opening and closing as she fought to move away. He could hear her heart pounding, taste how dry her mouth was.

Suddenly his twisting body didn't hurt as much. Anger flared where the pain had been.

He refocused on the male figure standing over her, causing her all of that fear. He wasn't human, although at first glance he appeared it. His skin was too tight, too translucent, and from his back protruded two black, leathery wings.

'Rick?' Erica's wide eyes focused on him, her lips quivering, tears falling from her eyes, straight down her temples to the grass beneath her.

The creature hovering over her snarled. Its wings opened and Erica was lost from view.

'Ricci.'

The creature heard Rick's whisper and looked over its shoulder at him. Rick swallowed hard in the face of the red glowing eyes and pointed, dripping teeth. The creature gave him a curious look and then laughed, turning back to Erica and lifting a claw ready to slash at her.

Rick didn't know what this creature was or what was going on. All he knew was what he could see. That Erica was in trouble, that this thing might be about to kill her, and that Alfie couldn't help.

Rick squared his shoulders and, with a defiant roar that came from somewhere deep within, he lunged at the back of the creature.

Screaming, the thing turned and hit Rick with an arm, flinging him back. Just before Rick lost consciousness, he saw Erica wriggle free as white glowing figures began to emerge from the tree line behind her.

She was safe.

Rick exhaled and let the darkness overwhelm him.

Erica

Gripping Alfie's shoulders, Erica shook him, searching around them for the figure of Rick. Unsure if it had really been him. He had been there and yet not there, a blue, translucent form of Rick, appearing and disappearing from this reality as if the channel wasn't quite tuned in right. Still, it had been his attack that had made the Devil lose his grip on her, just before the Devil could claw at her. At her soul.

Erica didn't have time to listen to her heart pound or consider her swirling stomach. She needed to get everyone out of there, immediately. She gripped Alfie's shirt and willed him awake.

Rick had vanished, flung away by the Devil. Erica kept an eye out, wondering if he would reappear, but was soon distracted by something that had caught the Devil's eye. He had returned to a human form and stood close by, watching something over Erica's shoulder.

She turned to look and ended up falling backwards, scuttling across Alfie to lay protectively over him.

Out of the woods walked around fifty white, glowing figures. As they reached the treeline, Erica recognised the nearest figure and her breath caught in her throat, entangling with a sob that wrenched itself free.

Minerva winked at her granddaughter and then straightened her back to face the Devil.

'What is this?' he crooned.

The fae lined the edge of the woods, their glowing magic fading as they stopped to watch him. Beside Minerva stood Eolande, towering over her in an elegant long dress.

Erica gave Alfie another shake as she scanned the rows of fae.

'Did you do this?' she whispered to him.

Alfie opened his eyes and took a deep, sudden breath, reaching around to grab her.

'Erica,' he croaked.

'I'm here. I'm here. I'm okay. Alfie, look.'

Alfie searched her face with unfocused eyes.

'They came?'

Erica nodded.

The fae smiled and lay his head back, looking up to the sky.

'This isn't over,' she whispered. 'You need to

move. Come on.'

Alfie groaned and tried to sit up, clutching at his head. He looked up into the face of the Devil and flinched.

'I should have killed you,' came the growl behind Erica.

She readied herself for another attack and managed to hold in a yelp as that same blue fire crackled at her fingertips.

Alfie appeared just as shocked, looking from her fingers to her face with wide eyes. Then, Alfie laughed.

The Devil's expression fell, his eyes glowing with rage.

Alfie took Erica's blue fire hand, entwining their fingers, and just as the Devil reached out to swipe at them, he held up his free hand and a flash of white light pushed the Devil back.

There came a shriek from Jess as the Devil tumbled back towards her and Mullarky. The Devil regained his balance and growled, making the ground beneath them tremble and shake.

'I was summoned!' he bellowed. 'I was promised! And I will not leave here without a soul. But you!' He turned on Erica. 'You have made me angry, witch. Perhaps there is more than a soul here that I should take. I will take the brownie's mistress, and your friend, your lover, your grandmother.'

Erica's breath caught in her throat, her chest tightening.

'The Devil dragging me down to hell? Ha! I'd like to see him try,' came Minerva's voice.

As one, the rows of fae shifted, lifting their hands, their ethereal glow returning to light up the woods around them.

'Mullarky! Call off your new friends, or I will take your mistress's soul.' The Devil held up his fingers, ready to click them.

'Witches!' cried the unsteady voice of the brownie. He wasn't calling them off, rather it was a cry for help. *Do something*!

The Devil grinned and clicked his fingers, but there was no sound. He looked at his held up hand, dumbfounded, and tried again.

Behind him, Jess was slowly sliding backwards, pulling Mullarky with her as the brownie held his hands over his eyes.

'We apologise that you have been summoned for no reason,' Minerva declared, stepping forward with Eolande. 'But, as you can see, there is nothing for you here.' She opened her arms out, forcing the Devil to take a good look at the fae watching him.

'I never go home empty-handed,' he growled, glancing down to Erica and Alfie. 'I will take some-one or I will stay in your realm and bring the fires of hell with me.'

Erica almost laughed. Minerva smiled.

'There is always a first,' she said in a low voice.

The row of fae took a step forward and Erica witnessed the Devil hesitate. He lifted a hand to reach out behind him, towards Mullarky, and the brownie looked to the cottage. Gripping Jess, he locked eyes with Erica and whispered, 'Please.'

Erica, heart thumping, found her feet and stood over Alfie, still clutching his head. The blue fire trickled around her fingers still, and she had no idea what it was or what it was capable of. All she knew was that she needed to keep the Devil's attention away from that cottage.

He watched her rise, lowering his arm a little, waiting to see what she would do next. Erica was just as curious.

'Witches called me their god once,' he told her gently, the red in his eyes dimming a little.

'That's what the witch hunters called you,' Minerva spat, although Eolande held her back, stopping her from rushing to draw level with Erica. 'We have nothing to do with you, demon.'

The Devil looked up at Minerva in surprise.

'Demon?' he bellowed. Erica flinched, fighting the urge to cower back down close to Alfie. Feeling her thoughts, Alfie struggled to stand, holding on to her. 'I am an angel,' the Devil proclaimed.

'A fallen, twisted creature,' Minerva spat.

Erica risked glancing back to her grandmother with wide eyes. What on earth was she doing? You couldn't goad the Devil. No good could come of that, surely. Did she have a plan?

The Devil's eyes burned.

'I will drag you to hell with me, Minerva Warner,'

he hissed, stepping towards her, and in doing so, stepping closer to Erica and Alfie. They both stood their ground, Alfie a little shaky, neither willing to move out of his path and give him access to Minerva.

In response, the rows of fae glowed brighter and began to step closer to Minerva, creating a shield, encircling her, Eolande, Erica, Alfie and the Devil.

'I am older than your magic, older than your fae.' The Devil gestured to the fae that now surrounded him and some of them murmured, glancing at one another. 'What makes you think you can push me away?'

'Try clicking your fingers again,' suggested Minerva with a wry smile.

The Devil's expression darkened, as did his eyes.

'For a human so old,' he said quietly, 'you are reckless.'

Minerva's smile drifted.

'I am reckless because I am so old.'

For just a moment, it was as if they were two friends and the others didn't exist.

The Devil gave a short sigh through his nose and regarded Erica and Alfie, then back to Jess and Mullarky.

'Only the young and very old are reckless,' he murmured, as if to himself. 'You understand my predicament.' He turned back to Minerva.

How had this happened? The tone of the conversation had changed and Erica couldn't fathom whether the Devil had done that or Minerva.

'I do.' Minerva lifted her chin. 'You can't be seen to return empty-handed. It will appear weak. And the King of Hell, Prince of Darkness, cannot have that.'

The Devil glanced back to Erica, catching her eye.

We could work wonders together.

He didn't say it out loud, his voice was in her head. She shook it, trying to dislodge the words.

I can help.

Erica blinked and reached out to grip Alfie's hand. The fae looked at her curiously.

Give you the riches you need to pay your rent. Buy a house. Ensure your family is well cared for. I can send you clients. Help you build a thriving business. The Devil smiled. *All above board, you understand.*

'An agreement,' the Devil said out loud. 'And I will be on my way.' He glanced around at the fae. 'And your little army of magical fairies can step down.'

The fae, as one, bristled. Alfie stepped out in front of Erica, to position himself between her and the Devil.

The Devil watched, bemused.

'We will not trade our souls,' came Erica's voice. She hadn't expected it, but there the words were, spoken, out in the world.

Alfie's shoulders hunched up, ready for whatever

the Devil might send at him. Erica stepped into him, trailing her fingers down his back. *It's okay. Everything will be okay.*

'I wouldn't dream of asking such witches to *sell* their souls to me,' said the Devil thoughtfully. 'I would ask for something else.'

Erica frowned and glanced back to her grandmother.

'What else is there?'

The Devil gave her a soft smile and something inside her flipped and twisted and, to her horror, it was pleasurable. Erica stepped back and Alfie went with her.

We could do wonderful work together.

Erica shook her head.

'Stop it.'

'Stop what? What's he doing?' Alfie asked quietly.

'Get out of her head, fallen angel,' said Minerva in a voice loud enough to be heard by everyone present. 'You think that's how you get around me? You cannot have my granddaughter.'

'But it sounds so poetic,' said the Devil, his eyes still on Erica. 'So...delicious.'

I would give you the world.

Erica met the Devil's eyes.

'What would I have to give you?' she asked.

Alfie looked back to her with fear etched in every feature.

'What are you doing?' he hissed.

'Your loyalty,' said the Devil. 'Your obedience. That's all.'

'Oh, not a lot then,' snapped Minerva.

'And then you'd go away? Leave here. And everyone would have their soul intact?' Erica checked.

The Devil took another step towards her and nodded.

'As you wish.'

'No!' shouted Alfie.

'Erica!' came her grandmother's stern warning.

But how else would they be rid of him?

'I'm getting bored, witches,' said the Devil, holding up his hand. 'Make your decision.' He smiled gently at Erica. 'Make your move.'

39

Jess

What was the point in a small army of fae if all they did was glow?

'There has to be a way to get rid of him,' Jess whispered to Mullarky, who was watching the action in front of them with bated breath, his hands curled against his chest.

'I...I dinnae ken,' he breathed, shaking his head. 'Satan must have what he came for. And he dinnae come for the lad.' Mullarky glanced at Jess. 'He came for a witch.'

Jess sighed, sitting back.

'We shouldn't have come here. Alfie was right. We should have just let him have Connor. I promise, from now on, I'm listening to Alfie.'

'Shh!' Mullarky held up a hand to her in a panic. 'Dinnae make promises, lass. Nae within his earshot.'

Jess looked to the Devil, his back to them. Then

she relaxed a little.

'I don't think he wants me, as such,' she whispered. 'He wants Erica. She's stronger than me. And younger than Minerva. So I guess she can do more damage than either of us.'

'Makes sense,' said Mullarky.

'Still, why bring an army of fae if they just stand there?' Jess tutted and found her feet. 'Maybe you should go check on your mistress?' she offered. The windows of the cottage were still dark. 'I would have thought this would have woken her up.'

Mullarky shrugged.

'Her hearing is bad these days.'

'Still, maybe you should go to her.'

Mullarky shook his head.

'It willnae do nae good. She disnae ken I exist.'

Jess stared at the brownie and then blinked twice.

'What?'

Mullarky gave her a sheepish look.

'I came with the house, lass.'

'Fine. Whatever.' Jess pinched the gap between her eyes, trying to think. 'What do we do? You know him. He knows you. You've met before?'

The brownie settled back.

'Aye. When he came for James's soul.'

'But he said he doesn't come for any soul. He's here because of Erica.'

'And ye.'

'Debateable.'

Mullarky gave this some thought.

'He came then because of my mistress. She was a witch. She was watching from the cottage. I stood out here and when James had made his deal and left, Satan lingered. So we spoke and...'

'And?'

'He made a promise not tae come for my mistress.'

Jess turned on Mullarky.

'How did you get him to do that?'

Mullarky blew out air.

'We came tae an agreement.'

Jess stared at him until the brownie began to squirm.

'Och, fine! I agreed tae keep the crossroads intact, tae give him passage, tae stay here in this cottage.'

'You promised to obey and stay loyal,' Jess whispered.

Mullarky nodded.

'Aye, I did.'

'Does he get your soul at the end of it all, then?'

The brownie bit down on a laugh.

'He disnae want my soul, lassie. I'm a tool. A pawn. And an idiot.'

Jess shook her head.

'You're no idiot. But you could have destroyed the crossroads after he'd gone. What would he do?'

Mullarky's eyes widened in shock and he shook his head.

'He cuid've... He wuid've...' He turned to Jess. 'Cuid I?'

Jess smiled.

'I don't know. You hear a lot of stories about tricking the Devil.'

Mullarky cocked his head to the side.

'Gotta be clever to pull that off. Those are just folk tales, told to make humans feel better about themselves.'

Jess shrugged.

'Fair enough. So Erica should take the agreement?'

'Nae! Absolutely not.' The brownie found his feet and began approaching the Devil.

'Mullarky! What are you doing? Where are you going?'

'I will make an agreement with ye, Satan!'

The Devil's shoulders heaved in a sigh and he turned to look at the brownie approaching him.

'You already have, Mullarky. What else could I possibly want from you? You can't promise me Erica Murray's power.' He did a double take. 'Can you?'

The fae surrounding them glowed brighter and then, in a burst of energy that sent Jess, Erica and Alfie back to the ground, the light was aimed at the Devil. Above the sound of the magic, and of the Devil's muffled yells, came Minerva's voice, chanting Latin.

It was Latin that Jess recognised.

'What—'

Jess pulled the brownie back to her and had to almost shout over the din. 'She's trying to banish him back to hell. Like we did with the demon. She said that probably wouldn't work.' But she guessed if it was a choice between a spell that might not work and Erica making an agreement with the Devil, it was worth trying the spell first.

That was when she realised that the Devil's yells had turned to laughter.

Heart in her throat, Jess jumped to her feet to do something, although she had no idea what. It was too late, anyway.

The Devil raised an arm and every single fae surrounding him flew backwards, including Alfie and Eolande. The witches were left exposed. After a moment of processing what had happened, Erica gave a shriek and ran to her grandmother just as the Devil pointed a clawed finger at Minerva.

She toppled forward and landed on the hard ground, the blanket of crisp leaves offering little protection.

Erica screamed.

Jess swallowed hard, watching Minerva's prone body for signs of life.

'You have made your move, and this is the last chance to make your decision,' said the Devil. 'Erica Murray, do we have an agreement?'

Erica, tears running down her cheeks, looked up at the Devil and shouted, 'No!'

Then, much to Jess's horror and amusement, Erica raised her middle finger at the Devil. Jess smacked a hand over her mouth.

The Devil growled.

'Another time, perhaps,' he said, with a hint of charm. He turned back to look at Jess, appraised her and winked at her. Jess's stomach twisted with nausea.

'I release you,' he said to Mullarky, and then he snapped his fingers.

The sound of the snap sent Jess to her knees.

When she looked back up, a silence had descended and the Devil was gone.

Jess found her feet immediately and ran full speed to Erica and Minerva, skidding down onto her knees beside her friend.

'Is she... I mean, is she...?'

'She's alive.' Erica sniffed, stroking Minerva's thin, grey hair. 'We need to call an ambulance.'

Jess nodded, pulling out her phone.

'He's gone?' she said, breathless, looking around as she lifted the phone to her ear.

'And we don't know what he took with him,' said Erica quietly.

'You don't need an ambulance,' said Eolande as Jess hung up from the call.

'She's unconscious. Who knows what injuries she had after a fall like that,' hissed Erica. 'She's going to a hospital. Right now.'

Eolande bent over Minerva and whispered

hushed, soothing words, running her long fingers over Minerva's head.

'I can mend her.' She looked up at Erica. 'If I take her home now.'

Jess watched, holding her breath, gripping her phone. Erica slowly stood and faced Eolande as best she could when the fae was so much taller than her.

'If you take her and anything happens to her, I will bring the fires of hell to your world and burn the place down. Do you understand me?'

Eolande glanced down to Erica's hands and nodded.

'I do.'

'Can you heal her?'

Eolande looked Erica in the eye and gave another nod.

'I can.'

There was a long pause as the two stared at one another, searching each other's eyes. Long enough that Jess leant forward and asked, 'Should I cancel the ambulance, or...?'

'Cancel it,' said Erica, breaking the spell and stepping away from her grandmother to give Eolande access. 'I'll come through and follow you soon.'

Eolande acknowledged her and lifted Minerva, with the help of another fae. She led the small army away, back into the woods. As they vanished from sight, Erica trembled and stumbled. Jess went to save her but Alfie got there first.

Looking around, Jess realised it was just the three of them left, as Mullarky went to check on his mistress. She turned back to Erica and took a deep breath.

'Okay. What the hell just happened? No pun intended. The Devil just left – why? What did he take? How will we know what he took? Are we all safe? Is my family safe? Why didn't the fae *do* anything, Alfie? How did Minerva know to come here? What the hell!'

The silence that filled Jess's sudden absence of words was a little heavier than before. She stepped back, hugging herself, suddenly wishing for a warm bed with Marshall's heavy arm across her, Ruby asleep in the next room and Bubbles protectively snoring on the landing between them.

'I have no idea,' said Erica, shivering as a cold wind blew through. Alfie put his arms around her.

'She's safe! She's fine!' came Mullarky's voice as the brownie left the cottage and rushed back to them. 'Soul intact. Fast asleep.' His smile fell as he looked up at the witches. 'Yer grandmother?'

'Alive. Just. Maybe. I don't know,' whispered Erica. 'The fae took her to heal her.'

'She'll be fine. Don't you worry,' said Alfie, kissing her hair.

'What was she even doing here?'

'I swear, I didn't know she would come,' Alfie told them. 'I explained the situation to Eolande.

She said she would bring reinforcements, to keep you both safe. There isn't much the fae can do against a fallen archangel who has made himself a god, especially one as old as the Devil. Evil has existed in the world longer than most people can fathom, and so he has existed, in one form or another. But I thought my kind's presence would be better than nothing, a distraction if nothing else. So you could run away. I didn't know Eolande would tell Minerva, if that's what happened. I didn't know Minerva would come.'

Erica shrugged.

'It's done now. It doesn't matter,' she mumbled.

'We should check on Connor,' Jess murmured after a pause. 'Find out if his girlfriend had the baby.' She shuddered, hoping the Devil hadn't been able to reach them, wherever they were.

'And what about Rick?' came Erica's voice. She looked up at Alfie. 'Rick was here, wasn't he? I didn't dream that.'

Alfie sighed and brushed hair from Erica's face.

'No,' he said. 'You didn't dream it.'

40
Rick

Hurtling through time, Rick landed with a thump and a throbbing in his chest from where he had been smacked away. Groaning, he tried to push himself up. Beneath him were floorboards. He looked around to find himself in a house, in a bedroom. Downstairs, he could hear voices; a woman and a child. Rick found his feet quickly, standing straight and trying to stay quiet. How had he gotten inside the house and upstairs? How would he explain this if he was found?

'I need a wee!' came a shout from a little girl.

Rick panicked and looked around the small bedroom. It was her bedroom, he realised, noting the clothes and big stuffed dog on the bed. Heart pounding, he went to leave but stopped when he heard footsteps on the stairs.

'Soon, we'll have a toilet downstairs and we won't have to go upstairs every time,' came the woman's voice.

'When?'

'I'm not sure, sweetheart. Definitely this time next year, though. I hope.'

Rick rushed behind the open door and tried to will himself small and thin.

The footsteps reached the landing and there came the creak of the bathroom door.

'Do you want me to help?' the woman asked.

'No, thank you.'

Rick clenched his eyes shut, hoping the woman wouldn't come into the bedroom.

'Gin?' a man's voice called through the house.

'Yeah?' the woman shouted back. 'Hang on, sweetheart,' she said through the bathroom door. 'I'll be right back.'

'Okay!'

The woman made her way down the stairs and Rick risked peeking around the door. As he did, the bathroom door opened and a little girl stepped out. She had her mother's eyes.

They stared at one another and then a smile touched Rick's lips.

'Ruby?'

Ruby grinned and waved, and then pointed to something on the landing. Praying that it was Jess or Erica in one of the other bedrooms, Rick came out of hiding and followed the girl's pointing finger.

On the other side of the landing, a shadow was forming.

'Bye!'

Rick went to turn back to Ruby and then heard the footsteps on the stairs again. He ducked back behind the door and watched Ruby's grandmother help her down the stairs.

'Ignore the shadow, sweetheart,' Ginny murmured as she went.

Once they were gone, he stepped out and found the shadow had grown into a figure. Rick studied it and then helplessly watched as the figure turned to look at him, the shadows drifting away and turning to colour.

He watched as the shadow figure became Erica.

They studied one another, Rick acutely aware of her breathing rather than his own. He swallowed hard, went to find some words and realised there were none.

Erica smiled at him, a sob wrenching through her as she frowned in curiosity, as if not believing her eyes.

'Rick?'

A grin broke through Rick's defences at the sound of her voice.

'How...?' he murmured, his eyes welling up as tears fell down her cheeks.

Erica covered her mouth with both hands and shook her head.

'I don't know. I don't know,' came her muffled voice.

'One minute you're on the ground and this thing

is attacking you, and Alfie is out, maybe dead, and the next I'm here,' said Rick, holding his arms out to gesture to the landing, the words coming in a rush.

'You're dead,' said Erica at the same time.

They stared at one another.

'What?' she asked. 'What was that?'

'I'm dead?' Rick murmured, patting himself down. He didn't feel dead, but then what did dead feel like if it wasn't standing on a random landing in a friend's house looking at the woman he loved? 'Are you dead too?' he asked carefully.

Erica gave a delightful little laugh.

'No,' she said. 'You don't remember? There was an incident. At work. Some guy with a gun. You were trying to talk him down and he...' Erica's bottom lip quivered and she shook the rest of the sentence away. 'And now you're here. On my landing.'

Rick stopped.

'Your landing? No, this is Jess's parents' landing. This is their house.'

Erica frowned.

'No, Rick. This is our house. Don't you remember? We bought it after we got married. We've spent the last year doing it up. We didn't get far, it's hard to renovate when there's a baby—'

'Baby?' Rick's voice caught.

Erica nodded.

'You don't remember?'

Rick stopped, an icy chill running over him. He lifted his arm and looked down at the device on his wrist.

'You're from a different timeline,' he breathed.

'What?'

'A different timeline.' He looked back up to her. 'In your timeline, your Rick was killed. In my timeline, well, here I am.' He opened his arms, this time to gesture at himself. 'Alive, well, and without you.'

Erica blinked.

'I'm dead in your timeline?' she asked gently, looking for the device on his wrist.

'No. You're happy. Just...not with me,' he said carefully, not wanting to ruin anything.

'Lying on the ground with something over me and someone dead close by?' she murmured.

Rick clenched his eyes shut.

'Not dead,' he said, knowing it to be true deep in his gut. 'Just...out cold.'

Erica gave a small, bitter laugh.

'Your Erica listened to her grandmother, didn't she.'

Rick nodded.

'You didn't?'

Erica shook her head.

'The fae are dangerous,' she said, hugging herself. 'I didn't want anything to do with them, other than Gran's lover, of course. Couldn't really help that. And then I met you, and...' She smiled at him. 'God, Rick, I miss you so much. What if this is all a dream?'

Tears stung at the back of Rick's eyes.

'I miss you too,' he murmured. 'I had you, and our son – do we have a son?'

Erica nodded.

'He's one next month.'

Rick's heart ached.

'I had you once, and then I lost you. Because I'm stupid.'

Erica shook her head fiercely.

'You're not stupid. You're wonderful and kind and loving and...maybe a little too trusting.' She grinned at him. 'You're amazing.' Her smile fell. 'This is a dream, isn't it. I've dreamt about you so often, it's never felt like this. Never. I sometimes wait here to chat to the little girl and she tells me about her family that sounds like Jess's—'

'Because it is Jess's. That's Ruby, her daughter.'

Erica's eyes lit up.

'Of course. She isn't called Ruby here. She's called Scarlet.'

There was a pause as they processed this information.

'Our son is called Freddie,' she added gently, glancing back to him. 'You're really you? Just from another timeline? Where it all went wrong and you lost me?'

Rick was hardly listening.

'Freddie,' he murmured to himself, smiling.

When he noticed the silence and looked up, Erica was holding out a hand to him.

'Come with me,' she whispered. 'Please.'

Rick's heart pounded.

This was everything he'd been hoping for. A new timeline, a new start. Only this was better, because it was with Erica and their boy.

He hesitated only for as long as it took to have that thought, and then he strode across the landing, took Erica's hand and stepped into her timeline and her world.

*

Ruby peered up the top few steps and watched as the shadow figures dissipated.

'Ruby? Where are you? I only turned my back for two seconds. Ruby!'

Giggling to herself, Ruby carefully went down the stairs and threw herself into her grandmother's arms.

'What were you doing?' Ginny asked.

'Just saying goodbye to Erica,' she murmured, pulling away and rushing to the kitchen where her grandfather was making cups of tea with Marshall.

'Erica?' Ginny glanced up at the stairs, following her into the kitchen.

'Erica's back?' Marshall asked as Ruby threw her arms around him. He picked her up, giving her a gentle hug. It was one of her favourite things about

Marshall; her father couldn't pick her up anymore.

'No. Shadow Erica. Upstairs,' said Ruby, pointing.

The adults gave each other wide-eyed looks, which Ruby ignored. It was their own fault for never listening to her.

Erica and Jess

'How do you know I didn't dream Rick?' Erica asked, trying to keep her voice level. 'How do you know everything? Do you know how infuriating that is? Trying to make decisions without you already knowing the outcome. Is that too much to ask? Why can't you at least make your gift useful? You could have told us about all of this. We could have stopped my grandmother coming. We could have stopped Connor. We could have—' Erica stopped herself as her chest tightened and a sob threatened to explode. She couldn't breathe. Sitting on the ground, near the empty crossroads, she put her head down and tried to get air back into her lungs.

Alfie hovered and then sat beside her, tentatively placing an arm around her, waiting for her to flinch away from him. She didn't. This wasn't his fault.

Maybe it wasn't anyone's fault. She wasn't sure. Exhaustion had hit her like a brick wall and right then she just needed her grandmother to be okay so she could go to sleep.

'I'm sorry,' said Alfie. 'I'm sorry. I should have told you more, but I didn't think you wanted to know the outcomes. And what was the point? Everything I tried to do, every way I looked at it, this was the outcome. Except for Minerva. I didn't see that. I don't know why.' Alfie frowned to himself. 'Sometimes I don't see everything. And what I see one moment will change the next because of one small decision made by someone distant.'

'Like Connor,' Erica murmured.

'Like Connor. Deciding that despite us all talking to him, he would still carry through with this whole thing.' Alfie sighed hard. 'Rick came to me a couple of months ago and asked for help with a way out.'

Erica looked up at him, her vision blurry with tears.

'A way out?'

'He'd stolen a time travel device from his bosses, who were blackmailing him, as far as I understand it, and he asked me for help in altering it.'

'Why you?'

'Because Minerva told him I would help.'

Erica laughed, wiping her cheeks dry.

'That makes sense. What did you do?'

'We altered the device so he could change timeline, but we were interrupted, the device was damaged and then he vanished. I didn't know what happened. And then I could only see snippets, nothing clear. Until he appeared with you.'

'You were out cold, Alfie. How did you see that?' Jess asked, moving to stand over them, hugging herself.

'I saw it,' Alfie assured them. 'He didn't look of this world. My best guess is that he was already between timelines.'

'Where is he now?' Erica asked quietly, afraid of the answer.

Alfie looked at her and waited until she met his eyes.

'With you,' he told her. 'In another timeline. He's happy.' Alfie reached out and took her hand. 'And Jess, you should tell your parents they won't have much trouble with those shadow figures from now on.'

'What? Why?'

Alfie smiled and stroked Erica's hand.

'They were an alternate timeline?' she asked quietly.

Alfie nodded and leaned forward to kiss her damp cheek.

'They were you,' he whispered.

Erica leaned into his warmth and Alfie wrapped himself about her, holding her close.

'It's over,' she breathed.

Alfie pressed his lips to her hair.

'If you want it to be.'

Erica closed her eyes and breathed the fae in.

'I do,' she murmured. 'Is Gran going to be all right?' she asked after a moment's thought.

Alfie kissed her hair again.

'Of course,' came his voice.

Erica closed her eyes and pushed her nose against his chest.

'Will the Devil come back?' she whispered.

Alfie didn't reply, but Erica was too busy drifting into sleep to be able to do anything about it.

She startled awake when her phone began ringing and vibrating in her pocket. Pulling away from Alfie, she forced her eyes to focus in the dim light from the nearby streetlight and found her phone. Shivering in the cold, autumn night, she found her way to her feet as she answered the unknown number.

'Hello?' She pulled her coat tight about her and stepped away from Alfie as he stood and made his way to Jess.

'Ms Murray? It's Adam Drescott, the manager of The Bank Hotel, where you're staying.'

'Oh, yes. Hi. Is everything okay?' Erica's stomach did a nauseating somersault.

'Yes, no, everything's fine. It's just...I've been having a good think and a chat with my parents, and then some more thinking, and I was wondering if we could have a chat about your services?'

'My...services?'

'The paranormal tour stuff?'

'Oh! Services. Yes. Of course. Sorry, it's been a bit of an evening.'

'Yeah, I wondered if you were out enjoying Halloween and the fair. But I know you're checking out tomorrow and wondered if you'd like that meeting before you go. I thought now might be good as the fair is closing. I probably should have messaged you. Sorry. I didn't think. I got a bit excited, if I'm honest. I've been down in the cellar and, well, you know.'

Erica smiled to herself.

'Of course. That's great that you're excited. And actually, tomorrow would be perfect. My business partner can come along before we all head home. Would you be able to do late morning?'

'Brilliant! Eleven?'

'Can you do ten?' asked Erica, rubbing away the headache growing in her temple.

'Perfect. I'll meet you at the bar.'

They said their goodbyes and Erica hung up, staring down at her phone's screen. Out of the corner of her eye, something glinted despite the lack of light. Frowning, Erica lowered her phone and approached the thing on the ground. Bending, she picked up the gold pocket watch, rubbing her thumb over it to wipe away the dirt, watching the second hand give a quiver as she did so.

When she looked up, there was just the darkness

and the woods, and Jess, Alfie and Mullarky stood in a huddle chatting. As if nothing had happened. As if there had been no fae, no Connor, no Devil.

No Rick.

Erica closed her hand around the pocket watch and considered Alfie's words.

Rick was happy. In a new timeline, with her and, presumably, the child she would never have. She could leave the guilt behind, she could leave the choices behind. Of course, there was always the chance she would bump into her time's Rick, but somehow she doubted that would make much difference now. They'd already met and set about their different life paths.

From a few steps away, Erica studied Alfie in the darkness. It was finally time for her to put Rick aside and focus on herself and what she wanted.

Alfie turned to her and smiled, as if reading her thoughts. So she gave him what they both wanted and screamed in her mind just how much she loved him.

Alfie grinned and held out a hand to her. She approached the huddle and showed him what she'd found.

'I think this is yours,' she murmured.

Gently, Alfie took it from her and slid it into his pocket, and Erica wrapped her arms around his waist. Even though he wore no coat on that cold night, he was still warm. He would always be her warmth and comfort.

'Who was that? Is everything okay?' Jess asked. Erica smiled.

'We have a new client meeting tomorrow at ten.'

Jess blinked and then laughed.

'Okay. Great! So, is that it? Are we done?'

'No,' said Alfie. 'Not entirely. The Devil took something when he left, but I can't tell what.'

'Okay. But right now, are we done? When will we know about Minerva?' Jess asked Erica.

Erica, still wrapped up with Alfie, shrugged awkwardly.

'Eolande will let us know, I suppose.' She glanced up at Alfie, who nodded. 'I'll let you know as soon as I hear,' Erica told her. 'Go home, be with Marshall and Ruby.'

Jess smiled and glanced down at Mullarky.

'Will you be okay?'

'Aye, witches. You'se did me proud. I cannae thank you'se enough.' He gave a strange little bow and then a polite nod to Alfie, who nodded back. Then the brownie turned and disappeared into the shadows, back towards the cottage.

'It still doesn't feel like it's over,' Jess murmured as they watched him go.

'Well, I for one have had more than enough. Now, take me into your world and to my grandmother,' Erica told Alfie. 'Then maybe we'll make it back to the hotel in time to finish our weekend, but I doubt it. See you tomorrow at ten, at the hotel bar.'

Erica peeled away from Alfie to give Jess a quick hug, and then they went their separate ways. Alfie led Erica towards the woods when she stopped and looked back.

'We should take Jess home.'

'No need,' said Alfie, and they watched as the figure of a brownie broke away from the shadows of the cottage and caught up with Jess. The two could be heard chatting as they found the path and walked back towards the high street and quietness of the closing fair.

'Good,' Erica murmured. When she turned, she found Alfie with his palm to the ground. 'What are you doing?'

The ground below them trembled and then there came the sound of stone cracking.

'Breaking the crossroads,' said Alfie. 'I don't know if it'll work, but I think this town has seen enough of the Devil. Come on, let's go check on Minerva, see if she's awake yet.'

Erica took Alfie's hand and followed him into the dark quiet of the woods to find the doorway that led to his world and the path that led to his village, and did her best not to think about bed or sleeping.

*

Everything always looked different in the daylight. Jess had recounted the story of the Devil to Marshall and her parents while Ruby lay asleep upstairs. She wasn't sure if any of them had slept that night. Connor kept popping into Jess's head and she wished she had a phone number for him. Part of the night had been spent searching for him online, for a glimpse of a baby update on social media. There had been nothing.

'I'm worried about Connor,' she told Erica as they walked out of the hotel, having shaken hands with Adam and agreed a contract.

Erica stretched and murmured an agreement.

'Only way to find out if everything's okay is to go to his flat,' she pointed out.

'Yeah, except, I don't know about you but I can't tell if someone's had their soul stamped "property of the Devil". Can you?' Jess asked, glancing sideways at her friend.

Erica smiled.

'Nope. But I know a couple of people who can and one them is just over there.' She gestured up the street to Alfie, hands deep in his pockets, staring into the window of a coffee shop. He looked up as Erica pointed him out, and smiled.

'How come he looks like he had a good night's sleep?' Jess mumbled.

'Fae magic,' said Erica. 'Trust me, he didn't. We didn't leave Eolande's until the early hours of the morning. Sort of fell into bed and just lay there. We ended up talking until dawn.' Erica looked at her friend. 'I'm knackered, Jess. Staying up until dawn is for young people, especially if that included an evening fighting off the Devil.'

Jess laughed.

'I think a lot of what we do is for young people,' she complained, stretching her neck.

'We're going to pay Connor a visit. Come with us and tell us if his soul still belongs to him?' Erica asked Alfie as they reached him. He fell into step with them, slipping his hand around Erica's.

'Of course,' he said, and let them lead the way.

'We should do something for him, whether the Devil has his soul or not,' said Jess as they left the high street. The fair workers were busy packing everything away and the air was filled with shouts and yells and the beeping of large machinery being moved. 'Because he still needs a job to provide for his family. And, you know, to make him feel better about himself. Selling your soul to the Devil in exchange for a job cannot be good for your mental health.'

'Well,' said Erica, stepping around someone. 'How about we offer him a job?'

Jess's heart skipped and she turned on her friend.

'Really? Because I was wondering the same thing. If we start doing tours at the hotel, that's quite a way for us to travel, but it's so local for him. Except...'

'Except?'

'I'd feel a bit guilty. I could do the tours and then visit my parents, couldn't I,' said Jess.

'Except you don't do the tours, Jess. I do. And I can teach Connor what to do, easily. You can keep checks on it all when you do visit.'

'But, you need the extra money for your rent,' Jess said carefully.

'Nope. I told you, I'm moving in with Alfie.'

Jess squealed, throwing her arms around Erica.

'I'm so happy for you both.' She grabbed Alfie and gave him a hug, breathing in his warm scent, a mixture of wood, earth and leaves, and for that moment, she struggled to let him go. 'Woah,' she murmured when she managed to convince her arms to disengage.

Alfie gave her a look, but Erica laughed.

'Finally, I get it.' Jess gave her friend a playful nudge.

They continued towards Connor's flat, Erica and Alfie holding hands, and Jess trying to calm her beating heart and steer her thoughts back towards Marshall, waiting for her back at her parents'.

42

Connor

Connor didn't remember the drive to the hospital that day. Only that as he'd been leaving the flat, closing the front door behind him, the women and man from the night before had approached. They'd talked. And then he'd gotten in his car and suddenly, somehow, he was walking through the maternity ward to his girlfriend's bed. She was sitting on the edge, dressed, ready to go home and cradling their newborn son, wrapped in a soft rainbow blanket.

'Hi,' he murmured.

She looked up with bleary eyes.

'Hi.'

He sat carefully beside her and they spent a minute watching their new son sleep.

'I have news,' whispered Connor.

'What news?'

'I have a job.'

Maggie looked up at him in a move that would

probably have been quicker if she'd gotten any sleep that night.

'A job?'

Connor nodded, unable to keep the grin from his face. With his thumb, he quickly brushed away the tears pricking his eyes. 'All being well, I'll start in a week or so.'

'What's the job?'

Connor struggled for a moment.

'At the hotel, at the top of the high street.'

She looked at him curiously.

'I didn't know they were hiring. Doing what?'

'They're not. Not really. They're hiring a company to do some work there, and the company is hiring me to do the work.'

'Connor. We haven't slept for twenty-four hours and last night I pushed a baby out of me. Now we've got to somehow take this little one home and look after him and I have no idea how. This is not the time for games. You still haven't told me where you were last night, even though you said you'd stay home. You promised, in fact. And I can't raise this baby with someone who plays games with me. I need you to talk to me and be honest. Please.' Her voice broke at the end, and Connor's heart did a sickening lurch with it.

'You won't believe me,' he told her as she soothed the baby, grumbling at the sound of her rising voice.

'I don't care,' she sang, soothingly. 'Tell me anyway.'

'Last night I went to the crossroads by the witch's cottage to summon the Devil and trade my soul for a job, or money, or both.'

Maggie slowly turned to stare at him. She searched his eyes and then frowned.

'Why on earth would you do something so stupid?' she said through tired, gritted teeth.

'You believe me?'

With a small shrug and a laugh, she went back to staring at her new baby.

'I believe that you believe that. How did you know I went into labour? You just said someone told you. Who?'

'The Devil.'

She pursed her lips.

'Fine. Don't tell me. What about this job, then?'

'Remember those two women who came to the flat?'

'Yeah?'

'They were there last night. Trying to stop me. Only they got there too late, I guess. I ran off when the Devil told me the baby was coming—'

'—Please stop talking about the Devil—'

'—Sorry. Anyway, I guess they sorted it out, somehow. They visited me just as I was leaving to come pick you up, and they offered me the job.'

'And the job is?'

'Running ghost tours at the hotel.' Connor snapped his mouth shut and waited.

His girlfriend laughed.

'Well, that isn't so bad.'

'No?'

'No. Actually, it sounds more interesting than waiting tables or cleaning or maintenance, which is what I thought you were going to say. Does it pay well?'

'Surprisingly.' Connor nodded. 'Enough. And maybe it'll lead to other things.'

Maggie smiled down at their baby.

'Maybe.' She leaned into Connor. 'We'll be okay, you know. I'll be back at work after my maternity leave, and things will be slow but I'll pick up my career again eventually. Work my way up.'

'I know, but now we'll be comfortable instead of living pay check to pay check. And maybe we'll be able to move to somewhere bigger with both of us working,' Connor murmured, stroking his son's soft, wrinkled head.

Looking up at him, Maggie reached, flinching with pain as she did so, to gently kiss his chin. Connor turned and caught her lips in his.

'You didn't sell your soul, did you?' she whispered.

'No.'

'Or anyone else's soul?'

'No.'

'So, we can just be a happy family now?'

Connor wrapped his arms around her and the baby.

'A happy, tired family.'

Maggie laughed gently and lifted their baby to her lips.

'That's all I really wanted.'

43

Jess

Marshall was strapping Ruby into her car seat as Jess checked the bedrooms for anything they might have left behind. Not that it mattered; she'd be back during the week for a meeting with Adam and Erica, to do an official survey of the hotel, likely with Connor in tow. There almost didn't seem much point in going home but Marshall had work to get back to and Ruby had school. Bubbles followed her from Ruby's bedroom to the one she shared with Marshall.

'Everything all right?'

'Yup, think we have everything.' She turned to her mother and picked up the bags. Ginny lifted one and then glanced at the corner on the landing. Jess followed her gaze.

'That's where it happened?' she asked.

'You try not to see these things. Hope that maybe if you don't acknowledge them, then it didn't happen, but then your granddaughter says things like "Shadow Erica" and you just can't unhear it.'

Jess smiled.

'I've told Erica. I'm not sure if she wanted to know, but I also think she needed to. To put her mind at rest. Not that Alfie would lie to her.'

'He's a strange one, isn't he,' Ginny murmured. 'I'm glad we'll have fewer shadow figures, though. It'll be nice to have the house to ourselves for once.'

'I did say he was strange,' said Jess, smiling and leading the way down the stairs. 'Dad says he'll miss the shadows.'

'Your dad doesn't know what he's talking about.'

Jess laughed.

'Funny, isn't it. How you found Dad, so interested in the paranormal when you didn't have the faintest idea you could be a witch. And then I found Marshall, who's the reason I now run a paranormal investigation agency with Erica. And how Esther met Erica's dad.'

'What's funny about it?'

'Oh come on, Mum. All these men who get excited about these things about us, that in some cases we're not even entirely aware of ourselves. It's like they were sent to support us with it all.'

Ginny tried to hide her warm smile, but Jess caught it.

'Erica didn't find that, then?'

'Well, I suppose. In a way. Except that Alfie is...'

There was a pause as Jess stopped herself. Ginny

placed the bag she was carrying down by the front door and turned on her daughter.

'What *is* Alfie', Jess?'

'He's a fae, Mum.'

'Which means what, exactly?'

'Scary, magical fairy folk that live in a world adjacent to ours and that sometimes sneak over here to seduce and lure people away. Usually young people. Like teenagers. Which is where Erica was this spring, chasing a teenager and a fae through the woods in Alfie's world. And there's a doorway to that world in the woods by the witch's cottage, so be careful walking there, all right?'

Ginny's eyes widened a little at the suggestion.

'Have you been to their world?'

'Nope.'

'Will she marry him, do you think?'

'She will.' Jess was certain of it. 'And I'm not going to a wedding there. Ruby is certainly never going into that world. No. Ruby will meet someone like Marshall or Dad. Someone excited and supportive and entirely human who loves her more than anything and will put up with the odd spirit. But hopefully no demons.'

Ginny watched her daughter affectionately.

'Are we not mentioning the Devil anymore?' she asked carefully.

Jess shook her head emphatically.

'Absolutely bloody not. Never again. Alfie broke the crossroads, so it shouldn't be a problem anymore. Maybe.'

Ginny nodded and they both stared down at the bags at their feet.

'Back to normal, then,' said Ginny.

'Yup.'

'Jess?'

'Hmm?'

'I know I said you could have a small wedding, that we wouldn't mind. Well, have the wedding you want, sweetheart. Whatever you want. With who-ever you want invited. No matter what, it'll be perfect. I know it will. As long as we're there to celebrate with you.'

Jess melted a little and stepped into her mother's arms.

'I wouldn't have it without you,' she whispered into her mother's ear. 'Thank you.'

Mother and daughter smiled at one another, until Bubbles barked at them both and then pushed past to run at Marshall, preparing her bed in the back of the car.

'Someone's eager to get home,' said Eddie, walking over to hug his daughter.

'Any more word on Minerva?' Ginny asked.

'Not yet. But we'll see you Saturday?'

'Wouldn't miss it,' said Eddie, pushing past to say goodbye to Marshall with a handshake and a pat on the back.

As Marshall drove home, Jess leaned back and

closed her eyes.

'Hey, your mum said that cottage by the woods might be up for sale soon,' came Marshall's voice.

Jess opened her eyes, a crease between her brow.

'How does she know that?'

'Said a little birdy told her.'

'A little brownie, more like,' Jess muttered.

'I thought it might be a good investment.'

Jess turned to look at her fiancé.

'You what?'

'You know, buy it, do it up. Nice little project, like your parents are doing. It's a proper pretty little cottage. We could rent it out.'

'Oh, to Connor and his family. Although I doubt he'd want to rent the cottage that looks out over where he summoned the Devil,' Jess corrected herself. 'So perhaps not. You want to be a landlord now?'

'I don't know. I've always wanted to get into property development.'

'And how on earth are we going to be able to afford to buy it?'

Marshall shrugged.

'Another mortgage, working some more hours. A smaller wedding...' he trailed off.

Jess laughed.

'Funny you should say that.' She recited what her mother had said about the wedding.

'Well, that's great. And we didn't even need an argument or a big discussion,' he said, taking a left turn. 'Just needed some guy to summon the actual Devil.'

Jess snorted.

'Thing is, after all that, I feel like we need a big celebration,' she murmured.

Marshall gave her a sideways look.

'Uh-oh.'

'Yeah. I keep thinking about who we would invite and the list keeps getting longer.'

'I don't think we should invite Connor.'

'Well, no, but there's Erica's family and Alfie and Eolande. Your family and friends. My parents. Mullarky, perhaps.'

'And how do we explain the fae and a brownie to my family and friends?'

Jess hesitated.

'Maybe we need two parties.'

Marshall sighed, but grinned nonetheless. He reached out and took Jess's hand.

'You know what? Whatever you want. As long as we become husband and wife, and it doesn't cost too much, let's do it. And let's look at the cottage, yeah?'

'No harm in looking,' said Jess, lifting his hand to her lips, her insides swirling pleasurably with the possibilities.

44

Erica

Erica's parents' house was alive with people. The two Labradors lay in a heap with Bubbles, panting after chasing each other around and asking for food from anyone who would listen. While the banner in the living room had been taken down, Minerva wandered around the party wearing a cardboard crown so that everyone would know it was her birthday they were there celebrating. She'd invited everyone she knew and most had been able to make it. Her coven from the residential home where she lived most of the time, and a handful of the staff who supported the residents there. Eolande and some of the other fae spoke graciously with the residents, and Minerva was quick to check on her neighbour after one fae attempted a seduction. Jess made a point of not letting the fae get too acquainted with her parents. At one point, everyone had wanted to hear the tale of the witches against the Devil. Minerva had embellished some of it, but no one could deny that it had taken its toll. For the first time, Minerva was starting to look closer to her age of ninety.

Esther had made a large cake to follow the buffet and there had been more food than anyone could eat. Minerva had done a toast, thanked everyone and then, a few hours later, her friends, neighbours and the majority of the fae had left, leaving only family in the house.

They sat around the living room as freezing November rain pounded against the windows. The Labradors were curled on the sofa with Erica's father as he tried not to snore along with them. Bubbles sat on Marshall's feet, only because Jess was snuggled up next to him, leaving no room on his lap. Ruby was on her second helping of cake, sitting on the other side of Marshall, kicking her legs happily.

Erica and Alfie sat squashed together on a love seat in the corner of the room, murmuring to one another every now and then. Erica's mother, doing her best to ignore her daughter and Alfie, bustled between the living room and kitchen with a glass of wine in one hand and the rest of the bottle in the other, topping up everyone's glasses. Ginny and Eddie took up the last sofa, sitting properly, although their smiles showed up how much they'd had to drink. Esther had offered them the spare room, so they'd relaxed and showed everyone who asked photos of their house renovations so far.

'Sit down, for the love of everything, you're exhausting me just watching you,' Minerva chastised.

Esther did as she was told and sat beside her husband, pushing Bramley, the youngest dog, over. He repositioned himself so that his chin rested on her lap and she stroked his ears absent-mindedly.

Minerva and Eolande exchanged a look, which wasn't a good sign. Erica spotted it first and looked at them expectantly. Minerva sighed and stood, with Eolande's help.

'I'd like to say something!'

A silence descended on the room and everyone looked to her.

'I know I've already said this, but I'll say it again,' she started. 'Thank you, Esther, for such a wonderful party. The cake especially was amazing.'

Ruby giggled to herself, putting another large forkful in her mouth.

'And now that it's just family here, there's something I need to tell you all.'

Erica's heart leapt into her mouth and she quickly exchanged a look with her mother. No, Esther didn't know what this was about either.

'Would you like us to leave? We can pop out for a bit,' Ginny offered, going to stand.

'Absolutely not, sit back down,' Minerva demanded, her voice not as frail as her body. 'We're all family here. We're all witches here.' She gave Ginny a wink and Jess's mother sat back, flushing a little.

'As I was saying, and I want no arguments' – she gave Esther and Erica pointed looks – 'I have made the decision to leave the residential home.'

'Mum?'

'And move in with Eolande. In her world.' Minerva turned to the fae sitting behind her and smiled, taking her hand.

'Mum...'

'If it wasn't for Eolande and her kind, in her world, I would be dead now.'

Erica's mouth went dry.

'We would have gotten you to a hospital, Gran. Jess had already called for an ambulance.'

'And what good would that have done, my love?' said Minerva kindly. 'I'm ninety. What could they have possibly done that the fae could not do better?'

Erica sat back and Alfie gave her a gentle hug.

'No, it's time for me to retire and live out the rest of my days in a beautiful world with the woman I love. I've been thinking about it for a while, waiting for the right time, and now here it is. The Devil almost killed me, but even he could not take me. And now my beloved granddaughter is also moving to the fae world.' Minerva gave Erica a warm smile. 'We can look after each other,' she added gently. 'And of course, I will come back regularly,' she added to Esther. 'I want to watch Ruby grow up, and I want to see Bramley and Bubbles grow up. I want to be at your wedding,' she said to Jess and Marshall. 'And yours.' She looked back to Erica and Alfie.

Erica's stomach twisted pleasurably and Alfie's thumb brushed lovingly over her arm.

'We humans age slower in the fae world,' said Minerva, before Esther could protest. 'We heal faster there. Their medicine is so far ahead of our own. This really is what's going to happen,' she told her daughter. 'And it's going to be okay.'

Esther, tears in her eyes, put down her glass of wine and descended upon her mother. They held each other silently, until Erica could take it no more. She untangled herself from Alfie and joined the women, tears burning at her eyes.

'I'm not going anywhere for good,' Minerva murmured to them both. 'When you need me, just think hard, and I'll be there.'

Erica pulled away.

'But...that must mean...'

Minerva grinned.

'Yes, that is the other part of the announcement. Eolande and I are getting married. And you're all invited, of course. It will take place at the cemetery, so everyone can attend.' Everyone meaning the spirit of Erica's grandfather. Erica nodded, brushing away tears.

'Perfect,' she murmured, giving her grandmother another hug. 'Congratulations.' She turned then and hugged Eolande without warning.

The fae's eyes widened abruptly and she sat with her arms out awkwardly before exchanging a look with Minerva and gently patting Erica's back with the tips of her fingers.

'Welcome to the family,' Erica whispered to her, and felt something deep inside Eolande relax. When she backed away, the fae wouldn't meet her eyes, blinking hurriedly instead.

Grinning to herself, Erica gave her mother a stern look and then picked up the bottle of wine Esther had brought in, topping up some glasses for a toast.

'Mum, are you sure? You can always move back in with us.'

'And die? No, love, I've still got a lot of living to do,' said Minerva. 'But thank you for the offer. You'll come to the wedding?'

Esther laughed, making Eolande jump.

'Of course! I wouldn't miss it.' She found her glass of wine and held it up. 'Congratulations, Mum. Ninety years old and you don't look a day over...eighty-five...'

'Got the Devil to thank for that,' Minerva mumbled, holding up her glass.

'And welcome to the family, Eolande,' Esther added, grinning at the fae.

Eolande smiled awkwardly, her cheeks blushing as everyone raised their glasses in toast. Minerva lowered herself to sit beside Eolande, and Eddie asked a question about fae weddings.

Erica took the opportunity to excuse herself and disappear into the kitchen. She leaned against the worktop for a moment before getting a glass of water.

'Alfie hasn't popped the question yet, has he?'

Erica jumped and turned to find Jess had followed her.

'No. He hasn't.'

'Good. Can't have three weddings back to back. You Warner and Murray women, stealing my thunder.' Jess stuck her tongue out and Erica laughed.

'Don't worry, I can't see me and Alfie getting married for a while yet. And even then, it'll only be so I can go between worlds easily.'

'You know that's not why Minerva and Eolande are getting married, don't you,' said Jess quietly.

'I have my suspicions that it's because they love each other so much that it's time they bound themselves to one another,' Erica mused. 'Much like you and Marshall.'

Jess poured a glass of juice into a small cup for Ruby.

'Can you believe that only two years ago, we were both single, in jobs we hated, I didn't have a dog and you weren't talking to spirits? I wasn't even entirely convinced spirits were real.'

Erica beamed.

'We've come a long way.'

'A ridiculously long way.'
They grinned at each other.
'And that's the best bit, isn't it,' said Erica.
'What's that?'
'That this is just the beginning.'

Epilogue

It was still dark, dawn only a few hours away, when Mullarky slunk out of the shadows around the side of the Victorian house and found a saucer of milk waiting for him on the back doorstep.

He stepped across the newly laid patio and carefully lifted the saucer. Once he'd drained the milk and licked his lips, the back door opened slowly and Mullarky looked up.

'I wondered if you'd like something a little stronger? Tea, perhaps.'

Smiling, Mullarky nodded and entered the house, sitting where instructed at the kitchen table.

'The new patio looks good,' he told Ginny as she busied herself pouring boiling water into the two cups.

'Thank you. I'll let Eddie know. He's very proud of it. And Marshall, too, of course.'

'The young ones have gone home?'

'They have. I mentioned the cottage to Marshall.'

Mullarky thanked Ginny for the tea as she placed it in front of him.

'Oh? What did the lad say?'

'Nothing much, but he seemed thoughtful.'

'It's a good idea. A witch should live there.'

'I still can't see Jess agreeing to it. It doesn't seem the modern place to bring up a child, but Marshall certainly didn't seem against it.'

'Well, it's a start.' Mullarky sipped his scalding tea, enjoying the burning sensation on his tongue. 'Yer sure ye dinnae want it?'

'I think I've had enough property excitement to last me a lifetime with this house,' said Ginny, sitting opposite him and looking up at the walls affectionately. 'I'm not sure I could cope with such an old cottage. The upkeep must be enormous.'

'It's true that Mauve hasnae been able to keep up with the maintenance, which is why I fear for the worst,' said Mullarky sadly, staring down into his drink.

'It'll be all right,' Ginny told him. 'If you like, I can pay her a visit? Help in some way?'

Mullarky shook his head.

'My mistress disnae ken I exist, so I dinnae think that would be possible. Although I'm so very grateful for the suggestion. Nae, I fear I'll be in need of a new mistress soon.'

'Well, don't look at me.'

Mullarky smiled.

'Yet ye still leave out milk for me.'

Ginny smiled back.

'Being a mistress and being a friend are two different things.'

Mullarky settled back into his chair, enjoying a warmth in his chest that didn't come from the tea.

'Aye. Been a while since I had one of those.'

'Well, you have one now. Biscuit?'

'D'ye still have the shortbreads?' Mullarky asked, his dark eyes widening.

Ginny gave a soft chuckle.

'Of course. I'm glad you enjoyed those.' She stood to fetch the biscuits, arranging them on a plate that she placed in the centre of the table. Mullarky reached for one and bit into it, letting the crumbs fall into his lap.

'Dinnae worry, lass, I'll clean it up.'

'You really don't have to.'

'That's what the milk is for. An offering.'

'Of friendship, Mullarky. You must stop cleaning around here.'

Mullarky paused in his eating.

'You cannae mean that. I'm a brownie. Helping around the house is what I do. Especially for a witch.'

'Of course. And right now, your mistress needs you more than I do. Also, stop calling me a witch.'

'But ye are a witch.'

'I am not.'

'A reluctant witch.'

Ginny pursed her lips.

'Stop it, Mullarky, or I shall call you Brownie instead.'

Mullarky laughed, sending out a spray of shortbread crumbs. He apologised and wiped his mouth.

'I like to help. Ginny,' he added, a twinkle in his eye.

Ginny sipped her tea and smiled.

'Have another biscuit,' she told him.

***

GINNY AND MULLARKY RETURN
in their own cosy mystery series coming soon.

Erica and Jess will also return soon.
Join us in the woods to find out when. Sign up at
www.jenice.co.uk

Join us in the woods

for news, early access and freebies at

www.jenice.co.uk

If you enjoyed this book

Authors love getting ratings and reviews. It's one
of the best ways to support authors you enjoy,
along with telling all your friends.
I would really appreciate it if you could leave a
rating or review wherever you get your books.